SHIELDING GILLIAN

Delta Team Two, Book 1

SUSAN STOKER

DEDICATION

In January 2018, Mr. Stoker and I filmed an HGTV show called Mountain Life. I got into a conversation about my career with the producer, and she was pouting because she'd never seen her name in a book. Well, Gillian, this one's for you!

CHAPTER ONE

Gillian Romano closed her eyes and rested her head on the seat. She was exhausted...but in a good way. The event that had taken months of her life to plan had gone off without a hitch. She'd been extremely nervous as it had been in Costa Rica, but because everything had gone smoothly, she knew she'd most likely have a lot more business coming her way.

The CEO of Pillar Custom Homes out of Austin, Troy Johnson, had contacted her almost a year ago to inquire about her organizing all aspects of an appreciation trip for the company's most prestigious clients.

She'd said yes—then immediately freaked out. As an event planner, Gillian was used to organizing weddings, birthday parties, and nonprofit galas in the Killeen and Austin areas. Mr. Johnson had gotten her name from the president of a local animal shelter, who'd hired her the year before to throw their annual fundraising dinner. The president had been using Pillar Custom Homes to build his house, and he'd passed her name along.

Mr. Johnson had invited a dozen of his esteemed clients and their families, as well as some of the most influential names in Austin real estate. Gillian had been responsible for all aspects of the trip. From flight and transportation arrangements, to booking the private hotel suites and selecting entertainment options for the four-day trip. It had been the most difficult thing she'd ever done—especially considering the fact she'd done most of her planning remotely—but everything had turned out beautifully, if she did say so herself.

Smiling, Gillian let out a long sigh of contentment. She'd seen the last of the guests off the day before and had spent one day in the beautiful Costa Rican resort soaking in the feeling of a job well done and getting in some well-deserved R&R.

She was now heading home and couldn't wait to tell her best friends—Ann, Wendy, and Clarissa—all about how beautiful Costa Rica was and how well the event had gone.

Her eyes popped open when she heard an odd sound up in the first-class section of the plane. Looking over the seat in front of her, she saw that almost all of the passengers in first class were standing. She wasn't alarmed—until she heard one of the women let out a sound that made the hair on Gillian's arms stand up.

It was a keening mixture of disbelief and terror.

Before she could do more than furrow her brow, a man appeared at the front of the coach cabin. He was holding a rifle. He pointed it up in the air and said something in Spanish, which made people all around Gillian shout out in horror and several began to cry.

Frozen in fear, Gillian couldn't believe what she was

hearing when the man switched to English and said, "On behalf of the Cartel of the Suns, my name is Luis Vilchez, and my friends and I have taken over the plane and will be landing in our homeland of Venezuela. Stay calm and don't do anything stupid, and you might live to see another day."

Gillian blinked. Her plane was being *hijacked*? How was this happening? She never in a million years would've thought after 9/11, when airlines had tightened security, that this would happen.

But then again, she wasn't in the United States. Hadn't she been surprised when she realized that she'd forgotten to put the small pocket knife Clarissa had given her for protection into her checked luggage, and she'd made it through the Costa Rican security with the knife in her purse?

But how did he get a *rifle* onboard? Was he a passenger?

Looking closer, Gillian realized he was dressed like one of the flight attendants. Though, now that she thought about it, she figured he could've probably smuggled the weapon onto the plane any number of ways...especially if he had help from someone who worked at the airport.

He nodded at someone in front of him, and when Gillian turned to look behind her, she saw there were three other men standing in the aisles with wicked-looking rifles as well.

Shit, shit, shit.

Swallowing hard, Gillian startled when there was another scream from the first-class area, and she whipped her head back around. The man who'd addressed the plane looked behind him then turned to face the coach passengers again. He pointed his rifle at a woman sitting in the first row. "You. Collect everyone's passports."

The woman stood up and looked visibly shaken.

"Get your passports out now!" the hijacker said loudly. "You will give them to this woman." When everyone remained frozen in fear, he scowled and, without further hesitation, turned to the man sitting in the aisle seat in the bulkhead row and shot him in the head.

The man fell over, and there were more screams and shouts of terror from her fellow passengers.

Gillian knew she was in shock. She couldn't make a sound. Couldn't do anything more than stare wide-eyed at what was happening right in front of her.

"I said, get your passports out...*now!*" the hijacker yelled in both Spanish and English.

The young couple next to her leaned over and immediately began to rummage through their bags, and Gillian did the same. She held out the small blue book as the woman selected to collect them walked down the aisle. Her hand shook as she passed it over, and for just a second, she caught the other woman's gaze. She looked absolutely terrified.

In all the confusion and panic amongst the passengers, Gillian hadn't thought much about what the hijacker had said previously—but now she did. They were going to Venezuela. She wasn't really up on current events, but even she knew the country was in serious turmoil at the moment. And the guy had said he was with a group, "cartel" something or other.

That usually meant drugs.

Too scared to take her eyes off the hijacker, Gillian felt herself breathing fast. This was really happening. The men who'd taken over the plane had already hurt people. Killed someone.

She felt the plane take a hard right, and ridiculously, she put out her hand to brace herself. It wasn't as if she was going to fall out the window or something.

Either the pilots were in on the plot to take over the plane, or the hijackers had gotten to them—they really were turning around and heading back toward South America.

She briefly thought about pulling out her cell phone to see if it would work, but Gillian had no idea who she could call. Nine-one-one? No, that wasn't an option. Her friends? What would they be able to do?

"Women in the front, men in the back!" a new voice demanded from behind her.

Gillian turned to look and saw the other hijackers were separating the passengers. The woman next to her whimpered, and her husband whispered something, obviously trying to calm and reassure her.

The man's arm was wrenched upward by one of the hijackers as he was shoved toward the back of the plane. Gillian stood immediately and let herself be pushed forward. She stumbled into the first-class cabin—and froze at the carnage around her.

Almost all of the men and women had been killed. Sometime in the general chaos, perhaps while the passports were being collected, their throats had been slit.

She saw three flight attendants lying motionless as well.

She had one second to be thankful the plane wasn't full before her arm was grabbed in a bruising hold. Looking up in panic, Gillian stared into the stone-cold brown eyes the hijacker who'd so calmly shot the man in the bulkhead row.

"*You*. You will be our spokesperson with the authorities," he declared.

Gillian shook her head, but no words would come out. She didn't want anything to do with this. She wanted to huddle in a corner and be invisible.

The man leaned into her, and his body odor assaulted Gillian's senses. He smelled like sweat and onions, and she forced herself not to gag. "You have two choices," he said calmly. "Be our spokesperson or die." Then he let go of her arm and stood back. He lifted his rifle and placed the barrel against her forehead. It was hot and felt like it was burning a hole right into her skull.

Swallowing hard, Gillian whispered, "I'd be happy to talk to whoever you want."

His lips quirked upward in an evil, satisfied smile as he lowered his weapon. "I thought you might." Then he grabbed her arm again and shoved his way between terrified women and children and hauled her to the area reserved for flight attendants, where the crew prepared food and drinks for the passengers.

He pushed her down, and Gillian gladly scooted until her back was against the side of the plane. "Might as well get comfortable, we've got a bit of time before we get to Caracas," the hijacker told her.

Gillian closed her eyes—but she couldn't block out the sounds. Women crying, the hijackers threatening passengers, the occasional terrifying shot from one of the guns.

People were dying all around her...and Gillian was ʉtterly helpless. She hated the feeling. But she also knew ɛre was nothing she could do if she was going to live through this, except try to stay calm and do as she was ordered.

* * *

Trigger grimly flipped through the folder of information he'd been given before he and the rest of his Delta Force team got onboard the flight to Caracas, Venezuela. Two days ago, a flight heading from Costa Rica to Dallas had been hijacked and flown to the South American country.

Now the plane had been parked on the tarmac for almost forty-two hours, the hijackers waiting for their demands to be met.

The group claimed to be associated with the Cartel of the Suns, who were involved in the international drug trade. It was an organization allegedly headed by high-ranking members of the military forces of Venezuela, as well as some of the most influential government employees as well. Not too long ago, in fact, the nephew of the first lady of the country had been arrested for trying to smuggle eight hundred kilos of cocaine from Venezuela to the United States for the cartel.

Trigger didn't give a fuck about the drugs *or* about the man the hijackers were attempting to free from prison. Hugo Lamas was a border patrol agent in Venezuela who'd been imprisoned earlier that year for taking bribes and allowing millions of dollars' worth of drugs to pass through his checkpoints.

What Trigger *did* give a fuck about was the remaining twenty-four American citizens on the plane. Twelve women, ten men, and two children. He was also worried about the dozen or so citizens from Costa Rica, Mexico,

Canada, Japan, Colombia, Panama, Nicaragua, and India onboard.

The entire Delta Force team thought the demands were bullshit. There was no way the Cartel of the Suns cared about one border patrol agent; not enough to hijack an entire plane. But at the moment, Trigger didn't care what their real agenda was. All he cared about was figuring out how to get onto that plane and take out the assholes who thought it was okay to terrorize innocent civilians.

Reports from Venezuela were that bodies had been dumped out of the plane onto the tarmac. The hijackers weren't fucking around. They weren't just threatening to kill people, they'd already done it. And with every hour that passed, more and more lives were in jeopardy.

The Deltas were called in to assist because they specialized in close-quarter rescue missions. These kinds of rescues weren't exactly Trigger's favorite. The chance of more people getting hurt was extremely high. He hated knowing passengers would most likely die in order for them to get to the hijackers. It was likely the assholes would use men and women as shields to try to survive.

"What are ya thinkin'?" Lefty asked.

Sighing, Trigger turned to his friend and teammate. "I'm thinking this stinks to high heaven."

Nodding, Lefty agreed. "I know. It doesn't add up."

"Nothing adds up," Grover chimed in. "I mean, the Venezuelan government hates the US. And with all the rumors that they're heavily involved in the Cartel of the Suns, why would they call us in to kill their own people?"

"Unless this group *isn't* their own people," Brain said.

Everyone nodded.

"That makes sense," Trigger said. "They could be

pissed off that someone hijacked the plane using their name, and they want to send a message."

"But at what cost?" Oz asked.

"They don't give a shit about innocent lives," Doc scoffed. "They don't care about anything but staying in power and making money. Many of them don't care about their *own* countrymen and women starving and suffering, so they certainly won't care about a bunch of foreigners."

"And I have no doubt they invited us in so if things go sideways, they can blame us," Lucky added in disgust.

Trigger ran a hand through his hair and sighed in agitation. "It doesn't matter why we're going, just that we do whatever it takes to get as many people as possible out of this alive."

The rest of the team nodded in agreement.

"What's the latest intel?" Trigger asked Brain.

The other man flipped through his notes and said, "It looks like they've got one of the passengers communicating with the negotiator."

"Smart. So we can't use voice-recognition software," Lucky said.

"Right," Brain agreed. "They also don't seem to be in a huge hurry. They've done the usual thing—bring us food and water or we'll start killing passengers—but otherwise, they just seem to be hunkered down and waiting."

"For what?" Grover asked.

"No clue," Brain replied.

"Who's the passenger doing the talking?" Trigger asked.

Brain shuffled some more papers. "FBI gathered background info on all the US passengers on the manifest. The spokesperson is identified as Gillian Romano. Thirty ye old, single, event planner from Georgetown, Texas. She checks out clean. Five-seven, blonde hair, green eyes, a hundred and eighty-five pounds. Got her undergraduate degree from UT-Austin and worked a series of entry-level jobs before starting her own company about four years ago. Both parents are living and still together; they live in Florida. She was in Costa Rica for seven days, apparently in charge of a big shindig put on by Pillar Custom Homes out of Austin. The guests all left the day before she did."

"You think she's in on this somehow?" Lefty asked.

"No," Brain said immediately. "I've got some of the transcripts of the calls she's had with the negotiator, and she's way out of her league. She's doing as good a job as she knows how, but the ass-wipe she's been talking to definitely hasn't helped."

"We taking over negotiations?" Doc asked.

"Fuck yeah, we are," Trigger answered for Brain. He'd also seen the transcripts. Gillian Romano was clearly scared, but she'd still done what she could to keep the hijackers calm and to get the passengers what they needed to be comfortable. He supposed her skills came from being an event planner.

"We're landing at the same airport, on the one runway they've still got open," Brain informed them. "But we aren't allowed to step foot off the airport property. The government doesn't want us in their country, and especially not out wandering around."

"Assholes," Oz said under his breath.

"So what's the plan?" Doc asked.

Trigger cleared his throat. "Get there. Get the asshole ff the phone with Ms. Romano and see if we can't pull as ch information from her as possible. Ideally, we'll pose as delivery men for supplies. We'll take out the hijackers and get the passengers to safety."

Grover chuckled. "Well, *that* sounds easy...not."

Trigger didn't even smile. "It won't be. We all know it. Those assholes could get tired of waiting. Most likely this is all a red herring, and they're a diversion from whatever their real agenda is. We have to stay on our toes. Trust no one. They landed in Venezuela for a reason, but whatever that is doesn't matter until those passengers are safe. Understand?"

Everyone immediately agreed. Their mission was hostage rescue. Nothing else. It was up to the CIA, FBI, DEA, and whoever else was involved to figure out the reasons behind the hijacking.

But even as the team fell silent, lost in their own thoughts about the upcoming mission, Trigger couldn't help but feel uneasy. Everything felt off about this op. And getting into an airplane undetected was impossible. Innocent civilians were going to die, there was no getting around that fact.

Trigger's thoughts returned to Gillian Romano, the appointed liaison for the hijackers. Just by reading the transcripts, he could tell she was smart. She was doing her best not to panic, which he admired. Not a lot of hostages he'd dealt with over the years kept as level a head as Gillian. While he hadn't heard her voice, and he couldn't read her emotions through her words, he could still tell she was terrified. And for some reason, that bothered him.

It was ridiculous. Trigger had no idea what she looked like or who she was as a person. She could be a harpy, or some vain chick only concerned about how many selfies she could post on social media. But he didn't think so.

Maybe he'd been hanging out with Ghost and his team for too long. Maybe he'd been wishing a bit too hard that he'd find a woman he could love and cherish as much as the other team cared about their women and families. He couldn't deny he was ready. At thirty-seven, he felt as if his life was passing him by. He wanted what his friends had.

He wanted someone to be there when he got home after a hard mission. Someone he could laugh with, completely let down his tough façade with, and who could make him feel as if the dangerous job he was doing was worth it.

He'd always thought he had plenty of time. But now he was closing in on forty. That wasn't old by any stretch, but Trigger still couldn't help feeling as if a vital part of life was eluding him.

Shaking his head, Trigger tried to get a grip. In the middle of an impossible op, which would most likely end in the deaths of way too many people, was not the time to start thinking about his love life...or lack thereof.

Pushing the inappropriate personal thoughts out of his head, Trigger did his best to formulate a plan. He knew he'd be the one taking over for the negotiator. He was good at it. The rest of the team would scope out the area and glean as many details as possible, so they could figure out the safest way to storm that plane.

We're coming, Gillian, Trigger silently promised. *Hang on just a bit longer, we're comin'.*

CHAPTER TWO

Gillian tried not to hyperventilate. She wanted to be anywhere but here. She didn't want to be the negotiator for the monsters who'd taken over the plane. She didn't want to be the person responsible for whether others lived or died. But she didn't have a choice.

The hijacker who seemed to be in charge—the one who'd told everyone his name was Luis—had shoved a cell phone into her hand after they'd landed and told her to talk to the person on the other end.

She'd been speaking with the condescending asshole assigned to communicate with her and the terrorists for almost two days, and he was acting as if she were a stupid little girl who didn't understand the situation.

But Gillian understood more than *he* did. She understood that when he didn't immediately agree to send water and food out to the plane, someone would die. And they had. Another one of the hijackers, Jesus, had shot a man in the temple and shoved him out of the plane. She'd never forget the thud the body made when it hit the concrete below.

The food and water had been delivered not too long after that.

She'd told the man on the other end of the line that the hijackers wanted someone named Hugo Lamas released from prison, and all he would tell her was that they were working on it. Gillian was afraid that soon, "working on it" wouldn't be good enough. Luis was getting impatient and wanted to see proof that the government was doing something to release his friend.

Luis grabbed her upper arm yet again, and Gillian winced. She had bright purple bruises all over her arm because the hijackers liked to manhandle her. He leaned close and once more threatened her. "Tell them we're getting impatient. They need to quit fucking around and release Hugo. We've got eyes on the prison and know they're just stalling. Also, tell them that this plane needs to be refueled. Once Hugo is released, we're out of here. If they keep stalling, more people will die. All of this could be done and over with if they just do what we fucking say!"

Gillian stared up at the man in shock. His beard was growing shaggier by the day, and while she didn't flinch from his stench anymore—everyone on the plane now smelled pretty rank—she couldn't help wincing at the new information.

"You're going to let us all go before you take off though, right?" she asked.

Luis smiled. But it wasn't a nice smile. It was evil and threatening. He ran his fingers down Gillian's cheek and said, "I think I might just take you with us. You've been such an obedient and good girl."

She jerked her head away from his touch, but Luis moved fast, fisting her long blonde hair in his hand and yanking her head backward. He licked up her cheek before moving to whisper in her ear.

"Don't think you're any better than me, girlie. Your blonde hair and tits might get you whatever you want back in America, but you're in *my* world now. And if I want you, I'll have you. If I want to kill you, I will. You'll do *exactly* what I say, when I say it. Got it?"

Gillian's mouth was as dry as cotton. She'd been terrified of the men since they'd taken over the plane, but she hadn't ever been worried that they'd try anything sexual... until now. She nodded as best she could with her head still immobilized by his hand in her hair.

"Good." He untangled his fingers and ran his hand over her head. "You know, if you were nicer to me, then I might be kinder to the others."

Gillian shivered. She definitely didn't want to be "nicer" to him...but if she could free some of the other passengers, it might be worth it.

Deep down, Gillian had a feeling none of them would be getting out of this alive. The hijackers had shown a complete lack of concern for anyone's well-being. They'd killed the flight attendants and the first-class passengers, and had been constantly threatening the rest. They couldn't outright kill them all just yet, they needed them as bargaining chips for the Venezuelan officials, but if they weren't given what they wanted, Gillian knew they wouldn't hesitate to kill more.

Gillian desperately wanted to live. She wanted to save as many of the other passengers as well. In just two days, she'd formed an intense bond with the women around her.

Like Alice, the woman who'd been sitting next to her on the flight. She wasn't dealing very well with the situation at all. She'd been crying for two days straight.

Or Janet and her seven-year-old daughter, Renee.

And especially Andrea. She was about Gillian's age and had been on vacation with some girlfriends in Costa Rica. Her friends had all been on other flights, and she'd ended up on the hijacked plane. Andrea also happened to live in Austin, and despite—or maybe because of—the overwhelming situation they'd found themselves in, she and Gillian had clicked.

Although the women had been separated from the men, Gillian had seen the fear in the men's eyes as well. The group of four guys who looked to be in their early twenties were definitely freaked out. And one older gentleman had a constant look of terror on his face and frequently put his hand on his chest, as if in pain. She didn't know many of the names of the men, but that didn't mean she didn't want to save them if at all possible. No one asked to be in this situation.

The last thing she wanted was Luis, or Alberto, or Henry, or any of the other terrorists killing more passengers when they didn't get what they wanted.

"I'm doing everything I can to make sure the authorities know that you're serious about getting your friend Hugo freed," she said quietly.

"He's not my friend," Luis growled.

Gillian swallowed hard. "Maybe if you give a little, show a little compassion to the other passengers, they'd work faster to get your demands met."

Luis smirked. "You think?"

Gillian nodded.

"So...who do you think I should let go? You?"

She shook her head. "I don't know. Maybe Janet and her daughter. Or Alice. Andrea. One of the men."

Luis laughed. "Why don't I just let them all go?"

She didn't dare agree or disagree. She had a feeling Luis was just fucking with her now. He turned from her without another word, and Gillian sighed in relief—but it was short lived.

He hauled Andrea up from the floor and pulled her in front of Gillian.

"You think I should let her go?" he asked harshly.

Gillian could only stare at him with huge eyes.

"Well? Do you?" he barked.

She nodded slightly.

"No," Luis decided. "She's hot. And much more my type than a spoiled, fat blonde bitch like you."

Before Gillian could get offended that he'd called her fat—she wasn't fat; she preferred the term curvy—Luis had bent Andrea over his arm and lowered his mouth.

Andrea frantically attempted to fight him off. She pushed against his chest and tried to turn her head, but Luis wasn't having it. He used his free hand to roughly grab her chin as he forced his mouth down on hers.

Gillian closed her eyes, but she couldn't escape Andrea's keening whimpers.

She would never get used to the violence the hijackers used against the civilians on the plane. She hated it, and wanted to do whatever she could to make it stop.

How long Luis forced himself on Andrea, Gillian didn't know, but the sudden ringing of the phone in her hand sounded loud in the stifling-hot plane.

Luis straightened, shoved Andrea away from him, and turned back to Gillian.

He flicked open a knife he kept on him at all times and held it to her throat. "Answer it. And make them understand we're serious. You can tell them if they get us food and water within the next two hours, I'll release ten hostages. You can even pick them...as long as it's not your friend Andrea. Or the bitch with the kid. People care a lot more about children than adults. I need her to bargain with. You can choose eight men and two women."

Gillian hated Luis more with every word out of his mouth.

She glanced at Andrea, who was repeatedly wiping her mouth as she quickly moved back to her spot on the floor.

Taking a deep breath, she nodded.

Luis pressed the knife a little harder to her neck. "And we need fuel for this plane. They need to start working on that as soon as possible. But don't say anything that will make me have to kill more people," he warned. Then he took the blade from her neck and pointed it at little Renee. "I'll start with *her*."

Gillian nodded once again and put her back against the door to the cockpit and slid to the floor. Isaac, another hijacker, sat on the flight attendant's seat nearby so he could listen to her side of the conversation as Luis walked toward his fellow hijackers, who were guarding the men huddled in the back.

"Hello?" Gillian said shakily after she brought the phone to her ear.

"Gillian Romano?" a deep voice asked.

Surprised when she didn't hear the nasally, high-pitched voice of the man she'd been talking to for the last two days, Gillian simply said, "Yes."

"My name is Walker Nelson. I'm taking over the negotiations."

Gillian wasn't sure what to think. On one hand, she was glad she didn't have to talk to the other asshole, but on the other hand, she had no desire to start over and explain from scratch what Luis and the others wanted. But as if he could read her mind, Walker reassured her.

"I've been debriefed about what's been going on. Rest assured that we are well aware of the demands the hijackers have made and the Venezuelan government is working on getting Hugo freed. How are you holding up?"

Gillian blinked. "What?"

"How are *you*? I know this can't be easy. And for what it's worth, I think you're doing an amazing job. You just need to hang in there a bit longer."

She wanted to cry. She didn't think the other guy had purposely made her feel as if she was fucking everything up, and yet some of the things he'd said when he was frustrated had done exactly that. The fact that *this* guy had started out their conversation with something positive made her want to curl into a little ball and cry. She'd always considered herself a strong, independent woman, but right now, she'd kill to have someone hold her and tell her things were going to be all right.

"Gillian?"

"I'm here," she said, her voice cracking. "I'm okay."

There was a slight pause, then Walker said, "You're not, but you will be. Are they listening to your side of the conversation?"

Gillian's mind spun with his topic change. "Yes."

"All right, I'm going to need you to get creative. I need as much information as you can tell me about what's going on inside that plane. How many hostages there are. Where they are. Anything you can tell me about the hijackers. I'm sorry that too much time has gone by without someone getting in there and freeing you, but hopefully now things can change. Okay?"

"Okay," she whispered. She felt hope rise within her. This Walker guy sounded like he knew what the hell he was doing, unlike the other guy. "You're American, right?"

He chuckled, and the soothing sound seemed to travel through her body, warming her all the way to the tips of her toes. "Yeah. Currently stationed in Texas."

Stationed. That meant he was military. Which also meant he was probably some sort of special forces guy.

Gillian wasn't an idiot. Living as close to Fort Hood as she did meant she came into contact with a lot of military service members. She knew there were several teams of Delta Force operatives stationed at the base. She closed her eyes and prayed harder than she ever had before that Walker was one of those super-soldiers.

"Gillian?"

"I'm from Texas too," she said softly.

"I know," he returned.

Gillian cried out in pain when Isaac kicked her leg, hard. "Ow!"

"What are you saying?" Isaac barked.

"It's a new negotiator," she told him. "He wants to get to know me."

"Tell him we want more food and need gas. Ask about Hugo," Isaac demanded.

"He already told me they're working on getting Hugo

freed. He said there's a lot of red tape and it's taking a while to work with the Venezuelan authorities. But they're working on it," she said quickly when he pulled his leg back to kick her once again. "And I'll tell him about the food, water, and fuel. I haven't had a chance yet," she told the hijacker.

Feeling braver than she had before, just because a kind voice was on the other end of the phone—she already felt safer with him organizing things, than she had with the other guy—she said, "In America, it's customary to get to know someone before you just start demanding things. I'm going to tell him what you want, but letting me talk to him for five minutes isn't going to mess up your timeline."

Not surprisingly, Isaac glared at her. *Very* surprisingly, he nodded. But he leaned forward and dug his fingers into her calf brutally as he said, "Fine, but if we don't have more food soon, it'll be your fault that someone else dies." He squeezed her leg once more, then let go and sat back, his dark brown eyes boring into her.

"Shit, are you all right?" Walker said into her ear. "Did he hurt you?"

"I'm okay," Gillian repeated. She wasn't, but there wasn't anything Walker Nelson could do about the throbbing in her leg or the fear making its way through her bloodstream. She knew she didn't have a lot of time to get information to this guy, and she hoped like hell he'd be able to figure out her clues. She wasn't exactly a pro at spy stuff, but she'd do her best.

"My dad was a pilot," she began. "But he died. My mom worked for the same airline as him, and that's how they met. She was a flight attendant. My dad wooed her by bribing the caterers to deliver her presents. The first gift he got for her was a stuffed animal. Cheesy, but it worked because she agreed to go out with him." Gillian knew Isaac was listening to every word, and she was afraid she was being too vague. But Walker's next words reassured her.

"Right. I know your parents live in Florida and weren't a pilot or flight attendant. So if I'm reading you right, you're saying the pilot's deceased and you think the hijackers got weapons smuggled onboard before the plane took off?" Walker asked calmly.

Gillian relaxed a fraction. He understood. Thank God. "Yeah."

"How many are there?"

"I have six brothers. I'm the youngest," she said.

"Got it," Walker reassured her. "All armed?"

"Yes."

"Guns?"

"Yes."

"Knives?"

"Yes."

"You're doing amazing, Gillian."

"My mom told me stories about how they liked to fool around in the plane after all the passengers had left. This would never happen today, but back then, they had no problem sneaking back on a plane after its flights for the day were over. Mom always wanted to be up front, in first class, but dad preferred the back of the plane."

"Okay...I know you're trying to tell me something, but I'm not understanding," Walker said. "I'm so sorry. Keep going. I'll figure it out."

Gillian refused to get discouraged. She was actually giving the authorities information they could hopefully use, not just getting yelled at by the negotiator and the hijackers. She forced a chuckle, as if Walker had said something funny. "So you know how it is. My brothers were all very protective of me. They always let me have the best seat. I was always in the front in the car, and when we went to shows, they put me in the row ahead of them so they could keep their eye on me."

"So you're in the front of the plane?" Walker asked.

"Uh-huh."

"Got it. They've separated the women and men, putting the women near the front of the plane and the men in the back, right?"

Gillian wanted to cry in relief. He'd understood her lame clues. "Exactly."

"Good job. We knew from the thermal imagers that there were two groups of hostages, one in front and one in back, but we didn't know you were separated by gender."

With every word out of his mouth, Gillian felt better. Heat signatures meant they had some fancy electronics and they could watch what they were doing.

"I'm going to get you out of this," Walker told her.

Gillian closed her eyes. She knew he couldn't promise her that, but she appreciated him saying it anyway. "Okay."

"I am," he said, more firmly now.

"I hope so," she whispered.

Isaac kicked again, and she yelped when his foot made contact with the same part of her leg he'd kicked and dug his fingers into not too long ago. "Get on with it," he hissed.

"That fucker better stop hurting you," he growled. "Are you okay, Gillian?" Walker asked in her ear.

Gillian closed her eyes and soaked in his concern. A

the hell she'd been through over the last couple of days, his words were a balm for her battered soul.

In just the few minutes they'd been on the phone, Gillian was already forming an emotional attachment to a man she'd never seen, a man she was relying on to rescue her. But she couldn't help it. His kindness meant everything.

"What happened?" Walker asked urgently.

Snapping out of her thoughts, Gillian blinked.

What the hell was she thinking? The man was doing a *job*. Any attachment she was feeling was because of the situation, nothing more.

"We need more water," she blurted, not taking her eyes from Isaac's foot. She wanted to be prepared next time he decided to kick her. "And food. And they want this plane fueled up."

"Wait—what? They're going to try to fly that plane out of here?" Walker asked.

Gillian ignored him. She didn't know what the hijackers had planned. All she knew was that there were ten people who could escape this nightmare if she played her role correctly. "They said they'd let people go if we got food and water soon, but if we don't, they're going to kill someone else. And they mean it."

"Take a breath, Gillian. I know they mean it."

She ignored him and continued on, talking as fast as she could to make sure she got as much information to him as possible. "Last time, they shot one of the men and threw him out of here. I heard his body land on the armac."

"Gillian," Walker said firmly, "take a breath. There's

food and water waiting. It'll be delivered before an hour's up. The deaths are on *them*, not you."

She tried to relax, but she couldn't. Something else occurred to her. "I don't know how it works, but the toilets are all backed up. They're full or something. This isn't one of their demands, but please, if it's possible, can they be cleaned out?"

"I'll see what I can do," Walker reassured her.

"Hang on," she told him, then looked up at Isaac. "He says they have food and water coming."

"And the fuel?"

"Walker?" she asked into the phone. "He also wants this plane fueled."

"Since that's a new demand, it has to go through several layers of approval, but I swear I'll work on it."

It wasn't what Gillian wanted to hear, but she found herself nodding anyway. "All the fuel trucks were moved away from the airport," she told Isaac, making things up as she spoke. "I don't think they have a problem refueling the plane, but it can't happen immediately."

Isaac growled and gestured to Carlos, another hijacker nearby. They spoke in Spanish to each other for a quick moment, then Isaac nodded. "Fine, but tell them that not fueling us up isn't an option. The longer it takes, the more people we'll kill. Ten, fifteen...maybe more...depending on how I feel."

"I heard," Walker said in her ear. "Tell him it'll be done."

"He said okay," Gillian told Isaac shakily. "He'll get the plane refueled."

"Good. Give me the phone," he ordered.

In the past, Gillian hadn't had any issues giving up the cell phone after she'd passed along their demands. But for some reason, this time she hesitated. Walker Nelson felt like a lifeline. Like if she hung up with him, she'd be signing her own death warrant. Her fingers tightened on the cheap plastic.

"Don't give up," Walker said into her ear. "We're here and watching. You're doing an amazing job and you'll be out of there before you know it. I can't wait to meet you face-to-face."

With those words ringing in Gillian's head, Isaac—obviously tired of waiting for her to comply with his order—swung his fist forward, punching her in the side of the head.

She cried out and went flying sideways. In the confined space in front of the cockpit, she didn't have far to fall. Her head bounced off the wall.

Gillian curled into a ball on the floor, holding her head in her hands, both sides throbbed, from Isaac's fist and from smacking against the wall.

The hijacker leaned down and picked up the phone she'd dropped and clicked it off, putting it in his pocket. He turned away from her without another word and headed for Luis, who was standing in the middle of the airplane.

Gillian crawled back over to where the other women were huddled in the first-class cabin and did her best not to cry.

"What'd they say?" Andrea asked. "What's going on?"

"Hopefully they're going to fix the toilets," Gillian informed the others.

"And food and water?" Alice asked.

"That too. The hijacker also said that some of us might be released."

There were gasps of excitement from the women around her, and Gillian wanted to feel happy that some of them would hopefully get out of this horrific situation... but all she could think about in that moment was Walker.

She'd heard his outraged curse when Isaac had hit her, right before she'd lost her grip on the phone. And he'd said he wanted to meet her.

As much as she tried to remind herself she was just connecting with another stranger because of the stress of the situation, she couldn't make herself care. She wanted to live through this awful situation, if only to meet the man who'd somehow made her more determined than ever to survive.

Trigger gripped the table in front of him so hard it felt as if he was going to break it. He'd been impressed by Gillian before, but now that he'd spoken to her, he was even more so. There was no doubt she was afraid, but she was hanging in there. She was clever, and even under the horrible circumstances she'd found herself in, she'd stayed strong, determined to help him as much as she could. He'd expected to have to explain how to give him clues without letting on she was doing so, but she didn't need any explanation.

They'd learned there were six hijackers onboard, and the men and women had been separated, with the women toward the front of the plane and the men at the back. The hijackers had also claimed some hostages might be released, and he had a hunch that was because of Gillian negotiating on their behalf. The request for the plane being refueled was new, but not entirely surprising. However, if the hijackers thought they'd survive their little stunt and be allowed to fly off into the sunset, they were more idiotic than they seemed.

But at the moment, all Trigger's thoughts were on Gillian. He recognized the sounds of someone being hit, and he wasn't happy at all that the woman on the other end of the phone had been the recipient of violence. He wanted her and the other innocent civilians off that plane. *Now*.

"Brain?" he asked his teammate, who'd been sitting next to him listening to his conversation with Gillian. "Did you get anything?"

The other man shook his head. "Not yet. I need to play back the recording and isolate the conversations in the background. It'll take a bit."

Trigger nodded. Brain was a language savant. He was fluent in at least thirty languages and he could pick up new ones without too much difficulty. His job was to listen to the background noise and glean any intel from conversations the hijackers were having with each other.

"The food and water is ready to be delivered," Grover informed him. "And we'll tell the authorities about the request for fuel."

"I've already got the waste people mobilizing," Oz added.

"It's got to feel like hell on earth inside that plane," Lucky muttered. "Between the heat, the toilets, and the fear..." His voice trailed off.

Trigger was more than aware of what the people inside

the plane were going through. He hadn't been in their exact situation, but close enough.

He felt a hand on his shoulder and knew Lefty was standing behind him. "She's going to be okay," his friend said quietly.

Trigger shook his head. "We don't know that. I said the same, but I have a feeling she knows as well as we do that there are no guarantees here. This whole thing stinks to high heaven."

"I agree," Doc said. "On one hand, this is a textbook hijacking, but it seems like overkill. The Cartel of the Suns is run by the Venezuelan government. Why would they have to resort to hijacking a plane from Costa Rica?"

"Right?" Lefty asked. "They could just get one of their contacts in the military or prison system to arrange for Lamas to escape."

"Regardless, our job is not to figure that shit out," Trigger told his team. "We were called in strictly to rescue those hostages. Not to solve the world's political issues. We need to concentrate on how we're going to get into that bird and save as many innocents as we can."

Everyone nodded in agreement.

"Gillian said in return for the food and water, they might let some hostages go," Trigger said. "Lefty, you and Grover are with me. We'll put on those overalls the airport staff wear and we'll be the ones to deliver the supplies. Hopefully we'll get a glimpse of some of the hijackers and can assess the situation onboard in the process."

The others nodded.

"Brain, keep working, let us know if you find out anything."

"Will do," the other man confirmed.

"The rest of you will be at the ready, covering our asses out there. I have an itchy feeling at the back of my neck that this is going to move faster than we think," Trigger warned.

"The faster we're out of this country, the better," Oz said. "Ever since we landed, I've felt as if we're being watched."

"Same," Lucky chimed in.

"The US government has arranged a flight for the surviving Americans to get out of here the second this thing is over," Brain added.

"Right. I think it was more the Venezuelan government wanting them gone so there would be no reason for the US to have a presence here for any longer than necessary," Doc said dryly.

Trigger tuned out his teammates. They weren't saying anything he hadn't already thought himself. All he could think about was the way Gillian's voice had trembled with fear—or pain?—as she spoke with him. She was taking more than her fair share of licks from the assholes who were enjoying toying with her...and the negotiators. On the surface, their demands were reasonable and made sense, though he couldn't help but suspect there was something else going on.

But at the moment, his only goal was to rescue the hostages. One blonde in particular.

CHAPTER THREE

Trigger drove the small airline cart toward the silent plane sitting on the tarmac. It loomed large and foreboding. There were no other planes or vehicles around it and no lights on inside the cabin. The sun had gone down and darkness was quickly setting in. The plane was parked well away from the terminal and there was no cover for Trigger and his men as they approached with the requested food and water.

The concrete under the back hatch was stained red with the blood of the men and women they'd dumped outside. The entire first-class cabin had been assassinated, the bodies disposed of after they'd landed. And there had been at least one other passenger murdered and dumped since they'd arrived in Venezuela as well. Trigger wasn't going to let that happen again, not if he could help it.

It was eerily quiet as they approached the airplane, but when they parked under the right side, near the entrance the catering companies used to restock the plane, the hatch slowly opened.

Looking up, Trigger saw a shadowy figure dressed all in black standing near the opening—but he couldn't take his eyes away from the woman who also appeared.

Gillian. He'd bet his life on it.

Her long hair was hanging limp around her pale face. She had on a pair of jeans and a dark blue wispy shirt that fluttered in the slight breeze of the evening. He watched as she took a deep breath, as if enjoying the fresh air, before the man standing next to her shoved the barrel of a rifle into her side.

She flinched away from him and looked down at him, Grover, and Lefty.

The last crew who had delivered supplies had brought a ladder with them and used that to reach the hatch. It wasn't ideal, but since it worked once, Trigger figured they might as well not cause any suspicion by asking for a different delivery method.

"Do you have the food and water?" the woman called down.

Trigger nodded.

"And the toilets?" she asked.

"After these are delivered, they'll start draining the tanks," Trigger said, adding a Spanish accent to his voice.

The man standing next to her said something too low for Trigger to hear, and she nodded. "Just like last time, one of you has to climb up the ladder and hand me the boxes. You can't come onboard, and if you do anything suspicious, you'll be shot. Then they'll kill one of the hostages as well in retaliation."

Her voice trembled slightly, and Trigger's adrenaline poured through his body. He knew he could leap into the plane before the asshole standing guard could kill him, but there were still five more hijackers. They'd certainly take him out before Grover or Lefty could get inside. Not to mention, it would put all of the civilians in danger.

He had to be patient. The moment would come for the hijackers to die, but now wasn't that time.

The woman licked her lips and got down on her knees in front of the opening. "Okay. Just move slow. Don't give him a reason to shoot you or anyone else. Please."

This was definitely Gillian; he recognized her voice. He nodded at her and turned to his teammates. Lefty and Grover met his gaze and they communicated easily without words. They would play this safe, but if the shit hit the fan, they were all ready to act. They had several weapons hidden on their bodies and could draw and shoot in seconds if need be.

Trigger set up the ladder and climbed a few rungs. He reached down and took the box Lefty was holding for him, then stepped up the rest of the way to the opening of the plane.

"I'm Gillian Romano, and that's Andrea Vilmer," the woman said as she reached for the box.

Trigger nodded. He approved of her doing what she could to share the names of the people still inside. She reached for the heavy box and the hijacker next to her backed farther into the plane, so Trigger couldn't get a good view of his face.

Frustrated that Gillian and Andrea had to do the heavy lifting of the boxes, Trigger could only watch as they and the other women nearby struggled to move the boxes from the hatch into the bowels of the plane.

"Thank you, Janet. Maybe there's something swee￼ there for your daughter, Renee," Gillian said as she h￼

another box to a woman behind her. "This one's heavy, Alice," she cautioned as another box was handed to another woman. "Maybe Leyton and Reed will help move the boxes to the back for the men. I know Charles will appreciate getting the water, with his cough and all."

With each box she handed off, Gillian recited names. Maria, Camile, Rebecca, Mateo, Alejandro, Muhammad... she'd done an amazing job of remembering the names of the other hostages on the plane.

Trigger was impressed. Intentional or not, she was doing her best to not only humanize the other captives, but to let him know who was still alive inside the plane. He wished he could reassure her. Tell her that he understood what she was doing, that she was so strong and he admired her. But he couldn't. All he could do was keep handing her the damn boxes filled with food and water.

He wasn't ready for Lefty to hand him the last box. It hadn't taken enough time. He hadn't been able to see enough of the inside of the plane...and he definitely hadn't had enough time with Gillian.

"This is the last one," Gillian told the man in the shadows as she handed it off to someone behind her. "You said if they delivered the supplies within two hours, you'd let ten people go."

Trigger wanted to tell her not to antagonize the hijacker, but he had to keep his mouth shut. It wouldn't be hard for the man with the rifle to realize he wasn't a native Spanish speaker and that something was up. He had a part to play, just as Gillian did. But that didn't mean he liked it.

Refusing to budge from the ladder, he stilled, waiting ~e what would happen next.

~e man gestured to someone inside the plane and

before Trigger knew what was happening, a man in his mid-thirties was standing at the opening of the plane, looking down at him.

"Be careful," Gillian was saying. "Don't fall as you go down the ladder."

With no choice, Trigger had to back down the ladder as the first hostage made his way off the plane.

As each person arrived at the bottom of the ladder, Lefty and Grover pointed them back toward the terminal. Each one took off as if the hounds of hell were at their feet, and Trigger couldn't blame them. It was obvious they were relieved to be away from the plane and from the hijackers.

But something was bothering him about the civilians who'd been chosen to be set free. Typically in hijackings, the freed were often women, children, or the infirm. Only two of the hostages set free were women, the others all men. Healthy, relatively *young* men.

People who might be able to put up a struggle and possibly overcome the hijackers.

Trigger understood the thought process behind letting the young, healthy, and strong free, and it pissed him off. Looking up at the hatch, he saw Gillian once again come to the edge. For a second, he wanted to encourage her to scramble down the ladder. To get the hell out of there. But somehow he knew, even if it was the right thing to do—which it wasn't—she wouldn't do it. She wouldn't bail and leave the others behind.

For just a moment, their eyes met. Her brows came down, she licked her lips, and he saw her mouth his name in question.

He nodded once—then a black-clad arm reached

around Gillian's chest and almost took her off her feet as she was wrenched backward. She let out a small sound of surprise as she was hauled away.

The hatch slammed shut, and Trigger heard the lock engage as it was secured.

"Fuck," Grover swore as he and Lefty grabbed the ladder and secured it back to the utility cart they'd driven out to the plane.

"You couldn't see much, could you?" Lefty asked.

Trigger shook his head. "No. They played it smart. Using the forward door meant the galley blocked the view of the rest of the plane."

"I'm assuming that was Gillian?" Grover asked.

"Yeah," Trigger confirmed.

"I heard some of what she was saying," Lefty said. "She was trying to give us as much information as possible as to who was still alive onboard, wasn't she?"

Trigger nodded. "I think so."

"We've got the passenger manifest," Grover reminded the men. "We've already got the names of everyone onboard."

"Right, but not who was shot and who wasn't," Trigger told his friend. He'd found that people reacted in very different ways to danger. Some froze in terror. Others freaked out. And the very rare few seemed to remain calm and process the situation carefully...like Gillian. She was obviously frightened, but had pushed her feelings to the side to try to help others.

"It was pretty ripe in there," Lefty muttered. "I could smell it even from where I was on that ladder."

For some reason, his friend's words irritated Trigger. "It's not like they can help it," he bit out. "It's fucking hot during the day and they're not running the engine for power. And let's not forget the toilets weren't meant for the number of people using them for days on end."

"Whoa!" Lefty said, holding up his hands. "I wasn't criticizing. Just making an observation."

Trigger took a deep breath and held on as Grover drove them back to the terminal. "I know, sorry."

"Hugo should be freed sometime tonight. We'll stall them by saying the paperwork is still being done or something, but we should be ready to make our move early in the morning," Grover said.

Trigger nodded. That was the timetable he was working toward as well.

The knowledge that by this time tomorrow, the standoff would be over, should've made him feel better. But instead, the unease deep within him continued to grow. For the first time in a very long time, he felt as if the enemy was three steps ahead of them. It wasn't a comfortable feeling...

Especially considering his thoughts about Gillian Romano.

It was crazy. He didn't even know her. Not really. But then again, he knew the important things. That she was smart and considerate. She worried more about her fellow prisoners than she did herself. She was brave...and all he wanted to do was hug her and tell her everything would be all right.

It wasn't like him, but Trigger couldn't get the woman out of his mind. She impressed the hell out of him, and that didn't happen very often. He wanted to get to know her better. Wanted to know every little thing.

But...he was a Delta. Ghost and his team might've

found women to spend the rest of their lives with, but they'd been damn lucky. Finding someone who could put up with his job and the danger it brought, and who would be all right with never knowing where he was or what he was doing, was damn near impossible.

No, it wouldn't be fair to Gillian to even ask her to do that.

But damn, did he want to.

Taking a deep breath, Trigger turned his mind back to the task at hand. He was getting way ahead of himself. There was no guarantee he or Gillian would get out of this situation alive. And she probably wouldn't want anything to do with anyone who was even close to this clusterfuck, not that he could blame her. She'd probably want to put it firmly behind her and get on with her life.

Trigger mentally recited the names that Gillian had used so he wouldn't forget them. He needed to talk to Brain and see if he'd been able to isolate any background conversations from his earlier phone call with Gillian. And he and his team had to plan the best way to raid that plane so the least number of innocent civilians were killed in the process.

His head throbbed, but Trigger ignored it and pressed his lips together. He'd get Gillian out of that plane one way or another.

* * *

Gillian wanted to cry when the hatch of the plane was secured. The air had been so damn refreshing, she hadn't even minded being forced to haul in all the heavy boxes.

But it had been the man at the top of the ladder that

had given her the biggest boost. At first she hadn't paid much attention to him, concentrating more on the slight breeze and fresh air. But when she finally noticed that he was paying *very* close attention to *her*, she took a second glance.

He had dark hair and his biceps strained the fabric of the one-piece jumper he'd had on. His gray eyes were piercing in their intensity, and she swore he was exuding confidence and positivity as if they were pheromones. But the thing that made her truly believe he was the man she'd been talking to on the phone was his lack of fear. The men who'd delivered the last batch of food and water had been falling all over themselves to unload the boxes and get the hell away from the plane.

This man, and his buddies, had given off the opposite vibe. Gillian had a feeling if Luis had made any threatening moves behind her, the man at the top of the ladder would've leaped into the plane and taken him out.

Feeling buoyed by the man's confidence, she'd started using as many names of her fellow hostages as possible. If this was her Walker, she wanted him to know exactly who was onboard.

Her Walker?

Gillian shook her head in exasperation. He wasn't hers. She had to get her shit together. He was just doing a job. Once this was over, and hopefully that would be sooner rather than later, he'd go home and forget she existed.

But a part of her didn't want to believe that. She felt as if she'd connected with the man, but again, that was stupid. He was probably one hundred percent focused on the mission. Namely, rescuing all of the hostages on the plane. She wasn't anyone special, and the sooner she got that through her thick skull, the better.

It was a ridiculous fantasy that he'd felt even a tenth of the emotional pull toward her that she did to him, but it was a hell of a lot better than thinking about her current situation.

She'd actually mouthed his name right before the hatch had shut, needing to know if it was really him. He'd nodded slightly...then Luis had grabbed her and manhandled her back inside the plane.

She sat on the floor with her back against the cockpit door, watching as Alberto and Jesus handed out water and food to the other women. Leyton, a Hispanic man who looked to be in his early thirties, was tasked with schlepping some boxes to the back of the plane for the men being held there.

Turning her attention back to the women, Gillian sighed. She'd hoped they would let Janet and her little girl go. Or even Alice, who hadn't been dealing well since being separated from her husband. But instead, as promised, they'd only freed two of the women. Gillian hadn't known them well; they were older and hadn't said one word to anyone, as far as Gillian knew.

They'd also let eight men go. Mostly young men, who hadn't even looked at the women they'd had to pass on their way out. It made a weird kind of sense to Gillian. The women weren't as strong as the men, and were less likely to plan any kind of revolt.

The hijackers might see Gillian and the others as weaker than they were, but they weren't. They just had to use different weapons than their muscles.

Gillian vowed right then and there to do whatever it

took to thwart their plans, whatever they were. If they thought they were going to take off to safety, they were dead wrong. She'd have to find some way to sabotage the plane. She'd watched Luis close the hatch; maybe she could disable the door somehow. They couldn't take off if the door wasn't latched, could they? She didn't know, but it was worth a shot. She'd also work harder to give Walker as much information as she could.

"I need my cock sucked," Luis announced.

Gillian started badly. She'd been lost in her own head, thinking about Walker and how she might be able to fight back, when the hijacker's words interrupted, loud and threatening.

She shrank back against the door and stared at him with wide eyes. He was standing in the middle of the aisle about six rows back, where the first-class cabin ended and the economy seating started.

He was looking at all the women huddled together as if he were shopping and trying to pick out the ripest fruit.

"You," he said, pointing at Andrea, who was sitting on the floor in one of the rows.

She let out a quiet sob and shook her head.

"Get your ass up, now!" Luis ordered.

Ever so slowly, Andrea stood. Her head hung low and she stared at the floor.

"Well? What are you waiting for? Get over here!" Luis said with an evil smirk.

No one said a word. Gillian could hear Janet and the others crying, but no one stood up to the hijacker or came to Andrea's aid.

Gillian's mouth opened—she had no idea what she was going to say; it wasn't as if she was going to volunteer herself—but it was too late. Luis had grabbed Andrea's arm and was roughly towing her back down the aisle.

Luis pulled her into one of the exit rows, probably because it was wider and had more room. He shoved her to her knees in front of him. Gillian couldn't see Andrea any longer, or what she was doing, but she could guess. All she could see was Luis from the chest up. Guilt surged that she was so grateful when the seats blocked her view.

Luis was looking down, and he still had that awful smirk on his face. As Gillian watched, Luis said something to Andrea, and she imagined him holding the other woman's head in his hands as she undid his pants. He stood still for a minute or so—then he threw his head back, as if he was thoroughly enjoying what was happening.

Gillian could tell by his swaying movements that his hips were thrusting forward and back, faster and faster, and she could just imagine what poor Andrea was enduring. Carlos and Jesus were watching raptly from the back of the plane, and she realized Henry was stroking himself as he sat in the jump seat next to her.

Shivering and closing her eyes at last, Gillian couldn't watch anymore.

Luis was horrible. Him *and* his buddies. As if this situation wasn't bad enough, now they were forcing themselves on the hostages? Was she next? Or poor Janet? Alice? What about beautiful Camile? It was too much. Hadn't they all endured enough?

A commotion made her eyes pop open, and she watched as Luis hauled Andrea back up the aisle. His pants were zipped but the button was still undone, and he had a satisfied look on his face. It made Gillian physically sick.

Andrea held a hand over her lips and refused to meet anyone's eyes.

"If you all don't behave and do exactly as you're told, you're next," he said as he threw Andrea back into her spot on the floor. Then he motioned to Alberto and Isaac, and the three of them sauntered down the aisle to have a private conversation in the relative privacy of the middle of the plane, where he'd just forced himself on Andrea.

Henry said something under his breath in Spanish that made the others laugh, and Gillian was glad she couldn't understand him. She had a feeling he'd said something derogatory about Andrea, or maybe about the women in general.

Gillian wanted to go to Andrea. Wanted to ask if she was all right. Reassure her that they'd get out of this alive, that they just had to be strong. But in her mind, the words just sounded hollow. She thought about how *she'd* feel if that had been her Luis had grabbed. She wouldn't want to hear any platitudes from anyone.

Closing her eyes, Gillian tried to dredge up soothing thoughts about Walker once more, but found it was impossible. All her fears and worries were overwhelming her, and she couldn't think about anything other than what Luis and his buddies might have in store for the rest of them.

Eventually, she did her best to get some rest, even if it was filled with nightmares.

It felt as if she'd only been asleep for seconds, but in reality, it had been hours when Gillian was painfully woken up with a kick to her side.

Crying out, she sat up immediately and flinched at the light shining in her eyes.

"Time for another call," Luis told her brusquely. "We need to know when Hugo will be freed and when the plane will be refueled. They're taking too long, and we've been sitting around waiting on them long enough. It's currently one in the morning. They have until five a.m. to have this plane fueled and to set Hugo free."

"What happens at five?" Gillian asked.

Luis smirked and leaned down. "People start dying," he said succinctly. "One every fifteen minutes until we have proof that our comrade is free. Make sure they understand. We're starting with your friends. Maybe with that little girl."

"No!" Gillian exclaimed. "Please!"

Luis grabbed hold of Gillian's hair and jerked backward. He held his knife to her exposed throat and growled, "Then make them understand we're not fucking around! You do that, and everyone lives. You fuck up, and they are all dead! You'll be last. I'll make you watch every person on this plane die. Got it?"

"Yes," Gillian whispered. She had no doubt he'd do exactly as he threatened.

Luis nodded then threw the cell phone into her lap as he stood. "And don't try anything stupid," he warned. "We're listening." And with that, he stood back and stared menacingly down at her.

Gillian's fingers were shaking, but she clicked the phone on and went to the most recent calls. She pressed on the last number received and waited for someone to pick up. Her heart was in her throat, and for a second she thought no one would answer since it was the middle of the night, but finally she heard Walker's voice.

"Yeah?"

"It's Gillian."

"Hey." His voice immediately changed from the gruff, menacing tone he'd used to answer to a gentler timbre. "You all right?"

"Yeah. I'm supposed to give you a message."

"Okay, but first, take a breath."

Gillian frowned. "What?"

"Take a breath, Di. I can tell you're stressed way the hell out. Just breathe."

"Di?"

"Sorry, that just popped out. Diana Prince. You know, Wonder Woman's alter ego? You remind me of her. Staying calm under pressure, looking for ways to help even when the odds are stacked against you. I didn't see a golden lasso earlier, but you might be hiding it somewhere."

Gillian was literally speechless. She couldn't think of a damn thing to say in response.

"Are you breathing? Somehow I don't think you are."

She let out the breath she was holding with an audible whoosh and, amazingly, she heard Walker chuckle on the other end of the line.

"Good. Now, tell me what those assholes want us to know."

And just that quickly, she was sucked back into her current situation. Looking up, Gillian saw Luis and Henry staring down at her with their arms crossed over their chests. She was definitely at a disadvantage sitting at their feet, but she tried not to let that intimidate her.

Hell, who was she kidding? She was way the fuck intimidated.

"They said you have until five in the morning to have the plane refueled and Hugo released. Otherwise they're going to start killing people. One every fifteen minutes." She gave him the message quickly, feeling bile rise in her throat at having to say the words out loud.

"The authorities are waiting for the sun to rise to start refueling," Walker said calmly. "I can tell them they need to start doing it sooner. And I believe Hugo is being released in around two hours. Are they listening?"

Gillian nodded but couldn't get any words out.

"I'm sure they are," Walker said. "Go ahead, tell them what I said."

How Walker could sound so calm and reassured, Gillian had no idea. She cleared her throat and passed along the message.

Luis and Henry immediately began talking to each other in Spanish.

"I don't—"

"Hush," Walker said swiftly through the phone.

Startled that he'd been so abrupt, Gillian swallowed hard and held the phone tightly to her ear. She wasn't sure what to say, or why she was still holding the phone. She should hang up. She'd passed along the message. But no matter how upsetting it was that Walker had been so terse, she couldn't bring herself to break their connection.

She could hear him breathing on the other end of the line, and concentrated on that. She tried to time her own breaths with his. Surprisingly, it calmed her. He wasn't huffing and puffing and wasn't acting nervous or freaked out.

Luis and Henry finally stopped arguing, and Luis stomped away toward the back of the plane. Henry ran an agitated hand through his hair, and he grunted before he too walked away from where Gillian was sitting. He didn't go far, only to where the first-class cabin stopped, but it gave her a bit of privacy.

"Walker?" she whispered.

"Sorry about that, Di."

"What happened?" she asked.

"I needed to hear their conversation," Walker told her.

Then Gillian understood. "What'd they say?"

"I don't know. But my teammate will figure it out. He's on his way, and he'll listen to the recording of our call when he gets here."

"Is that guy really going to be freed soon?"

"Yes," Walker said simply.

"And the plane refueled?"

"I take it no one is listening to you right now?" Walker asked.

"No, Henry's pouting. Oh! Luis, Jesus, Alberto, Carlos, Henry, and Isaac. Those are the hijackers' names."

"Good girl," Walker said, the admiration easy to hear in his tone. "And this is going to be over soon."

"They really *will* start killing people," Gillian warned him. "They said they would start with the women."

"I believe you, but it's not going to come to that."

"Promise?" She knew it wasn't really fair to ask that of him, but she was desperate. Her heart fell when Walker didn't immediately respond. "Sorry. Ignore me, I—"

"I'm not a fortune teller, sweetheart. I wish I was. I wish I could tell you for sure what was going to happen in the next few hours. All I *can* tell you is that I'm doing n very best to get you, and everyone else on that plane, out of there in one piece."

"Please don't let them take off with all of us inside this plane."

"No way in hell," Walker said fervently.

She believed him. "I watched as Luis secured the door. I'm sure I can do something to open it, or to make it not close right. They can't take off without the door being latched, right? Maybe when the plane is refueled, someone can leave a gun or something in a secret compartment that I can get to and take them out. I can—"

"Diana Prince, right down to your toes," Walker interrupted.

"What?"

"We've got this, Di. All you have to do is go with the flow, keep your head down, and not put yourself in the line of fire. Okay?"

"Okay. Walker?"

"Yeah?"

"That *was* you with the food and water, wasn't it?"

"It was."

Gillian felt a little stupid. Of course it was. He'd confirmed it with his nod earlier. But her emotions were all over the place. She was exhausted, stressed, and freaked out. Not to mention, she had a feeling she smelled atrocious...she couldn't really tell, since everyone around her smelled awful too. She hated that Walker had seen her at her worst. She wanted to impress him. Wanted to look like the kick-ass women in the movies who could live through the worst and still manage to seduce the hero.

"I thought so," she said lamely when the silence went too long.

"What's goin' through your head?" he asked.

Gillian closed her eyes and rested her forehead on her knees. She hurt. All over. She was exhausted and terrified. And she was apparently vain enough to want Walker to like her...when they were in a middle of a freaking *hostage situation*. She was certifiably insane. "Nothing."

"You want to know what I saw when I climbed that ladder?" Walker asked softly.

Gillian shook her head, but said, "Maybe."

He chuckled softly—then blew her mind. "I saw a woman who was at the end of her rope, but who was still holding on. Not only that, but I saw a leader. Someone who everyone on that plane probably looks up to. Someone who might be scared, but was doing her best to power through it for the good of the rest of the team. I saw a woman who I admired, and who I vowed right then and there wouldn't become a statistic or a quick blurb on a news story." And then, after a beat, "I saw a woman I wanted to get to know better."

His words felt good. Damn good. Taking a deep breath, she asked, "You want to know what I saw when I looked at *you?*"

"Sure, Di, tell me."

"Hope."

They were both silent for a moment. "I like that way more than I should. Hang on just a little longer, Gillian. Stay alert, and be as calm as you can. All right?"

"Yeah." Something occurred to her then. Something she should've thought about before. "Walker? You said you're recording when I call you?"

"Yes."

"What if I give them the phone back and pretend to hang up, but don't?"

"No."

"But—"

"No. If they realize what you did, they'll hurt you."

"They're going to hurt me anyway. They've *already* hurt me. So far they've just been toying with me, but I know the second they have the chance, Luis or one of the others will take great pleasure in making me suffer. But if you can hear their conversations, then you might be able to catch them if they fly away."

"You're more important."

Gillian knew she'd replay those three words over and over in her head for the rest of her life...however short it might turn out to be.

She'd had her share of boyfriends, but for the most part, she'd never felt as if they'd put her first. She'd dated a musician who'd moved to LA to pursue his career. She would've gone with him...if he'd asked. He didn't. Then there was the accountant who she hadn't seen for three months around tax time. Also, the guy who loved sports so much he never asked her over when his favorite team was playing because she would distract him.

Walker didn't even know her, and he was putting *her* above capturing six ruthless terrorist hijackers.

"I'm doing it," she told him. "I hope to be able to officially meet you soon, Walker Nelson. Be careful." Then, without waiting for his response—because she had a feeling he'd be able to talk her out of it—she clicked out of the phone app and turned off the screen. As it faded to black, she prayed her plan would actually work and the ‸sholes who were keeping them hostage would actually say something incriminating, and that Walker and his friends would hear them.

She held the phone face up and waited for Henry to realize that he'd left her alone with his cell. Surprisingly, it took another few minutes. When he did, he raced back up the aisle and snatched his phone from her hand. He shoved it in his back pocket and smacked her across the face. "What'd you tell him?" he barked.

"Nothing!" Gillian protested. "I hung up when you left."

"You'd better not be lying," he hissed as he stood over her threateningly.

"I'm not! I swear!"

Kicking her once more, Henry then turned and left. Gillian caught Andrea's eye and tried to smile reassuringly. She wanted to tell her and the others that help was coming. That hopefully this would all be a bad memory soon, but she didn't dare.

She hoped Walker was being honest with her, and that the hijackers' friend would be released. Maybe then they could all get out of here with their lives.

CHAPTER FOUR

Trigger stood on the edge of the tarmac. Every muscle in his body was tense. He'd heard Gillian get smacked around and hated hearing the fear in her voice. But he couldn't deny what she'd done would be helpful. Maybe not right now, but later, once this was over, the officials could listen to the hijackers talking and learn what their plan had been. From what he could tell, the hijacker who'd taken the phone hadn't realized it was still on, and he prayed the recordings would be audible.

For now, however, they had a plane to storm and hostages to rescue. That was their main objective. Why they were there in the first place.

And they were out of time. It was oh-four-hundred and the deadline the hijackers had given was quickly approaching. Hugo Lamas had been freed, but the second the vehicle had left the prison grounds, it had been hit with a rocket-propelled grenade. Hugo, and everyone else in the vehicle, had been blown to bits.

No one knew who was behind the hit. Was it the

Cartel of the Suns taking care of one of their own so he wouldn't talk? Was it someone in the military or government who didn't want him released? A rival drug gang? No one had any answers, and that made Trigger and his team antsy. Whoever was behind the assassination either had inside information about his release or had been watching and waiting. Either way, if Luis and the other hijackers got wind of the fact their friend had been killed, who knew what they might do in retaliation.

There was no more time to stall. The men on the plane were expecting their friend to appear, and when he didn't, they were going to start killing innocent civilians. It was the Deltas' job to prevent that.

"Everyone know their roles?" Trigger asked through their hands-free radios strapped around their necks. When they spoke, it triggered the connection to open.

"Ten-four."

"Yes."

"Gotcha."

The answers were immediate and confident. Trigger's adrenaline was coursing through his veins. They were ready to storm the plane. He and Lefty would go in from the same door the food was delivered through. Grover, Brain, and Oz would breech through the back hatch, Doc would take out the emergency exit door on one side at the wings and Lucky would take the other side. They were hoping the simultaneous breech would cause mass confusion with the hijackers and they'd be able to take enough of them out before they could retaliate by shooting the hostages.

It was risky as hell, but with no other good way onto the plane, it was the best plan of action, and someth they'd practiced in training over and over. They were ready. Trigger just hoped Gillian and the others were.

"The refueling truck is about ready to go," Doc said. "Everyone stand by. We'll use it as cover and once we're at the plane, we'll spread out. One, two— Fuck! What the hell?"

Trigger looked toward where the refueling truck sat idling—and saw a twin-engine Beechcraft Queen Air come racing around the corner of the terminal. The propellers were running, and it was clear it wasn't simply a clueless pilot oblivious to the situation. It could hold up to twelve people—and it was headed straight for the hijacked plane with no signs of slowing.

Their carefully constructed plan had just gone to hell.

Trigger's head swung back toward the hijacked plane when he heard the sound of one of the escape slides inflating.

"Fuck, fuck, fuck," Trigger muttered, motioning for his team to move out.

Before they could get to the plane, people started exiting. Two at a time. A man and a woman. The second the first pair made it to the bottom of the slide, they began running toward the small Beechcraft.

They had no idea what the hijackers looked like, so he didn't know if the people running were their targets or not.

Two-by-two, more and more people slid down the escape slide and ran toward the smaller plane now idling nearby.

The first couple swerved around the plane and headed for the terminal behind it.

Parking the plane right in the middle of the path the

hostages would take to get to safety was fucking brilliant. It made distinguishing the bad guys from the good guys that much harder.

It was clear the hijackers never had any intention of flying the large plane out of there. They were going to catch a ride on the smaller, more maneuverable aircraft, one that could fly under radar and disappear without a trace into Central America.

Trigger ran next to Lefty as the team headed for the panicked passengers focused on escaping the hell they'd lived through for the last three days.

"They're using the passengers as cover," Trigger told his team. He knew they were already aware, but it still needed to be said. "Shoot to kill, but make sure the person you're shooting is actually a hijacker!"

They had a lot of open ground to cover before they could get to either airplane, and Trigger had never felt more like a sitting duck than in that moment.

A loud gunshot sounded and as one, all seven Deltas hit the deck and rolled. They had no cover, but they wouldn't just stand around waiting to be shot either. Within seconds, they were back up and running for the plane. No one knew who was firing or from where, but they couldn't stop the mission now.

It seemed like it took an hour, but they finally reached the front wheels of the hijacked aircraft. They lined up, using the wheels and each other as cover. Trigger was in front, and he frantically searched for whoever was shooting at them.

The scene was complete chaos. Women were crying, men were shouting, and Trigger knew they needed to figure out who was a hijacker and who was an innocent civilian immediately.

"Grover, take out the pilot in the Beechcraft," Trigger ordered. "Doc, cover him. Lefty, you and Brain need to find a way to reroute the civilians...separate them from our targets. Oz and Lucky, you're on the hijackers with me."

Without a word, the men on his team fanned out. Trigger heard Lefty whistle as loud as he could as Brain began yelling for the hostages to run in the opposite direction from the Beechcraft.

As if the terrified men and women had merely been waiting for someone to tell them what to do, they immediately made a hard right turn and headed for the two men frantically gesturing at them to run toward them.

With the change in the tide of humanity, Trigger could easily make out who was a bad guy and who wasn't. But now there was a new problem—the hijackers were using the women and children as shields.

One man had a small child in his arms. He held a knife at her throat as he bolted for the small plane.

Another had the barrel of a rifle jammed into a woman's side as he forced her to jog toward the Beechcraft.

Then Trigger saw Gillian.

Her blonde hair stood out, even in the low light of the rising sun. A man had an arm around her neck and was attempting to walk backward toward their escape plane while randomly shooting at the retreating hostages and Trigger's team.

Something inside Trigger shifted, and a feeling he'd never experienced while on the job swept over him.

Fear.

Suddenly, he was terrified the man would get on the small plane with Gillian, and he'd never see her again. Never hear her voice.

Not. Happening.

His eyes narrowed and he focused on the man. Tunnel vision. Trigger knew what it was, but he didn't try to snap himself out of it. He had faith in his team. They'd cover him and take care of the other hijackers. The asshole who was hurting Gillian was going to die.

* * *

Gillian's head was reeling. When the hijackers had suddenly rounded up all the women and forced them to the back of the plane with the men, she'd thought they were going to let them all go. That the plane had finally been refueled and they were getting ready to take off. When they'd opened a hatch, her conclusions had been confirmed. She couldn't help but smile.

But then Luis had spoken into a handheld radio she hadn't seen before and started pairing up the hostages. One man with one woman. He shoved the first couple out of the door and down a slide, without giving them any warning. Then he did the same with the next. And the next. Then Henry grabbed Alice and jumped out behind one of the pairs of hostages.

What in the world was happening?

She looked out the hatch and saw a small plane coming toward them—fast.

And it clicked.

The hijackers weren't going to leave in the larger

aircraft. They had a buddy who was picking them up and taking them away in the twin-engine plane.

Gillian was so stunned, she'd stopped paying attention to what was going on around her, so she wasn't prepared when Alberto grabbed her arm and hauled her against his body. He squeezed her arm so tightly, Gillian couldn't help but cry out in pain.

"You're coming with me," Alberto hissed. "And if you run, I'll shoot you. Understand?"

Gillian could only nod.

He pushed between some of the other hostages waiting anxiously for their chance to escape the plane and hauled her up behind Luis and Andrea. The other hijacker had a small pistol against Andrea's temple and was saying something to her in Spanish. When she and Alberto appeared behind them, Luis straightened but didn't remove the gun from Andrea's head.

"We're having fun, no?" he asked with a malicious smile. Then he leaned into Andrea and licked up the side of her face. "I'm taking this one with me. She sucked my cock so good, how could I not? Me and her are gonna have a lot more fun, aren't we?"

Gillian shuddered as Andrea closed her eyes.

"Come on," Luis ordered. "We don't have much time. Is everyone out?"

"*Si*, Isaac is behind me," Alberto said.

Gillian turned to look and saw Isaac was indeed standing behind them. Next to him was Leyton, the Hispanic man who'd helped with the boxes earlier.

"I'll go with her," he said when their gazes met.

She frowned in confusion.

Leyton reached for her arm. "I'll take her," he repeated.

Gillian had no idea why Leyton offered to go with her when it seemed obvious Alberto planned to use her as a shield. Then she saw Wade, Alice's husband, who'd been sitting in the same row as Gillian when everything had started.

"No, I'll jump with her," Wade said.

Gillian finally realized the men were doing what they could to try to help her. To get her away from the hijacker.

Leyton even reached forward and grabbed hold of her arm. For a short second, he and Alberto had a kind of tug-of-war with Gillian between them.

"You want to come with us too?" Alberto sneered, then put a hand on Leyton's chest and shoved. Hard. The young man fell back, but he didn't take his eyes off the hijacker. "Back off," Alberto said sternly. "And that goes for the rest of you," he continued, talking to the others who were gathered around them. "Do *what* we tell you, *when* we tell you, and you might live through this. Grow a brain, and I'll kill you right here and now!"

"We need to get out of here," Luis interrupted impatiently, before pushing Andrea forward. They both slid down the inflatable slide.

Before she was ready, Alberto jumped onto the slide himself, dragging Gillian with him. The second their feet hit the tarmac, he was yanking her upright and pulling her toward the small plane waiting for them.

People were running around everywhere. Confusion was rampant. The freed hostages didn't know which way to go. Some were heading for the small plane, but others had turned and were running off to the right, toward man wearing all black. Gunshots rang out, but there was nowhere to find cover.

Alberto wrapped an arm around her neck and pulled her against his chest. Gillian's hands went to his arm and she tried to pull it away from her throat. He was cutting off her air, and the only thing she could concentrate on was getting oxygen into her lungs. As they walked backward, Alberto raised his rifle and shot at the men and women running in the opposite direction, then laughed when screams sounded around them.

"Stop fucking around!" Luis yelled from behind them. "Get to the plane!"

Gillian fought then. She was not going to get on another plane with these heartless assholes. She knew if they got her onboard, no one would ever see her again. Not her parents, not her best friends, no one. They'd abuse her, hurt her, then discard her body deep in a jungle somewhere.

She wasn't just going to let that happen.

Alberto was obviously surprised by her struggles, because he stopped shooting and dropped his rifle. It was slung around his back with a strap, but he needed to use both hands to try to subdue her.

No matter how hard she struggled, though, Gillian couldn't escape Alberto's hold. It wasn't until she heard Luis swearing in Spanish that she realized they'd reached the smaller plane.

Before she could process what was happening, Andrea screamed. Poor little Renee was also crying from somewhere nearby.

Gillian distractedly noticed that Leyton must have owed them off the plane. He was standing nearby. He wasn't helping her, or Andrea, or even Renee. He was just standing there watching, almost as if he was in shock.

She wanted to yell at him to run, to get away from the plane and the hijackers, to save himself, but she didn't get the chance.

One second Gillian was standing, and the next, she and Alberto were on the ground. They'd smacked into Andrea and Luis, hard, and all four of them went down. The other couple was now under them. They were lying at the bottom of the three steps leading into the twin-engine aircraft, Luis yelling in Spanish and trying to get to his feet.

Renee was curled in a ball nearby, crying for her mom.

Everything was chaotic and confusing and happening too quickly for Gillian to process.

A loud gunshot rang out—and everyone seemed to freeze. The sound of glass breaking came immediately on the heels of the gunshot, and shards rained down on the foursome at the bottom of the steps.

"Dammit!" Luis shouted before he finally extracted himself from Andrea and stood. He turned to scramble up the stairs, but another gunshot filled the air, and the leader of the hijackers slumped against the very stairs he was attempting to climb.

Andrea screamed again.

Alberto wrenched Gillian to her knees, but before she could gain her feet, one more shot rang out...

And Alberto slumped against her.

She felt wetness splash against her face before she went down again, Alberto's weight pinning her to the ground.

Andrea continued to scream, Renee continued to

and Gillian had the uncharitable thought that she wished they'd just shut up. She could hear more screaming and crying all around her.

Struggling to get out from under Alberto, Gillian heard more gunshots, this time much closer. Flinching with every one, she decided to stay where she was. It was irrational, but somehow she felt safer hiding under Alberto's dead body than standing up and exposing herself to flying bullets.

It might've been two minutes or two seconds, she wasn't sure, but the sound of silence finally registered in her ears.

Then, "Gillian!"

She'd recognize that voice anywhere.

Walker.

Renewing her attempt to get out from under Alberto, Gillian tried her best to wiggle free. She struggled for only seconds before shoving the man's body off herself. Turning her head, Gillian looked into the concerned gray eyes of Walker as he ran toward her.

He looked very different than the last time she'd seen him. Gone were the gray airline coveralls. Now he was dressed in black, even had black makeup smeared on his face. He was holding some sort of rifle and he had something wrapped around his throat.

Reaching down, he hauled her up with one hand, keeping his rifle at the ready, and pulled her toward him.

Gillian went willingly.

He was hard all over, mostly because of the bulletproof vest he was obviously wearing, but even his biceps were as hard as rocks.

She'd never felt so safe in all her life.

She allowed herself a second to close her eyes and relax into him before the sound of Andrea's sobs forced her to open them once more. Looking to her right, she saw a man dressed much like Walker, helping Andrea to her feet. She looked terrified out of her mind. So much so, she couldn't even walk; the man had to pick her up to get her to safety.

Luis's body had been pushed off the stairs and he lie dead on the tarmac, next to the small plane. Another man, obviously with Walker, stood in the doorway of the plane. He was frowning, and he scared Gillian a little bit with his dour expression.

Turning, she saw that Renee was no longer lying on the ground. One of Walker's teammates was pointing her toward the terminal and telling her to run.

Gillian's ears rang. "Is it over?" she whispered, feeling stupid.

"It's over," Walker confirmed.

"Three dead inside, not including the pilot," the man standing in the plane said.

"There's three more out here. Good job, everyone," someone standing behind them said, scaring the hell out of Gillian.

"Easy, Di," Walker murmured, not loosening his hold on her.

It was a good thing, as Gillian knew she would've fallen to the ground without his support.

Looking around, she pointed to Luis. "That's Luis." Then she nodded to Alberto. "And the one who had me was Alberto." Turning, she looked at the dead man behind her. "And that's Jesus."

"We need her to ID the others," the man in the plane said.

"No," Walker replied.

At the same time, Gillian said, "Okay."

"You don't have to do this," Walker told her sternly. "Someone else can figure this goat screw out."

She shook her head. "I need to know they're dead."

Walker pressed his lips together. She could tell he wasn't happy, but he didn't try to talk her out of it. "Oz, drag them to the door. She can ID them from here."

The big man on the plane nodded and ducked out of sight for a moment. Then he was back, dragging Carlos's body by the upper arm.

"Carlos," Gillian said softly.

Oz nodded and repeated the action twice more as she identified Isaac and Henry.

Gillian knew she was in shock. This couldn't be her life. Was she really standing in the middle of a runway in Venezuela identifying dead men? Men bleeding from holes in their heads?

Sirens sounded in the distance, the sound jarring and unwelcome.

Walker kept one arm around her shoulders, but turned her so she was facing him. "Are you hurt?"

"Not really. I mean, I'm alive, I can't ask for much more. What just happened?"

"The hijackers were obviously never planning on leaving via the jet."

Gillian nodded. "The fuel was a decoy." The look of admiration in Walker's eyes was gratifying. She felt raw and off-kilter, but she also felt as if she could do anything if he kept looking at her like she was something special.

"Exactly. They let the hostages go in pairs as a distrac-
n. Since no one had seen what they looked like, we

didn't know who was a hijacker and who was an innocent civilian. It was smart. But after Lefty and Brain got the hostages rerouted, it was easy to distinguish who was running for the Beechcraft and who was simply trying to get away."

Gillian nodded.

"The other three made it to their escape plane and let go of the women and children they were using as shields. Looked like Luis was trying to pull Andrea into the plane with him when you and that asshole," he kicked at Alberto at their feet, "ran into them and tripped everyone. It gave us enough time to get to them before they could get inside. Grover killed the pilot, shot him through the window, and Oz went inside and took out the others. And now...here we are."

Gillian's head spun. She was more sure than ever before that Walker and his friends were some sort of special forces operatives. Everything had seemed to happen so fast after three of the longest days of her life. They'd just acted. Thank God.

"Where did Leyton go?"

"Who?"

"Leyton. He was one of the hostages. He followed us to the plane, then he just disappeared."

"I don't know, and right now I don't care. All I care about is that they're dead and you're not," Walker said.

"I think they were going to take me with them," she whispered. "Thank you for making sure that didn't happen."

"No way in hell was I going to let them do that," Walker told her. Then he slowly pulled her into him once again.

Gillian rested her cheek on his chest. He was taller than she was, but they still fit together perfectly. She knew she needed a shower, and she had Alberto's blood in her hair and on her clothes, but she couldn't bring herself to care. All she could focus on was the man holding her.

She'd never felt for *anyone* the way she felt about Walker at this moment.

She was well aware it was because she'd almost died. She was shaking with the adrenaline still coursing through her veins. But some distant, stubborn part of her whispered that this was real. That Walker *felt* something for her, and not just because he was doing his job.

"We need to get gone," one of his friends said gently from next to them.

For a second, Gillian gripped Walker tighter, then she took a deep breath and picked her head up off his chest. He didn't immediately loosen his hold. They stared at each other for a long moment before he reluctantly—at least, she thought it was reluctantly—dropped his arms.

Gillian swayed, and Walker immediately reached out and steadied her with a hand on her biceps. She flinched, and he frowned.

"What's wrong? Are you hurt after all? Let me see."

"I'm okay," Gillian reassured him. "That's just the same place those assholes liked to grab me and haul me around. It's just bruises. They'll heal."

She thought he mumbled something about how he should've killed them slowly, but then he brought his hand up to her face. His thumb rubbed her cheek, and she watched him taking her in slowly. His gaze flicked from the top of her head to her eyes, then her cheeks, and finally her mouth.

She couldn't help but wipe her tongue over her suddenly dry lips, and she loved that his pupils seemed to dilate at seeing the movement.

"What happens now?" she asked quietly.

"The US government has chartered a flight to get you and the other Americans back home as quickly as possible. Venezuela is not a country you want to spend any more time in than necessary right now. Much of the government is corrupt and it's dangerous as hell."

"Yeah, I think I found that out the hard way," Gillian quipped.

His lips quirked up into a smile, but he quickly got serious again. "I'm sure you'll be interviewed about what happened. You should see a doctor to make sure you're all right physically, as well."

"I will," she told him. "What should I say about you and your friends?"

"What do you mean?" he asked with a frown.

"I just...I guess I assumed you'd want your role in what happened here to be downplayed."

"Why would you think that?" Walker asked.

Feeling awkward, like maybe she'd misread the entire situation, Gillian said, "You said you were stationed in Texas, which means you're in the military. And since it's just you guys, and not a whole platoon of men, I'm also guessing you're special forces of some kind? And because of the relationship between the US and Venezuela, I'm further assuming what you did today should be downplayed."

When no one said anything, Gillian looked down at her feet. "Or I'm just a girl who reads too much. Nev mind, forget I said anything."

She felt a finger under her chin and looked up into Walker's eyes. "I knew you were a smart cookie. I'm sure the people who interview you will know who we are and what our role was, so you can be honest with them. But once you're home...yeah, it would be good if you didn't talk about us with the media or anyone else."

"What about my best friends? Ann, Wendy, Clarissa, and I tell each other everything. We're more like sisters than friends. I can keep most of the details secret, but they'll know I'm lying if I don't tell them something."

"Use your best judgement," Walker said.

"I like her," one of his friends said from behind them.

"Me too," someone else chimed in.

She saw Walker shake his head in bemusement at his friends, but he didn't take his eyes from hers. He leaned forward and said softly, "You're amazing, Gillian Romano. I'm in awe of your strength."

Then he straightened and took a step away from her.

Gillian shivered, even though it wasn't close to being cold.

She heard yelling, and turned her head to see at least a dozen men headed toward them wearing camouflage uniforms. She looked back at Walker and saw a mask had fallen across his features. He was back in business mode.

"Will I see you again?" she blurted. When he didn't immediately respond, she awkwardly said, "I mean, I live in Austin, and I'm assuming you're stationed at Fort Hood because, you know...it's Army, and really big."

She couldn't interpret the look on his face, but she was relieved to see his expression change. Get softer.

"Go with the Venezuelan officials," he urged. "Be safe,

Di. You never know who might just show up on your doorstep someday."

Everything inside Gillian relaxed. He didn't come right out and say that he'd see her again, but he'd insinuated it. She'd take that.

"Thank you all," she told the men standing around her. "I mean it. Thank you."

They all nodded at her.

The last glimpse she had of Walker was him turning around and walking away with his six friends and teammates surrounding him.

CHAPTER FIVE

Three Weeks Later

"What is up with you, man?" Lucky asked impatiently. "You've been in a funk for weeks now."

It was oh-six-hundred in the morning, and Trigger and his team were doing their customary five-mile warm-up run before starting the rest of their PT exercises.

"He's been that way since Venezuela," Grover added helpfully.

"Ever since he met *her*," Lefty added not so helpfully.

"Fuck off," Trigger muttered. He loved his friends, but they were a pain in the ass.

"Why don't you just call her already?" Doc asked seriously.

"You know why," Trigger said.

"No, I don't," Doc countered.

"Because of what we are," Trigger told him.

"What? Men?"

Trigger stopped running and glared at his friends as they all stopped as well and stared at him in confusion. "We're Delta," he said simply.

"And?" Oz asked when no one else said anything.

Trigger blew out a breath in frustration. "You all know as well as I do what that means. Our lives aren't our own. We could be called away this afternoon for who knows how long. We could be killed in action and no one would ever know how or where we died. We've all dated, and it never works out. Some women just want to screw a Delta. they love the *idea* of what we are and not really who we are as people. Not to mention, a lot of chicks get fed up with all the secrecy and eventually end it. I won't do that to Gillian."

"Ghost and his team have all made it work," Brain said matter-of-factly.

Trigger tried to come up with an argument that would make sense, but he couldn't. The fact of the matter was, he was jealous as hell of Ghost, Fletch, Coach, and the others. They *had* made relationships work. They had women who loved them, who they loved in return, and many of them even had kids now. Like Annie. The firecracker who had him and anyone she came into contact with wrapped around her little finger.

He sighed. "I'm afraid she's too good for me," Trigger said softly, hating to admit the truth. "I took a second look at the information we received from the FBI, and from what I can tell, she's smart, extremely hardworking, and dedicated to her job."

"And those are bad things?" Brain asked.

"Well, no, but you all know what military life is lik It's hard. I'm afraid I'd somehow...contaminate her. S' strong as fuck and independent to boot. She's got a loving family and friends who would do anything for her. I don't want to mess that up. You all know as well as I do that getting involved with us means the possibility of moving, and that means taking her away from her support network."

"Seems to me," Lefty drawled, "that's exactly the kind of woman you *should* want. That we *all* want. We need a partner who won't crumble when we're deployed. Someone who can mow the grass and figure out how to call for a fucking plumber when the toilet overflows. It's a *good* thing that she has a support system. And even if we do get moved out of Texas, she'd make a new support network, with other Delta wives. Besides, no one's saying you have to *marry* this chick. You like her, she obviously likes you. So what's *really* bothering you?"

Trigger hesitated. He knew what he was about to say would sound crazy, but these were his best friends. Men he'd die for, and they'd do the same for him.

"I think she's it," he said, putting a hand on his stomach, which was spinning and rolling.

"She's what?" Grover asked in confusion.

"I don't know how to explain how I know, but we clicked out there. It's stupid, I realize that. Certifiable. We don't even know each other. But something inside knows she could be *it* for me. And if I get to know her better, I'm not going to want to let her go. If she dumps me, it'll kill me."

No one said anything for a long moment, then Brain smiled. Huge. "Congratulations!"

The others chimed in with their own felicitations.

"Hang on, you guys," Trigger complained. "Nothing's

happened. She's probably totally forgotten all about me by now."

"There's only one way to find out," Doc said reasonably. "Call her."

"I don't have her number," Trigger backtracked.

"I'll find it for you," Brain volunteered. "And her address too."

"Talk to her, man," Lucky urged. "What can it hurt?"

"Why are you guys pushing this so hard?" Trigger asked. He couldn't deny he was happy for their support, but was a bit confused by it.

"Because none of us are getting any younger," Lefty said reasonably. "You especially."

Trigger punched him in the arm and everyone laughed.

"But seriously, we all love the Army and what we do, but we won't be Deltas forever. There'll come a time when we'll sit up and look around and be alone. And that sucks. I want to find someone smart, independent, and sassy as fuck. Someone who will kiss me and tell me to kick some bad-guy ass when I leave, and be thrilled to see me when I get back. Someone who won't cheat on me and won't decide that she's sick of waiting for me to come home.

"I want her to understand what I do is important to me. In return, I'll treat her like a queen. She'll be the center of my world, and I'll make sure she knows it. Relationships are hard as fuck, even more so for us. So if you feel as if this woman is the one who can be all that for you, I'll do whatever I can to make that happen for you. And I'll fucking kill anyone who tries to come between you and your woman."

Trigger wasn't sure what to say. He was deeply touched.

"What Lefty said," Grover quipped.

Everyone laughed again.

"I'll think about it," Trigger said.

Brain rolled his eyes. "I'll have her info to you this afternoon."

Trigger nodded, then took off running. He turned around and said, "You guys comin' or are you gonna let this old man kick your ass?"

That was all it took for the rest of the guys to dig in their heels and chase after him.

* * *

Later that afternoon, Trigger was sitting in his office when a knock sounded at the door. Looking up, he saw it was Brain.

"You know, you didn't *really* have to rush and get Gillian's info to me," he joked.

But Brain didn't crack a smile. "We need to talk," he said instead.

Trigger immediately stiffened. He nodded to a chair in front of his desk.

Brain sat, and he didn't make him wait. "You know how Gillian didn't turn off the phone connection that last time in the hopes that we'd be able to get something from the hijackers when they talked to each other?"

"Yeah," Trigger said.

"We got something."

Trigger leaned forward. "What?"

"As we realized there at the end, they had no intention of flying that big-ass plane out of there. They had a cartel ot picking them up in the Beechcraft to take them back o Mexico."

"Mexico?" Trigger asked in surprise.

"Yeah. They were with Sinaloa."

"Fuck," Trigger said, sitting back in his chair with a thump.

"They didn't want Hugo Lamas freed so he could escape with them. They wanted him killed to send a message to the Cartel of the Suns. Essentially, they started a war."

"And like any drug cartel, they didn't care who got caught in the crossfire," Trigger said in disgust. "The people they killed on the plane didn't mean shit to them. All they cared about was sticking it to the Venezuelans. Letting them know they got one over on them right on their own turf."

"Exactly. But there's more," Brain added.

"What?"

"There was talk of a seventh hijacker."

"What are you saying? That we missed a hijacker and he got away?" Trigger asked.

"Yeah, that's exactly what I'm saying. On the tapes, they were arguing about the Beechcraft. Luis was saying they were good because it could hold up to twelve people —and there was seven of them with the pilot, plus two more with the women he and Alberto were taking, leaving room for their 'amigo' and two more, if someone else wanted to bring along a 'plaything.'"

Trigger wanted to kill Luis and the other hijackers all over again. Alberto had planned to take Gillian with him. The thought of what would've happened to her if he'd gotten her deep into the Sinaloa Cartel territory was too disturbing to dwell on.

Brain went on. "But then another said something

about how it would be better for their 'amigo' to go with the rest of the hostages, to find out as much information as possible. To find out what the government and the Cartel of the Suns knew about the op. As far as I can tell before the call was abruptly cut off, they were still arguing about that. Half of those assholes wanted to let the mole stay hidden and camouflaged with the other civilians, and the other half wanted to extract him with them."

"So the CIA needs to look into the backgrounds of all the hostages who were on the plane. See who has connections to Sinaloa and Mexico," Trigger said.

"Not that easy," Brain said with a shrug. "Even if we *did* narrow it down, everyone's in the wind. They all went back to their countries and lives. Hell, our target could've used a fake name. But I think we've got bigger problems."

"Bigger?" Trigger asked.

"Whoever was in cahoots with the hijackers knows everything that went down on that plane. *Everything*. They're likely aware of how their friends were killed...and how Gillian was a big factor in giving us time to get to them and take out Luis, Alberto, the pilot, and the others. He or she might not be too happy that Gillian escaped... might even realize that she was giving us intel."

"But why single her out? There's no reason for it," Trigger asked. "There were a lot of other passengers on that plane who interacted with the hijackers."

"I talked to one of the agents who interviewed the hostages. Several said they saw Gillian struggling with Alberto, and saw them go down and trip Luis and Andrea. They also saw you and her hugging. It was the talk of the group. How impressed they were with Gillian and how brave they thought she was...but also how intimate the two of you seemed to be. As if maybe you knew each other before the hijacking, and *Gillian* was the reason the team was sent in. If I was an insider, I'd be pretty pissed off at her right about now. Especially after hearing all my fellow passengers praise her so highly."

Trigger stood so quickly, his chair fell to the floor behind him. "Address?"

Brain didn't quite smile, but his lips twitched as he pulled a piece of paper out of his pocket. "She lives on the north end of Georgetown. Shouldn't take you too long to get there."

"This isn't funny," Trigger said with a scowl.

Brain stood up. "Never said it was. No matter what hang-ups you might have about what you do and who you are, she needs to know that she could be in danger."

"I know."

"The Sinaloa Cartel doesn't fuck around. If they want her dead, it'll take a miracle to make sure that doesn't happen," Brain said solemnly.

Trigger ground his teeth. He turned to leave, but he had one more question. He looked back at his friend. "Did they really hijack an international flight just to kill some border agent who was working with a rival drug cartel?"

Brain sighed and shook his head. "Doubtful. As far as the DEA can tell, it was a distraction from their main goal. Smuggling eight hundred kilos of cocaine and meth out of Venezuela. Sinaloa stole it from the Cartel of the Suns. While the world's attention, and that of the leaders of Venezuela, were on the airport, they loaded up a ship with the drugs and sailed away without so much as a second glance from the authorities."

Trigger could only shake his head. All those deaths

because of drugs. Well, more accurately, because of money. He'd never understand it. "Thanks for the heads up," he told Brain.

His friend brushed off his thanks. "Your best bet is to move her up here to Killeen so we can keep an eye on her."

Trigger snorted. "You really think that's gonna happen? You *did* hear me say that she's independent and smart, right?"

Brain smiled fully for the first time. "Yup. You'll just have to convince her. Show her some...leg...or something."

Trigger rolled his eyes and turned to walk out of his office. He knew there wasn't a chance in hell of convincing Gillian to move in with him, even for her own safety. But he couldn't deny the thought of having her in his space was pretty fucking appealing.

* * *

Gillian stood in front of her bathroom mirror and stared at her reflection. She looked damn good, if she did say so herself. She was going out with Ann, Wendy, and Clarissa tonight and had dressed for the occasion. She had on a pair of tight jeans that hugged her ass and thighs, high-heel sandals with sparkly crystals, which made them look fancier than they really were. She also picked her favorite black wrap shirt, which hugged her boobs and gave her a ton of cleavage.

She'd used a heavier hand with her makeup than usual and put on her favorite necklace, a two carat—fake—diamond, which rested right in the middle of her chest, bringing attention to the aforementioned cleavage.

Her hair fell in curls around her face, and even though Gillian knew they'd probably come out by the end of the night, at least she'd start out the evening looking good.

Sighing, she leaned on her hands on the counter and bowed her head. Now, if only she *felt* as good as she looked.

Three weeks. It had been three weeks since her ordeal in Venezuela, and in some ways it still seemed like yesterday. Her parents had insisted on flying in to make sure she was all right, and the week they'd stayed had done her a lot of good. She wasn't used to being the center of attention, and talking to the press made her extremely nervous, but her mom had reassured her that the information she'd shared with the reporters was concise and clear without going into too much detail, which was a huge relief. She'd been embarrassed by the way a few of the other passengers had gushed over what a good job she'd done under pressure, but again, her parents being there was a good distraction from everything.

But, ultimately, even the affection and pampering her mom and dad had showered on her couldn't take away all the bad memories of what had happened.

She was still sleeping with the lights on in her apartment and she started at every little sound. She'd fallen back into her old routine, more or less, which was good... but a tiny part of her died inside when she didn't hear from *him*. She'd expected him to be busy right when she'd gotten back home, but with every day that passed without a phone call or even an email, she'd begun to think the connection she'd felt was one-sided.

She'd been so sure they'd connected on a level she'd

never felt with anyone else. He said he'd be in touch... hadn't he? She doubted the possibility more and more.

Intellectually, she knew it was unlikely she'd hear from Walker Nelson again. He'd just been doing his job. If he was special forces, he did that kind of thing all the time. Probably rescued hundreds of people. He was probably, even now, on another mission, rescuing someone else. Why would he want to get back in touch with *her*? Just because she'd felt a connection with him didn't mean he felt the same.

She was being stupid.

Gillian knew she was a romantic, and that was why she hoped every day when she got up in the morning that today would be the day. Walker would somehow find her number and call or text her, saying he wanted to see her again. Or he'd be waiting for her outside her apartment complex, leaning casually against the wall, and he'd tilt his chin up in greeting when he saw her.

Huffing out a breath, Gillian stood straight and smoothed her shirt. No, it was obvious that wasn't going to happen. He'd moved on, and she needed to as well.

Her phone dinged with a text, and she grabbed it from the counter and saw she had a few messages she'd missed while she was showering and getting ready.

The first was from Janet. She'd kept in touch after the hijacking, and Gillian loved hearing updates about her daughter Renee. At first the young girl had been traumatized, but after seeing a therapist, Janet reported that she was starting to be more like the girl she'd been before their ordeal. She'd attached a picture of Renee to the text. She was hanging upside down from a set of monkey bars. The smile on her face made Gillian grin. The text accompanying the picture said, *Because of you, I've got my girl back.*

She was uncomfortable with the praise. When all the hostages had been corralled together in a room in the airport in Caracas, waiting to be interviewed individually, they'd talked about everything that had happened. And when the CIA and FBI had arrived to interview them, they'd somehow given the passengers the impression—or maybe it was the hostages who'd given the *Feds* the impression—that Gillian had been their leader, of sorts.

That it was because of *her* that so many people had survived the ordeal.

Shaking her head, Gillian read the next text. It was from Andrea. She lived in Austin as well, but she wasn't ready to meet back up in person yet. Gillian knew she was struggling because of the sexual abuse she'd endured at Luis's hands, and how traumatized she'd been when Luis had tried to force her to go with him.

Earlier, Gillian had sent her a short text letting Andrea know she was thinking about her. Andrea had replied with, *Thanks. I'm doing better and I'll be in touch soon. I really do want to be strong enough to give you a hug in person.*

There was one more text, from Alice, the young woman who'd originally sat next to Gillian on the flight from Costa Rica. She and her husband had both survived and were putting their lives back together in Washington state. They didn't correspond often, but Gillian was glad to hear from her, even if it was only Alice saying that they'd moved into a new apartment complex, one with twenty-four/seven security.

As she was reading her texts, Gillian's phone vibrated with another incoming message. This time from Wendy.

. . .

Wendy: Have you left yet? Quit overthinking shit and get your ass to the bar. We've got your first margarita waiting for you!

Smiling, Gillian shot back a quick note letting her friend know she was on her way, then she turned her back on her reflection and headed out of the bathroom. She grabbed her crossbody purse from her unmade bed and put the strap over her head.

She was walking into her living area when there was a knock on her door.

Stopping in her tracks, Gillian made a conscious effort to slow her heart rate. She didn't often get people at her door uninvited, but it happened. There was a buzzer that people were supposed to use to get into the building, but sometimes they slipped behind another resident.

Cautiously, and as quietly as possible, Gillian tiptoed to her door and peered through the peephole.

Shocked beyond belief at the person she saw standing there, Gillian fumbled with the locks as she tried to turn them. Her hands were shaking, and she couldn't get the door open fast enough.

"Hi," she said when she was finally face-to-face with the man she thought she'd never see again.

"Hi," Walker Nelson returned.

Gillian inwardly sighed. If she thought he looked good dressed in his black commando gear with black paint smeared on his face, it was nothing compared to the vision that was standing on her doorstep right that second.

He was wearing a royal-blue short-sleeve shirt, which

only emphasized his muscular biceps. His forearms were thick as well, and Gillian had to force herself not to swoon right then and there. She'd always been an arm girl, and Walker's certainly didn't disappoint. He had on a pair of faded blue jeans that hugged his thighs. She tried not to stare at his groin too long, but noticed he filled out that part of his jeans just fine. Finally, he wore a pair of black combat boots that should've looked out of place here in Texas, but somehow seemed to fit him to a tee.

He had a five o'clock shadow that outlined his jaw, chin, and cheekbones. Gillian's fingers twitched with the need to touch it, to see if it was prickly or soft. His gray eyes had flecks of brown in them—and they were looking at her as if she were the only person in the world right that second. She wasn't ever the recipient of that kind of attention from men, and to have *this* man staring at her so intently she thought she would combust was a heady feeling.

They'd been staring at each other so long, Gillian suddenly felt embarrassed. "Um, come in," she said, stepping back and gesturing to her apartment with her hand.

"Thanks," Walker said, crowding her for just a second before passing her in the small foyer.

Telling herself to get a grip, Gillian tried to slow her heartbeat. She was giddy with excitement that Walker was actually here. That he'd tracked her down after all. Excuses to get out of her plans with her friends ran through her mind as she followed Walker deeper into her apartment. She tried to keep her eyes off his ass...without much luck. He filled out the back of his jeans just as well as he did the front.

She inhaled deeply to try to get control over hersel

and not jump on him, and his woodsy scent filled her nostrils. She didn't remember anything about what he smelled like when she'd last seen him, but that was probably because *she'd* smelled like a fish head that had been sitting out in the sun rotting for a week or more. At the time, she couldn't smell anything other than her own fear and sweat.

He stopped in front of the bar that separated her kitchen from the rest of the apartment and turned to face her. "You look great. Did I interrupt anything?"

Gillian was suddenly very glad she'd planned to go out with her friends that night. Otherwise she would've been wearing her fat pants—large, flowy cotton pants with an elastic waist—and no bra. Her hair would've been thrown up into a messy bun and she would've been mortified. At least now she looked her best.

"Thanks. And I was just heading out to a bar called The Funky Walrus to hang with my friends."

Walker smiled, and Gillian had to lock her knees at the sight. Frowning and serious, he was good-looking. Smiling? He was lethal.

"The Funky Walrus?" Walker asked.

Gillian chuckled. "I know, the name is weird, but then again, a lot of Austin is weird, so it fits. It's not a college bar, and most of the patrons are businessmen and women in their thirties and forties. It's low-key and laid-back, and we try to get together at least once every few weeks to catch up."

Walker nodded, and the ensuing silence between them stretched.

Gillian fidgeted. This was weird...and not at all how she'd imagined this meeting would go. She'd fantasized that she'd be witty and amusing, and Walker would tell her how he'd been thinking about her and he had to come see her.

Taking a deep breath, Gillian decided to make the first move. It seemed unlikely, but maybe Walker was nervous.

"I'm glad to see you."

"We need to talk."

They'd spoken at the same time, and Gillian flushed. Walker didn't sound happy about needing to talk to her, and he certainly didn't sound as if he were flirting, as she was trying to do with him. "Um...okay," she stammered.

He ran a hand over his head and sighed, and Gillian steeled herself for whatever he was about to say.

"I stopped by because we've gotten intel that there was a seventh hijacker on the plane. Using the audio that you managed to record—that last time we talked, and you kept the phone line open when you handed the phone back—it was determined that a hijacker was posing as a passenger. Luis and another hijacker discussed him, but didn't give us any clues as to who he might be."

Gillian blinked—and she felt her heart drop into her stomach.

The only thing she could process was that Walker *hadn't* come to ask her out, or to get to know her better. She'd been dreaming about him for three weeks, hoping against hope that the spark she'd felt between them hadn't been one-sided. With his first sentence, he'd effectively crushed any hope that there might be more between them.

"Oh..." It was all she could say. Her throat was tight and it was hard to swallow.

"I wanted to warn you, let you know that you could be in danger. There's no telling what this seventh person is thinking. We don't know if he might want revenge for his friends dying, or if he might think you heard too much while you were onboard, or might be able to identify him."

Gillian barely heard him. The disappointment and embarrassment she felt was overwhelming. She knew she should be more concerned that there was another hijacker out there, but her disappointment over the reason for Walker's visit had totally overshadowed everything else.

Her shoulders slumped forward unconsciously. "Well… thanks for letting me know," she said awkwardly.

Walker frowned. "Are you okay?"

"Great. Fine. Yeah, I'm good," she said a little too brightly, doing her best to pretend Walker hadn't shattered her fantasy about the two of them getting together. "I appreciate you telling me. I'll be on the lookout."

"I thought we might talk. Go over your memories of the passengers and see if we can't narrow down who the sleeper might be."

Spend more time with him? When all he wanted was information? No, thank you. Maybe later—like a year or two—she'd be able to sit across from him and have a perfectly professional conversation about that time she'd been hijacked and forced to act as a go-between for the hijackers and the negotiators. But today wasn't that day.

She nodded quickly, having a feeling she looked like a spastic rag doll. "Sure. Yeah, fine. But I can't right now. I'm leaving. I have a date…with my friends. My girlfriends."

Walker frowned. "I'm not sure that's the best idea right now. Not when we don't know who the seventh hijacker is or where he might be."

Gillian snorted. "He's not going to care about me. I'm nobody and totally harmless. Besides, I always lock my doors and strangers off the street can't just walk into the building. They have to be buzzed in by a resident. I'll be fine."

"*I* walked in off the street," Walker said flatly.

Gillian was desperate to get rid of him. She wanted to cry. Was *on* the verge of crying. And she'd rather walk over a bed of nails than let Walker see how upset she was. "I'll be careful," she told him firmly. "It was good to see you, but I really need to go now." She turned and walked toward her front door. She opened it and was about to leave when Walker spoke up behind her.

"Um, Gillian?"

She turned. "Yeah?"

"You're going to leave me in your apartment?"

Shit, shit, shit. She tried to play off her blunder. Shaking her head, she said, "No, I was holding the door for you."

He grinned as if he knew she was lying, but he walked toward her without a word. He stopped when he was right in front of her. Gillian didn't dare look up at him. She had a feeling he'd be able to see right through her bravado.

"Gillian?"

"Yeah?" she asked, staring at his Adam's apple as if it was the most fascinating thing she'd ever seen.

"Look at me."

Internally steeling herself, Gillian lifted her chin and let her gaze meet his.

"What's wrong?"

"Nothing," she said quickly—too quickly. "I'm just on my way out and you took me by surprise."

"Are you sure we can't go back inside and talk? I'm not comfortable leaving you like this."

For just a second, Gillian got mad. *He* wasn't comfortable? Of course it was all about him. She was just a stupid, romantic girl who'd foolishly thought they'd connected over an intense situation.

Most of the time she had high self-esteem. She was thirty and owned her own very successful business. She had great friends and people seemed to like her. She had a gift in that she could defuse almost any situation, which came in handy since she had to deal with stressful situations on a daily basis with her job.

But the one thing that eluded her was love. The kind that made a man put her first no matter what else was going on in his life. She was more than willing to reciprocate, and had put her all into each and every serious relationship she'd been in. But when push came to shove, the men she'd thought she loved had proven that she came second.

Taking a deep breath, and trying to ignore how good Walker smelled, she knew she was being irrational. But his words hurt all the same. She shook her head. "I'll be fine. I always am," she said, her voice filled with sadness she couldn't hide. Then she shrugged and slipped away from him into the hall. "Can you get the door?" she asked as evenly as possible.

Walker continued to frown, but he grabbed the knob and pulled the door shut. Gillian made quick work of securing the locks and gripped her keys tightly. "Well, thanks for coming by," she said, not able to be rude, no matter how devastated she felt inside. "Say hello and thanks again to your, um...team for me. I'm running late and really need to get going, or my friends are going to wonder where I am."

"I'll walk you to your car," Walker said firmly.

Pressing her lips together, she nodded. She counted each step as they took the stairs down one flight to the first floor. The silence between them was awkward, or maybe it was just Gillian who felt that way.

Mourning the loss of something she'd never had in the first place, she headed for her RAV4. Clicking the locks, she opened the door and turned to Walker once more. She wanted to ask him what was wrong with her. How it was possible she felt so connected to him when he felt nothing in return. But she merely forced her lips into a smile and said, "Be safe, Walker. It was good to see you."

"You too," he returned, his brow pulled down as if he was trying to figure something out. "I really think—"

"Bye!" Gillian interrupted, needing this to be over. She slipped into the driver's seat and shut the door. Blinking as fast as she could to keep the tears from spilling over, she forced a smile in the general direction where Walker had been standing, put the car in reverse, and backed out of the parking spot. It was a good thing she'd been to The Funky Walrus plenty of times and had the route memorized.

Gillian refused to look in her rearview mirror at the man who, without realizing it, had just broken her heart.

Trigger stared at the taillights of Gillian's SUV as she drove out of the parking lot.

"That didn't go as I imagined it would," he muttered to himself.

He wasn't sure what he'd expected when he'd driven to Georgetown to see Gillian. At first she'd seemed please⟨

to see him. And Trigger would never forget how his heart had skipped a beat when she'd opened the door.

She was absolutely fucking gorgeous. Not too tall, but not short either. Curvy in all the right places. His eyes had immediately been drawn to her tits. God, they were perfect. He'd wanted to bury his face between the fleshy globes and spend hours worshiping them, but he'd forced himself to be a gentleman and not stare too long.

Her jeans clung to her curves, and it took everything he had not to pop a woody right there in her doorway. She would've slammed the door in his face if she'd looked down and saw his dick pressing against his jeans like that of a prepubescent teenager.

She'd done something with her makeup that made her green eyes stand out, and in her heels, they were almost eye-to-eye. When she'd invited him in, and he'd walked past her, he'd smelled honeysuckle. He had no idea if it was her perfume or shampoo or what, but it made it hard as hell not to grab her and pull her into him and kiss her.

By the time he'd reached her small kitchen area, he'd gotten himself mostly under control, though the smile she'd bestowed on him had left his fingers tingling. He had no idea what he'd even said to her when he'd first entered.

He was more relieved than he cared to admit that she was going out with her friends, and not on a date. He'd been afraid he'd waited too long. Had lost his chance. Not that her going on a date would've kept him from pursuing her. He hadn't been sure about seeing her again, but once he had, he'd been determined to let her know *he* wanted to be the one to take her out. To take her to dinner. To watch her laugh at a funny movie. To hold her hand as they casu-ally strolled down the riverfront in Austin.

He'd wanted to get the business side of why he was there out of the way first, then he could let her know how he hadn't been able to stop thinking about her. How proud he was of her and how she'd handled herself in Venezuela. He wanted to tell her that he'd never felt a connection with a woman like he had with her, and even though it was crazy, he'd wanted to see if she felt the same.

But something had happened. Right after he'd told her about the seventh hijacker, she'd seemed to shut down. He'd seen the light fade from her eyes, and while he knew what he'd said was shocking, her reaction didn't seem to jive with what he knew about her.

Had she been terrified about the possibility of a hidden hijacker? Had merely talking about the incident sent her into a mental downward spiral? He had no clue.

She was polite but distant. The sparks that had been flying between them were suddenly doused, and he wasn't sure why. Then it was more than obvious she'd tried to rush him out of her apartment, that she'd wanted to get away from him.

Trigger hated that. *Hated* it.

Hell, in her hurry to escape, she'd nearly locked him *in* her apartment.

While it was good her apartment complex had rudi-mentary security, it wasn't going to keep a terrorist out. Trigger only had to wait three minutes for a resident to appear. He'd simply smiled at the man, and the guy hadn't even thought twice about letting him slip in behind him.

No, Gillian definitely wasn't safe here if the hijacker decided for some reason to target her.

But she'd made no secret of the fact that she wasn't all that fired up to see him again.

Sighing in frustration, Trigger wasn't sure what to do. He didn't want to go back to his place in Killeen. He'd spent the last three weeks thinking about nothing but Gillian, and leaving now felt too...final. If he left, he had a feeling he'd never see her again, which wasn't acceptable.

Taking a deep breath, Trigger argued with himself about his next course of action. Follow Gillian and make her tell him what he'd said that had turned her warm welcome cold?

Retreat and try again when he had more information about the hijacker? It would give him a reason to come back and see her.

Wait and make sure she got home all right?

Sighing again, Trigger headed for his car. He didn't know what to do, and for the moment he needed to think. He'd sit in his vehicle and try to work through how the evening had gone from one full of anticipation and excitement to getting the cold shoulder.

Trigger admired Gillian. He hadn't found out one thing about her that turned him off...which was highly unusual.

He liked being alone. Liked not having any responsibilities. But something about Gillian made him *want* to be tied down. *Want* to look after her. *Want* to have someone to worry about other than himself.

It was confusing as hell...and Trigger needed to come to terms with his feelings before he made a decision about what his next step would be.

CHAPTER SIX

"Let me get this straight," Wendy said. "He only came to see you because he wanted to tell you about this other hijacker?"

Gillian nodded miserably and took another large sip of her margarita. It was amazing how smoothly they went down when she felt like shit. She was on her third one and was definitely feeling the effects of the alcohol. She wasn't a heavy drinker, but she'd had the biggest disappointment of her life earlier and needed to drown her sorrows. "Yup. He said I looked great, and at first he couldn't keep his eyes off my boobs. But it became obvious real quick that he was only there because of business."

Gazing up at her friends, who were looking at her with sympathy, she blurted a little too loudly, "I mean, my boobs *are* on point tonight. My hair actually did what I wanted for once and I squeezed my ass into these jeans. And he didn't even *blink*."

"You said he was eyeballing your boobs," Ann said sympathetically.

"He was!" Gillian exclaimed. "But obviously he wasn't fazed." Her emotions had been swinging from indignation to sorrow all night, and suddenly she was exhausted. Putting her head on her forearm on the table, she said softly, "I thought he was the one."

"Oh, Gilly," Clarissa said sympathetically.

That was all it took for the tears Gillian had held at bay all night to spill over. She lifted her head and impatiently wiped them away. She looked at her best friends. "I love you guys. Clarissa, your husband is amazing. I remember that time you were sick when you were dating, and he took two days off work to be with you. When you didn't make it to the bathroom and puked everywhere, he cleaned it up without even making any kind of gagging sounds."

Clarissa chuckled. "I'm not sure that's the best example of how great Johnathan is."

"It *is*," Gillian insisted. "And *you*, Ann. You're my age and you already have two kids! The two most beautifulist and smart kids on the planet. They're polite and kind and that's because of you and Tom, and how you've raised them."

"They're pains in the asses sometimes, Gillian. They're not always polite and kind."

Gillian ignored her. "And Wendy..." Her eyes filled with tears again, and she closed them to try to control herself. "You and Wyatt are perfect together. Every time he looks at you it's obvious you mean the world to him. Remember that time we were all at that festival in downtown Austin, and that guy started heckling us? We were ignoring him but he wouldn't shut up. Wyatt went right over and told him if he didn't shut the hell up, he was going to find his nuts shoved so far up inside his abdomen it would take a crowbar to find them again. That was so romantic!" The last word came out as a wail, but Gillian couldn't help it.

"Gilly, that guy would've pounded Wyatt. He was half a foot taller and way stronger. Wyatt was being an idiot; it wasn't romantic. We're lucky the other guy thought it was funny and wasn't offended," Wendy reminded her.

Gillian shook her head. "But he did it anyway. Because he loves you," she said softly. "You don't get it. He'd do anything for you. *Anything*."

"I think she's had enough margaritas," Clarissa said dryly, trying to pry the glass out of Gillian's hand.

"No! I know exactly what I'm saying," Gillian protested, keeping hold of her glass. "I'm not you, so I don't know what you felt when you saw your men for the first time, but you've all told me something deep inside felt...*right*. The first time I heard Walker's voice, I knew."

"Knew what, Gilly?" Ann asked.

"That he was mine," she said simply.

Shaking her head at the skepticism she saw on her friends' faces, Gillian tried to explain. "I know it sounds insane. Crazy. Stupid. But I can't deny it. I thought we clicked," she said sadly. "I thought he felt it too. He gave me a nickname. He even told me he would show up on my doorstep."

"He didn't say that exactly, though," Wendy said.

Gillian waved her hand in the air. "Just about. It was more about the underlying meaning of his words. Every day since then, I hoped today would be the day. I hoped he'd show up and tell me that he missed me so much and couldn't stay away anymore. And then there he was! Beautiful. And he smelled sooooo good. But he wasn't there fc me. Wasn't there to tell me he couldn't live without me. He only came by because he felt *obligated*."

"You deserve the world," Clarissa said softly. "You deserve a man who will move mountains to be by your side. You're successful, and pretty, and so damn smart."

"If I'm that pretty, smart, and irresistible, then why am I sitting here alone and lonely?" Gillian said sadly.

She hated bringing the group down. Hated that her bad mood had ruined the night for everyone. Taking a deep breath, she took a long swallow of her drink before wiping the last of the tears from her cheeks. "You know what? Fuck him. It doesn't matter. He's probably an asshole anyway. Sure, he's probably really good in bed and we might've had amazing chemistry between the sheets, but he probably has no idea how to be a good boyfriend."

"Gillian—" Ann said, but Gillian spoke over her.

"Like, he'd probably insist we split the bill when we went out to eat, and would make me walk on the outside of the sidewalk so I'd get run over by a car first."

"Gillian, you should—"

It was Wendy who tried to interrupt that time, but Gillian was on a roll. "And he probably has a small dick anyway. That bulge I saw in his pants was probably a sock or something. And it wouldn't surprise me if he wanted blowjobs but refused to recip...resurp...suck on me in return."

"Gillian!" Clarissa hissed sharply.

"*What?*" Gillian asked.

"Was your Walker wearing a blue shirt, jeans, and combat boots when you saw him earlier tonight?"

Gillian's eyes widened. "How did you know? Except his shirt wasn't blue exactly. It was dark blue, kind of a royal blue, and it kinda shone in the light. I don't know what kind of material it was made out of, but it looked silky. I wish I could've touched him..."

"He's standing behind you," Clarissa said with a small grin.

Gillian rolled her eyes. "No, he's not. He's on his way back to his Army fort. He fulfilled his duty by telling me about the hijacker and now he's gone."

Clarissa and Ann both sat back on their side of the booth and smiled. Wendy turned at the waist and looked behind her. "Holy shit," she said softly. "If I wasn't dating Wyatt, you might have a fight on your hands, Gilly."

Gillian froze. She glanced over at Wendy on her left, who was still staring behind them. "Tell me you're kidding," she stage whispered.

"Nope," Wendy said with a grin.

"How long has he been standing there?" she asked Clarissa, thinking she was being quiet during her rant, when in fact, the tables closest to them could probably easily hear her thoughts.

"You're sitting there single and beautiful because you hadn't met *me* yet," a voice Gillian had dreamed about for weeks said from behind her. "When we go out, you'll never pay, and no way in hell will you walk next to the street—or sleep on the side of the bed by the door, for that matter. And just for the record, I don't have a sock in my pants, and I can pretty much guarantee that after I get a taste, one of my favorite things will be going down on you as often as you'll let me."

"Holy shit," Ann said, fanning herself with her hand.

Clarissa merely blushed, but her huge smile said she approved.

And Wendy could only stare with her mouth open.

If she hadn't been drunk, Gillian probably wouldn't have done what she did, but because she was feeling no pain and her inhibitions were down, she turned around and glared at Walker. "What are you doing here?" she blurted defensively. "Are you stalking me?"

He chuckled. "Seeing you again didn't go as I'd imagined it would in my head. I said something wrong and didn't know what. I thought maybe I could try again."

Gillian blinked.

"You came to see her only because of a seventh hijacker," Ann said helpfully.

"She thought you wanted to see *her*, but instead you were there for work," Clarissa added.

"Not cool," Wendy scolded.

"That's what you thought?" Walker asked, gaze locked on Gillian.

She couldn't look away from him, lost in the emotion she saw in his eyes, and nodded.

"I really did fuck up," he muttered. Then he came around the booth and squatted next to where Gillian was sitting. He put a hand on her leg, and she swore she could feel tingles shoot down her thigh. "I didn't come to see you tonight out of obligation, Di. The FBI could've sent someone to inform you about the seventh hijacker. I used it as an excuse to see you again. And I didn't call you before now because I wasn't sure you'd want to be reminded about what you went through. I thought maybe I'd be a bad memory for you."

"You were the *best* memory about that whole situation," Gillian blurted.

"Can we start again?" he asked, not looking away from her eyes for a second.

Gillian wanted to say yes. Wanted to jump at the chance. But she'd had just enough alcohol to be completely honest. She shook her head sadly. "I can't."

"Why not?" he asked.

"Yeah, why not?" Clarissa echoed. "Gilly, you were just sitting here telling us that you had a feeling he was—"

"I know what I told you," she said quickly, cutting Clarissa off then looking back at Walker. "I just...if I hurt *this bad* after a misunderstanding, and I don't even know you, if we start dating and you decide you're tired of me, or I'm too annoying, or too type A, too romantic and needy...it'll kill me." The last three words were whispered.

"I've thought about nothing but you for the last three weeks," Walker told her without hesitation. "I've wondered what you were doing and how you were dealing with what happened. Until I knew for sure you and the others had left Venezuela, I worried that you might get stuck there somehow. You can ask any of my friends; I've been distracted and a huge pain in their asses. And when I heard that you might be in danger, my first thought was getting to you and making sure you were safe. *I'm* the one who has to worry that you'll get sick of dating a soldier like me. You'll get tired of the not knowing where I am or when I'll be home. Believe me, Di, I know who the lucky one is here, and it's not you. It's me. It's definitely me."

Wendy nudged her shoulder when she didn't say anything.

Gillian looked at her friend, then back to Walker. He hadn't moved. Was still crouched next to her. His eyes hadn't left her face. He was wholly concentrated on her. It felt weird...and good.

"I'm drunk," she informed him.

His lips quirked upward. "I can see."

"I'll worry about you when you're gone, but I'm not going to sit at home and boo-hoo all day and night until you get back. I have a business to run. I have friends."

"Good," he said calmly.

"I haven't had a guy go down on me, so I actually don't know if I'll like it or not."

His smile got bigger. "You'll like it."

Gillian rolled her eyes and looked at Ann and Clarissa. "He's arrogant."

Clarissa shrugged. "Gotta love confidence in a guy."

"You always said you wanted an alpha man," Ann added.

Gillian looked back down at Walker. "Don't hurt me," she pleaded.

"I won't."

The two words were said with such confidence, Gillian couldn't help but believe him. "Okay."

Walker immediately stood and held out his hand. "Come on. I'll take you home."

"But I'm out with my girls."

"Go," Wendy said, pushing at Gillian's shoulder. "I think we can survive the rest of the night without you. Besides, after all this hot talk, I think I'm gonna get home and call Wyatt...see if he wants to come over."

"I'll make sure she gets home all right," Walker told her friends, and Gillian couldn't help but shiver at his tone. It was commanding and warm at the same time...and made her think about what they might do together when they got back to her apartment.

"Oh, but my car is here," she said with a shake of her head.

"You're not driving," Walker growled.

Gillian rolled her eyes again. "Of course I'm not. I'd never drink and drive. That would be the stupidest thing ever. I was gonna take an Uber."

"You're not taking an Uber either," Walker said.

"Why not?"

"One, because I'm here, and I'm taking you home. Two, because it's not safe to go on the internet and arrange to meet with a stranger in their car. Haven't you seen all the crime shows? Once you're in a car with someone who wants to do you harm, the likelihood that you'll end up dead in a cornfield somewhere is ninety percent or more."

Gillian narrowed her eyes at him. "Are you making that up?" Then, not giving him time to answer, she turned to her friends. "Is he making that up?"

"I have no idea," Ann said. "But now I'm going to think twice about getting into an Uber again. I'm not sure there are any cornfields around here, but the next time I see one, the only thing I'm going to be able to think about is whether there are any poor women in there who'd just wanted a ride."

"Good," Walker said. "Are you ladies all right to drive? I can call you a cab, or take you home if you prefer."

Clarissa smiled huge. "We're good. We all had our customary one margarita," she looked at her watch, "two hours ago. And we all ate. It's only Gillian here who decided she needed to get shit-faced and wasn't hungry."

Gillian saw the look of regret cross Walker's face, and she couldn't deny it sent shivers through her.

"Come on, Di. Let's get you home."

"What about my car?"

"We'll figure it out."

We'll. She liked that. A lot.

She stood up from the booth and would've face planted if Walker hadn't been there and put an arm around her waist.

"Walker?" Clarissa said when they were about to leave.

"Yeah?"

"Don't fuck with her. We might be women, and you might be some sort of super-soldier who can kick hijacker ass, but we'll find a way to make your life a living hell if you do anything to hurt Gilly."

Gillian was embarrassed, but when she looked up at Walker, strangely, he was smiling.

"Got it," he said. "And for the record, I'm not going to hurt her. I'm glad she's got friends like you three to have her back."

"Just don't forget it," Ann warned.

He nodded at them then looked down at Gillian. "Ready?"

Wrapping her arm around his waist, and not surprised when she didn't feel an ounce of fat under her hand, Gillian nodded. She stumbled alongside Walker as he led her out of the restaurant and into the parking lot. He helped her into his Chevy Blazer and even reached across her to snap her seat belt into place. But instead of backing up and shutting her door, he stayed in her personal space.

"What's wrong?" she asked nervously.

"Nothing," he said. "I'm just memorizing this moment."

Gillian frowned. "What moment?"

"This one." Then he lifted his hand to the side of her neck, turning her head toward him. He leaned forward, giving her time to reject his advance.

But there was no way in hell Gillian was going to reject anything this man wanted to give her. She leaned toward him, reaching out and grabbing hold of his bicep with her right hand.

Walker's lips brushed against hers gently. Once. Twice. Teasing little touches that made Gillian's toes curl. His tongue came out and licked her bottom lip, before he pressed his lips against hers once more.

As far as kisses went, it was chaste and way too short... but it was the most romantic thing anyone had ever done for her.

Walker rested his forehead against hers, and she could feel his warm breaths against her skin.

"Thank you," he said softly.

"For what?"

"For giving me a second chance," he said simply. Then he brushed his thumb against her cheek once and pulled back. He shut her door and walked around the front of the vehicle. He climbed in on the driver's side and started the engine. Putting one arm on the seat back, he twisted to look behind him before backing out of the parking space and heading out onto the road.

"That kiss was amazing," Gillian told him, her filter obliterated by the amount of alcohol she'd consumed.

"Agreed," Walker said with a smile.

"But I want more."

"Yeah?"

"Yeah."

"I'm happy to give you exactly what you want...when you're not three sheets to the wind."

Gillian frowned. "I know what I'm doing. I've never dranken so much that I can't remember."

"Dranken?" he asked with a laugh.

"Drunken, drunk, drank, whatever," Gillian said.

"Be that as it may," Walker said, "I've never taken advantage of a woman before, and I'm not about to start now."

Gillian pouted. "Not even if she wants you to?"

Walker laughed loud and long. Gillian was fascinated. She never would've guessed that he was a man to let go like that. She found herself smiling in return. Then she sobered. "This is weird. Is this weird?"

"No," Walker said immediately.

"It is," Gillian said. "I mean, we don't know each other, not really. And you saved me from being carted off on a plane to some drug lord's hideaway and being horribly abused and maybe forcibly addicted to drugs. And you *killed* people for me. Shot them! POW! Right in the head. And I got brains and ick on me. I looked like shit when we met. I hadn't showered in forever and smelled horrible. And even though I know it wasn't appropriate at the time, I couldn't help but wonder what you looked like without any clothes on. That's messed up, Walker. And how can I feel like I *know* you, when I really don't?"

"The first time I heard your voice, I got hard," Walker said matter-of-factly.

Gillian stared at him with wide eyes as he went on. "It •s so inappropriate. You were a hostage and scared out of your mind. You said, 'I'm here' and 'I'm okay.' And that was that. I fell hard. I volunteered to bring that food out to the plane just so I could get a look at the woman who'd impressed the hell out of me, and who'd made me feel more just with her words than I had in any serious relationship I'd been in before. If this is weird, then I'm okay with that."

"Walker," Gillian whispered.

He reached over and took her hand in his own. "Close your eyes, Di. I'll get you home safe and sound."

"I know," she sighed, and did as he ordered.

The entire car was spinning as if it was in the middle of an F5 tornado. It had been a long time since she'd had as much to drink as she had tonight. She'd started out the night depressed and sad, and somehow here she was... sitting next to Walker, who was taking care of her and making sure she got home all right.

Was this really her life?

* * *

Forty-five minutes later, Trigger was staring down at a sleeping—or passed out—Gillian. He'd gotten her into her apartment and shoved a T-shirt he'd found in her drawers in her hands and pointed her to the bathroom. He hoped like hell she'd be able to stay awake long enough to change, because he wasn't sure he'd survive if he had to strip off her jeans and shirt.

He'd been staring at her luscious tits the entire way home; her shirt had gaped just a bit, showing him a slice of creamy, luscious skin that he wanted to lick and taste. But she'd managed to put on the T-shirt, and while it covered her cleavage, it left her long legs bare. He had no idea if she was wearing underwear or not, and he closed his eyes as she climbed under her covers.

"Just push the button on the knob when you leave. It'll lock behind you," she slurred as she closed her eyes and hugged a pillow to her chest.

Trigger hadn't answered. He didn't like the thought of her only defense from someone who wanted to break in being a flimsy lock on a doorknob. Leaning over her, he inhaled deeply, and was rewarded with the smell of honey-suckle once more. Deciding the scent was coming from her hair, he lifted a strand and brought it to his nose. Yup...definitely her shampoo.

Gillian stirred under him, and Trigger dropped her hair and stood. Jesus, he was hovering over her like some kind of pervert. She coughed, and he tensed until she calmed once more.

She was hammered. He couldn't leave her. What if she puked in bed? If she choked? He had to stay for her own safety.

Trigger knew he was being ridiculous, but he couldn't make himself leave. He headed to the front door and threw the deadbolt and engaged the chain, along with twisting the little lock on the doorknob. Then he grabbed a chair from the small table in her kitchen and brought it back into her bedroom. He placed it on the other side of the room from the bed, and sat down slowly. He had a perfect vantage point of both Gillian and the living area of the apartment.

He had no idea if the seventh hijacker would decide to come for Gillian for some reason, but he'd be there if he did...at least for tonight.

Knowing he wasn't going to make it to PT in the morning—for the first time in his career—Trigger pulled out his phone and sent Brain a text.

Trigger: Something came up. I won't be in for PT in the am.

His friend immediately responded.

Brain: You okay?
    Trigger: Yeah.
    Brain: Gillian?
    Trigger: She had too much to drink. I'm making sure she's okay. Will be in later.
    Brain: She have any clues about the hijacker?

Trigger frowned. He hadn't even thought to ask her about that. One, she was drunk; she probably couldn't think straight anyway. But two, he realized that he had no desire to talk about the fucked-up situation in which they'd found themselves in Venezuela.

Eventually they'd have to talk about it. He needed to find out if she had any suspicions on who the sleeper terrorist might be. She'd spent more time with her fellow passengers than anyone else and probably had better insights than any kind of report could give him. But for now, all he wanted was to try to understand the crazy feelings spiraling inside him.

. . .

Trigger: We didn't talk about it.
    Brain: Seriously?
    Trigger: Seriously.
    Brain: You moving her to your apartment back here? :)

Trigger chortled softly under his breath. That was Brain's advice when they'd first learned about the seventh hijacker. And while it seemed like a better idea than ever right now, he knew Gillian would never agree. She was too independent and she had a life here in Georgetown.

As much as Trigger wanted to wrap her in woolen linen to keep her safe, he also never wanted to clip her wings. He *liked* her independence. He'd just have to find other ways to watch over her, to protect her from the evil in the world. It wouldn't be a hardship.

Trigger: No. I'll talk to you tomorrow.
    Brain: Later.

Trigger put the phone back in his pocket and leaned forward, resting his elbows on his knees and staring at Gillian. What was it about her that was so different from anyone else? He wasn't sure, but he was eager to find out.

CHAPTER SEVEN

Gillian woke up around six the next morning, wanting to die. She stumbled into the bathroom and saw her clothes lying in a heap on the floor where she'd tossed them after getting undressed the night before.

She used the bathroom then sat on the edge of the bathtub with her head in her hands. She felt like crap. Not bad enough to puke...she didn't think...but bad enough. She should've known better than to drink all that tequila. But the margaritas had gone down way too smoothly.

She remembered everything about last night.

It was still hard to believe that Walker had come to The Funky Walrus to see her...and that he'd said he felt the same crazy connection to her that she'd felt with him.

Gillian had no idea what to do now. She didn't have a way to contact him—she'd forgotten to get his phone number before he'd left last night. She'd look him up on social media, but she knew that would probably be futile. If he was who she suspected he was, he wouldn't have a

Facebook page. And he definitely didn't seem the type to have a freaking Instagram page.

Sighing, Gillian stood and went to the sink. She wasn't up for a shower, but she washed the makeup off her face and threw her now crazy, slept-on-wrong hair up into a bun. She shuffled back into her bedroom and pulled on a pair of black fat pants with huge yellow and orange flowers on them.

Deciding she was going to lie on her couch for a while and try to pretend she wasn't hungover as hell, Gillian headed out of her bedroom.

She froze in the hallway when she heard someone in her kitchen.

All of Walker's concerns immediately sprang into her mind. Maybe he hadn't been so far off the mark when he'd said he was worried about her. Was the mystery hijacker in her apartment right this second, ready to kill her when she showed herself?

For a second, Gillian was paralyzed with fear...then she inhaled.

And smelled coffee?

Would someone hell bent on murdering her stop and make coffee first?

Confused as hell, Gillian walked silently the rest of the way down the hall. She stopped in her tracks when she peeked into her small kitchen.

Walker Nelson was sitting at her kitchen table, drinking a cup of coffee, holding his phone in his other hand and reading something intently. He was wearing the same shirt and jeans as the night before, but now his hair was sticking up in the back, and on his feet were only a pair of white socks.

Gillian's heart lurched. He looked absolutely perfect sitting there in her space. She brought a hand up to her chest and pressed on her heart, feeling it thumping hard under her palm. God, this was so close to the fantasies she'd had over the last three weeks, it was uncanny.

She must've made some sort of noise, because suddenly Walker looked up and saw her lurking in her own hallway, staring at him. He put down his mug and phone and immediately stood. He stalked over to her, and all Gillian could do was watch as he neared.

Craning her head back to keep eye contact with him, she was shocked when he didn't stop as he got close. He invaded her personal space and put his hands on either side of her head.

"Good morning," he said softly, his rumbly voice making Gillian's nipples peak.

She knew if he looked down he'd see the effect he had on her body, but he kept his gaze on hers.

"Hi," she said after a moment. "What are you doing here?"

"There was no way in hell I was going to leave you last night. Not as drunk as you were."

"You never left?" she asked. It was a stupid question. Of course he hadn't. He was wearing the same clothes he'd had on last night, and it wasn't as if he would've left then driven all the way back to Georgetown this morning.

He grinned. "I never left," he confirmed.

"Where did you sleep?"

"On your couch."

Gillian bit her lip. "But it's not that comfortable."

Walker merely shrugged. "It's fine. I've definitely slept in worse places in my life. And it smells like you."

111

She had absolutely no clue what to say to that, so she just stared up at him. His gaze moved from her eyes to her hair, to her lips, down her body, taking in her shirt and crazy pants.

Gillian wanted to melt into a puddle on the floor in embarrassment. If she'd known he was there, she would've put on some real clothes. A bra. Done something to her hair...like brush it.

Just when she was deciding if it would be weird if she pushed him away and fled to her bedroom to change, he spoke.

"I thought you looked amazing three weeks ago, after everything you'd been through. And last night, you about knocked me off my feet when you answered your door. But this? Right now? I've never seen anything more beautiful in my life."

Gillian's stomached flip-flopped. "I'm hungover, not wearing a bra, just scrubbed the makeup off my face, which I should've done last night, and I think a mouse has taken up residence in my hair," she blurted.

"You're real," Walker countered. "You look mussed and relaxed. Exactly how I've pictured you in my dirty fantasies."

Gillian knew she was blushing, but couldn't help it. "And you look as perfectly put together as you have every time I've seen you. How do you *do* that?"

But he didn't answer her. Instead he asked, "Are you hungry?"

Gillian wrinkled her nose. "I don't know."

"I didn't want to cook anything in case the smell of eggs or bacon made you sick," Walker told her, and Gillian inwardly sighed. Fuck, he was perfect. How in the hell could someone be this perfect?

"A plain bagel," Gillian blurted. "Toasted. Dry. I think maybe I could eat that."

"Okay, Gilly, then that's what you'll have," he told her.

The sound of him using the nickname her best friends called her felt good.

He leaned down and kissed her forehead, his lips lingering for a long moment. Then he dropped his hands from her head and put his arm around her waist as he led her into the living area. He steered her to the couch and urged her to sit. Once she had, he shook out the blanket she always kept on the back of the couch and covered her with it.

"Stay put. I'll make your bagel."

Gillian watched as he strode into her kitchen. He opened her fridge and took out a bottle of water, breaking the seal on the top before walking back toward her. He handed it to her with a smile, then turned and went back into the kitchen.

She took a sip and watched as Walker started making her breakfast...such as it was. He looked completely at ease in her small kitchen. He knew where everything was and acted as if he'd been there hundreds of times before.

Lost in her admiration of Walker's ass as he moved around her space, she blinked in surprise when he sat next to her, a plain toasted bagel on a plate in his hand. She turned in her seat and gave him a small smile of thanks.

She nibbled a piece of the bread cautiously, happy when it settled and she didn't feel the need to puke it back up.

"We need to talk."

His words immediately made her stiffen. It was the same four words he'd used the night before that had sent her into a downward spiral.

"No, don't tense up," Walker said, putting a hand on her thigh and leaning into her. "Listen to me, okay?"

The bite of bagel she'd managed to swallow threatened to come back up after all. It seemed to be stuck in her throat, and she couldn't have said anything if her life depended on it.

"I told you this last night, but I don't know what you remember and what you don't."

"I remember it all," Gillian admitted softly.

"Right, well then, I'll repeat this so you hear it again. Yes, I came down here to Georgetown to let you know about the seventh hijacker. But that was just an excuse. I haven't been able to stop thinking about you. You impressed me three weeks ago. You were levelheaded and did everything right. You didn't panic when shit hit the fan. I wanted nothing more than to be there to reassure you and help you navigate the interviews and shit that followed.

"I've missed you, Gillian. Which isn't normal, considering I barely know you. I came down to deliver that message in person hoping that we could talk after. Get to know each other. So I could ask you out and see if you'd go to dinner with me sometime. I wanted to go slow, see if this obsession I seem to have with you is a result of the situation...or more."

Gillian knew her eyes were huge in her face, but she couldn't stop staring at Walker in astonishment.

"I knew I'd fucked up somehow when you left. I saw the light go out of your eyes, and it killed that I had done that. I didn't know how, but it was obvious. So I found out where The Funky Walrus was located and went there with the intention of apologizing for whatever it was I'd said."

Gillian huffed out a small laugh. "Yeah, and then you found me drunk as hell, saying the most embarrassing things."

"They weren't embarrassing," Walker said earnestly. "They were honest. I hate that you thought for even a second that you were just a job to me. You weren't. You *aren't*."

"It's okay," she told him.

"You're way too forgiving," he said with a small head shake, but he didn't give her time to say anything else. "It was probably creepy and wrong of me to stay last night, but I never would've forgiven myself if someone had broken in when you were vulnerable, or if you'd have puked and choked in the middle of the night. But I can't be sorry, because I got to see you like this..." His eyes dropped, and Gillian knew he could see her hard nipples through her T-shirt.

He cleared his throat and went on. "I want to date you, Gillian. Call you and talk into the wee hours of the night. Send you texts to let you know I'm thinking about you. Take you out to dinner and make out in my car in the parking lot when I drop you off. I want to get to know your friends, and to laugh with you. Eventually, when the time is right for us both, I want to hold you all night as you sleep after we've made love. I want to taste every inch of your body and have you explore mine in return. We've had a connection from the start, and as much as I want to get to know you intimately right *now*, I want to savor learning everything about you. Learn who Gillian Romano is. What makes her tick."

Every word out of his mouth made Gillian fall for him more. She wanted to shake her head, tell him no, that she didn't want to go slow. That she wanted to feel his hands and tongue on her right that second. But another part of her wanted what he'd described. Wanted the giddy feeling that came with getting to know a man. Wanted the phone calls and texts. Wanted the sexual tension.

She wanted to be wooed. Mostly because she had a feeling Walker would make her feel just like she longed to feel...as if she was wanted. And she had a hunch he'd never make her feel like she came in second.

"I...I'd like that."

His shoulders dropped as if he'd been afraid she'd turn him down. It was hard to believe that this man, this strong-as-hell, beautiful man, would be worried about *her* turning *him* down.

"But you need to know, I'm not a drama queen," she added.

"What do you mean?" he asked.

"I'm different from most women. I don't do drama. Women in general are really bad about that. They get jealous and bitchy and have to be all dramatic about it. They don't get their way, they cause a scene. They think they should be getting more attention than they are, so some dress more flamboyantly and outrageously. That's not me. I say it like it is, but don't do it for any kind of reaction. I prefer honesty to lies because it's just easier."

"I like that. It's a relief."

"But, Walker, if we do this...don't cheat on me."

He looked shocked at her words. "Why would you

even say that? I don't cheat. And I can't imagine, if we get together the way I want to be with you, that I'd ever be stupid enough to fool around."

Gillian shrugged. "Others have."

"Cheated on you? Then they were idiots."

His words were immediate and heartfelt, and they made Gillian relax a fraction. "They wanted something more than me, I guess. One also hit me. You do either of those things, and I'll be done with you faster than you can blink."

Walker sat up straight, and when he spoke, his tone was low and kinda scary. "Someone *hit* you?"

Gillian realized that she was about to have an extremely pissed-off alpha man on her hands if she didn't do damage control. Pronto. "Yeah, one guy. Once. It was the last time I saw him. I left his ass that day and pressed charges. My point is that I don't put up with shit like that. Especially not from someone I'm dating. I'm worth more than that. I'm a damn good girlfriend. Attentive and generous. When I'm with someone, I put them first. If they need me, I'm there, and I want to find someone who feels the same way about me. And cheating, stealing, and knocking me around isn't looking out for my well-being. It's not putting me first."

She could see that Walker was having a hard time letting go of the thought that someone had hit her. She gentled her tone. "It happens, Walker. Unfortunately, all the time. Walking down the street, men feel as if it's okay to whistle and cat call. They don't hesitate to ogle our boobs and tell us how turned on they are. A lot of them feel as if it's okay to smack a woman simply because they're a *man*, stronger and better than a woman because they have more muscles and a dangling piece of flesh between their legs they pee through. It doesn't make it right, but bad things happen to good women all the time."

"Not to you. Not anymore," Walker said in a possessive tone that made goose bumps break out on Gillian's arms.

"Okay," she agreed easily.

Walker took a moment to visibly try to control his extreme reaction to her admission that she'd been hit, then said, "I can't stay much longer as I have to get back up to Fort Hood. My team is gonna give me hell for missing PT this morning. I've never missed it before. Not once."

Gillian blinked. "Really?"

"Really," he confirmed. "You were more important than getting back to run ten miles with my friends."

That felt good. *Really* good.

"But, before I go, there's something else we need to talk about."

"The hijacker," Gillian said somberly. Even though her belly was churning with happiness, she knew they needed to discuss this.

"Yeah," Walker said, his face serious. "No one knows who he is, what he's thinking, or even where he is right now."

"But why would he care about me or any of the other passengers?"

Walker stared at her for a long moment, and Gillian could tell he was weighing what he should and shouldn't say.

"I need you to be honest," she said quietly. "I get that you don't want me hurt, but I need to know everything."

"Right. Everyone's working on this. The FBI, CIA,

DEA. The antiterrorist organizations from other countries. Everyone who was on the plane is being scrutinized, even you. Your friends might have people ask them questions about you. Your tax and business records will be combed through looking for inconsistencies. I'm very sorry."

Gillian shrugged. "I don't have anything to hide, Walker. I'm not thrilled, but the sooner they figure out I'm just me, the better."

He smiled briefly, then sobered once more. "There are more questions about this seventh hijacker than answers. Why was he hiding amongst the passengers? How pissed is he that his fellow conspiracists were killed? We know now that the hijackers didn't work for the Cartel of the Suns, but instead were from a rival drug syndicate, the Sinaloa Cartel in Mexico. They didn't want to free Hugo Lamas, they wanted him dead, which they accomplished. They embarrassed the Cartel of the Suns and essentially started one hell of a war."

Holy crap. She was hardly up on all the various cartels and hadn't really paid that much attention to them before she'd been hijacked, but even *she* knew about the Sinaloa Cartel, who occasionally made the local news. What she remembered about them was terrifying. "Why would anyone come after *me*?"

"To find out what you know. Because, when push comes to shove, you were a big reason why Luis and all the others were killed. You stalled them just enough, you put up a fight. Alberto wanted you on that plane, and because he wanted you, someone else might think there was a good reason."

"But Luis was taking Andrea," Gillian pointed out.

"I know. And that means she could be in danger too. She's being checked in on as well."

"Oh," Gillian said, her mind swirling.

"With all that said, I think the chance someone from the Sinaloa Cartel, or the Cartel of the Suns, coming after you is low. But I'm not willing to stake my life on it...or yours. You need to be very careful, Gillian. Don't go anywhere by yourself if you can help it. Don't take any chances. Always lock your door. Get a security system installed, or at least buy those motion-sensor cameras that are so popular nowadays. And for God's sake, don't take an Uber anywhere."

Gillian couldn't help but smile. "You really don't like those rideshare things, do you?"

"No," he growled. "You have no idea who's behind the wheel. What their driving record is, if they've been drinking or on drugs, or if they just got out of jail for sexual assault. Once you get in a car, you're vulnerable. You could be driven anywhere...out into the middle of nowhere and never seen again."

"Okay, Walker," she said, putting her hand atop his on her leg. "I'll be careful. Can I...do the other passengers know about the sleeper guy? I mean, I email and text quite a few of them. I don't know what I'm allowed to say and what I'm not."

"Some will be informed, others won't. The thing is, someone you're talking to could very well be the seventh hijacker, Gillian."

She shook her head. "No. I don't believe it."

She didn't like the look in Walker's eyes.

"No," she said again. "There's no way Janet is a terrorist. Maybe you think it's little Renee? Or Reed? Maybe one of the college boys? Alice, the woman who was so scared she literally peed her pants? Or Andrea, the woman Luis forced to suck his dick? No, *no way*."

"Breathe, Gilly," Walker said gently, turning his hand over so he could intertwine their fingers. "This is something else that you're going to have to do...talk to the authorities about the other passengers. Tell them everything that happened in minute detail. Even the smallest thing could be important, could be a clue as to who the other hijacker was."

Inhaling deeply, Gillian tried to control her panic. It was just now sinking in that someone she'd gotten to know, had bonded with over their horrific experience, might really have been on the side of the hijackers. "I don't know that much, Walker. The men were kept on the other end of the plane, you know that. I only briefly talked to most of them. Mateo, Charles, Muhammad... they all seemed nice. Now, I just don't know. Oh! But now that I think about it, Leyton was a bit strange. When Alberto was trying to pull me onto the plane, Leyton was standing nearby, just watching us. Not helping and not running away like the others. But honestly, I think he was just in shock. Everything happened so fast."

"Okay, Gillian, I'm not the one who needs to know the details, the investigators do."

She frowned at him. "You don't want to know?"

He shrugged. "I want to know whatever you want to tell me. But my job in Venezuela wasn't to solve the mystery of who had hijacked the plane, and why. It was to rescue hostages, and if that meant killing the hijackers, so be it. I'm not involved in the investigation. As of right this moment, my one and only concern is to make sure *you're* safe."

That felt really good.

"If you want to talk to me about what you went through, I'll listen. I've been through some pretty serious shit in my life, and I can help you deal with what happened if you need it. But starting today, I'm the man you're dating, not someone who's with you to pump you for information. Okay?"

Gillian nodded.

"But you have to know that if I think you're being reckless with your safety, or not treating this as seriously as you should, I'm gonna call you on it."

That didn't bother Gillian like it might've if it had been anyone else who'd said it to her.

"If I find out more information, I'll certainly pass it along, especially if it affects your safety. But as far as I'm concerned, we're just a man and a woman who are getting to know each other."

"I like that."

"Me too," Walker said with a smile. "And as a part of this getting-to-know-you shit, you need to know that I work weird hours. I don't have a nine-to-five job."

"I think I got that," Gillian told him with a wry chuckle.

"I don't think you do," he said seriously. "I could be called away on a job at any moment. I'll do my best to let you know, but there might be times I don't get a chance to call you...things can get crazy and intense for me that fast."

Gillian licked her lips and nodded.

"I might be gone for a few days, or a few weeks. I never know how long a deployment is gonna take."

"Okay."

"You think you can handle that?" he asked.

Gillian could hear the worry in his voice, and she hurried to reassure him. "Walker, as I said last night, I'm not going to pine away waiting for you to get back. I'll miss you, but I've got a life. A job that will keep me busy. And when I feel sad, I'll just get together with Ann, Wendy, and Clarissa and have a pity party, then continue on with my life. I've managed on my own for a decade. I'm not going to fall apart when you get deployed. I'm proud that you're serving our country. And..." Her voice lowered, and she couldn't help but glance around her apartment. She wasn't sure what she expected to see; it wasn't as if there were people around to overhear her. "I know that you're not a normal soldier."

"You do?" he asked with a small grin.

"Yeah. I've lived in this area long enough to know that typical deployments from the Army base are for like six months or longer. A team of seven regular infantry soldiers aren't sent to Venezuela to rescue hostages on a huge plane."

"You're right, they're not," Walker said simply.

Gillian nodded. He wasn't going to tell her exactly what he did, and that was all right. "I don't care, Walker," she said earnestly. "I care about you being safe and coming back from your missions safely, but you could be the president's personal bodyguard, and it wouldn't make a difference in how I feel about you."

Walker closed his eyes for a second and took a deep breath. When he opened them again, Gillian saw his pupils had dilated slightly. He leaned into her and nuzzled her hair by her ear.

"Honeysuckle," he murmured. "I'll never be able to smell it again and not get hard." Then, as if he hadn't just said one of the most carnal things she'd ever heard, he pulled back to look into her eyes once more. "Did I say I wanted to go slow?" he asked. "I think I'm an idiot."

Gillian laughed. She could tell he hadn't changed his mind, but it felt good to know he wasn't unaffected by her.

"All I ask is that you be extra careful until the authorities find out who that seventh hijacker is," he said. "It's unlikely that he'd come to Austin to try to do you harm, but until we know his identity, I'm not willing to take any chances."

"Okay."

Walker glanced at his watch. "You feel okay?" he asked.

She nodded, but said, "No. I'm not nauseous, but I don't feel all that good either."

He smiled and ran a hand over her hair. "Poor Gilly. What are you going to do today?"

"Sit here on the couch and binge watch shows that will lower my IQ ten points and try not to even think about ever drinking again."

"Sounds good. Can I call you later?"

"Yes."

"It's Thursday; you have plans for this weekend?"

"I've got a *quinceañera* party Friday night and a golf outing Saturday morning."

"Would you like to go out to dinner on Saturday night?"

"Yes."

He smiled. "How about I pick you up around four? There's a great place up in Killeen I'd like to take you to.

We can eat, then I'd love to show you around Fort Hood and where I work."

"I'd love that."

"Good. If it's all right with you, I'm gonna call a taxi and head over to the bar and drive your car back here before I leave."

"You don't have to do that," Gillian told him, shocked that he would even consider it. "I can go get it later."

"I know I don't have to. You feel like crap, and it's not a big deal for me to go get it."

She wasn't sure what to say. She'd already planned to either call one of her friends to pick her up or take a taxi to The Funky Walrus later to get her car. But she couldn't deny that she liked that Walker offered to do it for her. "Thanks. I'd appreciate that."

"Great. I'll take care of it for you then. Gillian?"

"Yeah?"

"I hope you know what you're getting into with me."

"I do," she said simply. And she did. She'd waited a hell of a long time for a man like Walker to find her. She was strong enough to be his woman...if he'd let her.

CHAPTER EIGHT

When Saturday night rolled around, Gillian was exhausted, but she also felt as if she'd had way too many shots of espresso. In just a few minutes, Walker would be at her apartment to pick her up for their date.

She'd gotten a bit too much sun at the golf party that afternoon, but she knew the pink would fade in a day or so. Gillian had asked Walker what she should wear, and he'd told her that jeans and a blouse would be perfect. He hadn't told her where they were going, but she trusted him.

It was about a forty-minute drive to Killeen, and Gillian was looking forward to simply talking more with Walker as they drove. True to his word, he'd called on Thursday night. They'd ended up talking for three hours, which surprised Gillian. It was her experience that most guys didn't like to talk on the phone that much. But there hadn't been one lull in their conversation. They'd talked as if they'd known each other their whole lives.

When she'd told Walker that he was the first guy who

hadn't seemed to mind talking on the phone for as long as they had, he'd told her that he wasn't like any of the men she'd dated in the past, and that normally he wasn't very chatty, but as far as he was concerned, he could talk to her for hours every night and be perfectly happy.

He always seemed to say the right thing, but Gillian didn't think he was merely saying what he thought she wanted to hear. Their conversation was too smooth, too easy to be faked.

He'd texted on Friday...several times. And each time her phone vibrated, she smiled in anticipation. Then he'd called her briefly that morning to see how the *quinceañera* had gone and to tell her he hoped her golf thing went all right.

It was a new experience for Gillian to have someone be so attuned to her schedule. Walker was enthusiastic and inquisitive about her job. He seemed to be fascinated by how organized she was and how many different kinds of events she arranged. He'd warned her to be safe and they'd finalized plans for the evening.

Since Walker had said jeans were all right, she took a chance and wore her favorite pair of brown and turquoise cowboy boots as well. She wore a turquoise shirt that matched and had braided her hair in two long braids that hung over her chest. She'd also dug some ribbon out of a drawer and tied each braid off with a piece.

She thought she looked cute...but it might be overkill. She definitely looked a little touristy in her cowgirl getup, but she felt good, so decided to go with it.

Gillian had just walked out of her bedroom when the buzzer sounded, letting her know someone was at the doorway downstairs. She pressed on the button. "Hello?"

"It's me," Walker said in his distinctive deep rumble.

Without another word, Gillian pressed the button to open the door and let him inside. She knew she had maybe two minutes before he'd be knocking. She took a deep breath, then another. She was nervous as hell, which was crazy, considering Walker had definitely seen her at her worst...twice.

She'd wanted to look nice for him tonight. To let him know that she was looking forward to spending time with him. The knock on the door came about a minute before she was expecting it. Smiling, happy at how excited Walker seemed to be for their date as well, she peered through the peephole, confirming it was him, before opening the door with a huge smile.

"Hi," she said brightly. "You got up here fast."

She barely got a chance to register what Walker was wearing before he was easing her into her apartment and closing the door. He backed her up against the wall next to her front door then reached out and took her face in his hands, tilting her head up. Gillian grabbed hold of his biceps and looked at him in surprise.

He didn't say anything, which kinda freaked Gillian out. "Walker?"

"Hmmm?" he murmured.

"Are you all right?"

"Good. Great, now that I'm with you."

She smiled uncertainly.

"Shit," he said under his breath. "I'm fucking this up." Then he took a deep breath, grimaced, and took a step away from her.

She shivered at the loss of the heat of his hands on her face. "What's wrong?" she asked, biting her lip.

His hand came up once more and he tugged her lip out of her teeth, then smoothed the pad of his finger across her lower lip. "Nothing's wrong. I just...I almost forgot we were taking things slow for a second. Seeing you almost broke through my restraint."

Gillian frowned. She looked down at her jeans and boots, then back up at him.

"You look amazing," Walker said softly. He picked up one of her braids and fingered it for a moment. "Every time I see you, you surprise me by being prettier than when I saw you last."

"Do I...is this okay for where we're going to dinner tonight? I know it's a bit much, but I love my boots and thought if you said jeans were okay, they'd probably do. And I haven't worn this shirt in a while. And after I'd gotten dressed, it just seemed more appropriate to put my hair up like this than to leave it down." Gillian knew she was babbling, but Walker's reaction had put her off balance.

"It's absolutely perfect," Walker reassured her. "As I said, I almost forgot my vow to take things slow when I saw you and did something I promised myself I wouldn't do."

"What's that?"

"Kiss you the way I've been dreaming about. Put one hand up your shirt and the other down your pants. Take you against the wall as I kept my nose buried in your hair to better inhale your sweet smell."

Gillian froze. *Holy shit*. Walker was way more intense than anyone she'd ever been with before—but she liked it. No, she *loved* that he knew exactly what he wanted and wasn't afraid to admit it.

"Shit, I freaked you out, didn't I?" he asked, taking another step away from her.

"No! I mean, maybe a little, but not in a bad way. I'm just not used to anyone being so honest, but I like it. And...as much as I feel connected to you...I...it's a bit soon for that. But..." She hesitated.

"What?" Walker asked. "You can tell me anything. Tell me to back off, that I'm moving way too fast, that I'm crowding you, that you need space...and I'll respect it."

She shook her head. "I was just going to say that while I might not be ready for all that right now...can I have a raincheck?"

"On the ravaging you against the wall?" Walker asked with a small smile.

"Yeah, that."

"You got it, Di."

They smiled at each other, and Gillian found she missed having his hands on her. She loved that she could make him act without thought. She had a feeling that didn't happen a lot with him. She reached for his hand and intertwined her fingers with his. "Take me to dinner?" she asked softly.

He squeezed her hand and nodded. Together they walked into her living area so she could grab her purse.

"I ordered one of those camera thingies online yesterday," Gillian told him. "It should arrive on Monday."

"Good."

"And I told both my neighbors that a former client was upset with me and if they heard anything weird from my apartment, that they should call the police."

She looked up at Walker and found he was staring down at her with a satisfied look. "Thank you."

"For what?"

"For taking this seriously. I know constantly thinking about your safety is a pain in the ass and can be kinda scary as well. But knowing you're taking this seriously makes me feel a hell of a lot better about being so far away from you."

Gillian had thought about that as well. They lived at least forty minutes from one another. If someone broke in or otherwise tried to hurt her, even if she was able to call him, there wouldn't be anything he could do in the short term. "I might be blonde, but I'm not an idiot," she told him. "The last thing I want is to end up a hostage again. It wasn't fun the first time and I have no desire to repeat it. If you think I might be in danger, I'd be stupid to dismiss your feelings."

"Good. Now, are you hungry?"

"Yeah," she said.

"You gonna be okay for an hour or so, or do you need a snack?"

Gillian chuckled. "I'm not exactly wasting away, Walker. I think I can hold out until we get to the restaurant."

Walker tugged on her hand until she fell against him with an *umph*.

"I *know* you're not disparaging your body, are you?" he asked.

Gillian shook her head. One hand was still in his, trapped behind her back where he was holding her to him. The other she rested on his chest as she looked up at him. "No. But I know what I am and what I'm not. And what I'm not is the size and shape of the women men seem to love to look at on the runways and in magazines. I'm okay with that, because I like to eat. I love chips and salsa, and I won't give up my chocolate."

Walker smiled down at her. "God, you're so refreshing," he said softly. "You really do say it like it is, don't you?"

"Yes."

"Right, well, I don't watch those fancy shows with people wearing ridiculous fashions, and I don't have time to look at magazines like *Maxim* and *Playboy*. What I *do* like is how you feel in my arms. Against me." He pushed harder on the small of her back until she was plastered against his chest. Gillian could feel his erection against her belly, and she swallowed hard.

"I'll be sure to stock up on chocolate so you can have some when you get the hankering for a snack. And chips and salsa is one of my favorite things to eat as well. Spicy or mild?"

"Medium," Gillian whispered, resisting the urge to wiggle against him.

"I like it hot," Walker said suggestively.

Throwing her head back, Gillian couldn't stop herself from laughing. When she had herself under control, she looked back up at him. "Why doesn't that surprise me?"

Walker was grinning down at her. "Because even after such a short time, you know me," he said.

They stayed like that for a long minute. Not speaking, simply enjoying being next to each other. Gillian could feel his heart beating fast under her hand and loved that he wasn't unaffected by their proximity.

Walker took a deep breath, then said, "And now we really need to get going."

"Right, I'm sure you made reservations," she agreed.

"Because of that too," Walker said.

Gillian couldn't stop the giggle that escaped. She loved that he wasn't bashful about letting her know how much he wanted her. She wanted him too, but she wasn't ready to sleep with him yet. She wanted to get to know him better. Her heart said he was the man she could spend the rest of her life with, but her brain was telling her to slow down and make sure.

They walked to her door together and he locked it behind them. They went down the stairs hand in hand and out to his Blazer. Once again, he opened her door and helped her put on her seat belt. Then he shut the door and walked around to the other side.

Gillian felt safe with him. As he pulled out of her apartment complex and headed for the road that led north to Killeen, she relaxed. The night was just starting and it had already been one of the best dates she'd ever had.

* * *

Trigger sat across from Gillian at his favorite barbeque restaurant in Killeen and realized he couldn't take his eyes from her. When he'd first seen her in her apartment, he'd acted without thinking. He'd had her pushed inside and up against her wall before his brain had engaged.

She looked adorable. Her braids, the boots, the tight jeans...it all made him want to take her right then and there. Luckily, he'd come to his senses. He never acted impulsively. That would get him killed on a mission, and over the years his common sense had taken over all aspects of his life. He was always methodical and cautious...except when it came to Gillian Romano, apparently.

He'd loved talking to her throughout the week. She was funny and entertaining. She didn't monopolize the conversation, and she asked him questions and had no problem answering his as well. He hadn't even realized they'd been talking for hours until he'd looked at the clock and had been shocked as hell to see the time.

She had a bit of sauce on her chin and, without thinking, Trigger reached over to wipe it off. Instead of being embarrassed, she merely laughed. "Am I covered in the stuff?" she asked with a smile as she brought a napkin up to her face.

"Naw, just a little bit on your chin," he told her with a smile.

The restaurant was crowded, as it was a Saturday night and they had some of the best barbeque in Killeen. Most of the patrons were soldiers from the base, but there were quite a few families there as well. It was an unconventional place to bring Gillian for their first date, but he wanted her to be comfortable. And there was nowhere more comfortable than here.

"Tell me about your team?" she asked as they chowed down on their smoked brisket and chicken. "I mean, I saw them all in Venezuela, but didn't really get to meet them."

"They're some of the best men I've ever known," Trigger said honestly. "They're hardworking, brave, and loyal, and they're also assholes."

Gillian chuckled.

That was another thing Trigger loved about her...she seemed to know when he was joking with her and when he was being serious. He'd once dated a woman who took offense to everything he'd said when he was being sarcastic or just kidding around.

"But seriously, they can be a bit rough around the edges, but I think we all are. We're all single, and have been most of our adult lives. The Army's been our mistress and it can be hard to change our mindset on that."

Gillian was giving him her full attention. "How long have you been in?" she asked.

"I'm thirty-seven. I joined the Army relatively late compared to some others. I graduated from college and started a job, then realized I hated being cooped up in an office all day. There was a recruiting station across the street from where I worked, and one day on my lunch break, I found myself in their office, talking to them about joining. That was about thirteen years ago."

"So you're a lifer then." It wasn't a question.

"Yeah, I haven't thought about when I'll retire, but I'll do at least twenty years," Trigger said. "I met my team in training." He had to be careful about telling her too much, but she'd already pretty much guessed that he was special forces, so he kept going. "Lefty, Grover, and I were in the same recruitment class. We slogged through mud, puked, got rained on, got shot at with rubber bullets, and nearly drowned together. We forged a bond that'll never be broken, no matter what we do in the future or where we go."

"Well, that sounds fun...not," Gillian said with a smile.

"It wasn't, but it was," Trigger said with a smile. "I knew I was going to be doing something that would make a difference in the world. Even if I couldn't talk about it to anyone, *I'd* know."

"Like rescue hostages from a hijacked plane in Venezuela," she said quietly.

"Exactly," Trigger agreed, reaching across the table for

her hand. He caressed the back of it with his thumb and didn't break eye contact with her. "We met Brain, Oz, Doc, and Lucky later, when we were teamed up together. Sometimes I feel as if I've known them all my entire life. We can finish each other's sentences and when they hurt, I hurt, and vice versa. It's a bond I always wished I had growing up. I'm an only child and always wanted a brother or sister."

"And now you have six brothers."

"I do."

Gillian smiled, then she licked her lips and looked down.

"What? What's wrong?" Trigger asked, holding on to her hand when she tried to pull back from him.

"I just...what if they don't like me?"

Trigger couldn't help it. He laughed.

When he got himself under control and looked back at Gillian, she was glaring at him. Once more she tried to pull her hand out of his grasp, but he held on.

"I'm not laughing *at* you," he reassured her. "I'm laughing because if anything, I'm going to have to worry about you deciding you like them better than me. They're going to love you; already do, in fact."

Her brows furrowed. "I haven't really even met them."

"Yeah, but I've talked about you. A lot."

"But we just met a few days ago."

Trigger shook his head. "Wrong. We met a few weeks ago. And the guys saw the kind of person you were *then*, and after me not being able to talk about anything but you for the last few days, they've gotten to know you even better."

Gillian flushed, and Trigger couldn't help but grin. He

squeezed her hand. "You have nothing to worry about, Di," he told her softly. "I think I have more to be concerned about. My best friends are all single. They're horn dogs and will probably annoy you to no end. They're a little uncouth and brash. You might meet them and hate them, and that wouldn't bode well for our relationship."

"I'm not going to hate them," she assured. "They're your friends...how could I?"

They were smiling at each other when someone called from across the restaurant.

"Trigger!"

He turned and smiled as he saw who was approaching. Standing, Trigger shook the man's hand and smiled at the woman at his side. Gillian had also stood, and Trigger introduced everyone.

"Gillian, this is my friend Truck and his wife, Mary. This is Gillian, my girlfriend."

Mary instantly looked like she had a thousand questions, but she managed to keep them inside as she shook Gillian's hand.

"It's good to meet you," Truck said. "We didn't even know Trigger *had* a girlfriend."

Trigger grinned and put his arm around Gillian's waist. "I do," he said firmly. Then he looked down at Gillian. "Truck is with a group of soldiers that we've worked with in the past. His team and mine are all friends. Seems like just yesterday that we were at Truck and Mary's wedding." Then he turned back to his friend and asked, "Are you guys excited to go get your kids?"

"Definitely," Truck said with a smile. "Feels like we've waited forever for the paperwork to go through to be able to pick up Aarav and Deeba. We've sent tapes of our voices and lots of pictures, but who knows how they'll react when they see us for the first time."

"They're adopting two young kids from India," Trigger explained to Gillian.

"Congratulations," she said with a huge smile.

"Thanks," Truck replied. "We're ready to have them home."

"Wait, are you Gillian *Romano*?" Mary asked out of the blue. She'd been smiling and nodding as her husband spoke, but it was obvious Gillian's name had just clicked in her brain.

Trigger tensed. He knew it was a possibility that Gillian could be recognized. Her name and picture had been in newspapers around the country after the hijacking. She hadn't given many interviews, but that didn't matter. She was a weird kind of celebrity.

He felt her tense next to him, but she answered politely enough. "I am."

"You're amazing!" Mary said immediately. "I read about what happened on that plane, and it sounds like it was so horrible. I mean, when I was held captive in the bank I worked at, I was terrified, but that was only for like twenty minutes. I can't imagine being in your situation for over two days!"

Trigger felt Gillian relax against him. "It wasn't fun," she told Mary.

"Understatement of the century," Trigger muttered.

"We can see you're eating, so we'll let you go," Truck told them. "Gillian, it was nice meeting you."

"Same," Gillian said.

Trigger shook Truck's hand again and said, "We still on

for that training exercise next week? Your team against mine?"

"Fuck yeah," Truck said with a grin. "May the best team win."

"Which'll be mine," Trigger said. "No way are we letting a bunch of old men beat us."

"We'll see," Truck said. "We'll see."

"Come on, He-Man," Mary teased. "I'm hungry, and if you two stand here beating your chests anymore, I'll never get fed."

Gillian giggled, and Trigger loved the sound. He gave Truck a chin lift and got one in return. Then he waited until Gillian was seated before taking his own once again.

"You guys seem close," she observed when they were eating.

"We are," Trigger agreed.

"I like Mary's hair."

"Don't you dare think of putting any streaks of color in yours," Trigger growled.

Gillian raised surprised eyes to his. "Why?"

"Because it's perfect the way it is. I love the color it is now. It reminds me of fields of wheat that grow in the Midwest."

For a second, Trigger thought he'd overstepped. He couldn't read the look on Gillian's face. But finally she smiled.

"Thanks. I wasn't really thinking about coloring my own hair. I just admire others who can get away with it."

They finished their meal without any further interruptions and Trigger was glad when they left the noisy interior of the restaurant behind and got back into his car. When they were both settled, he turned to her. "Want to see some of the base?"

"Sure," she said eagerly.

So for the next two hours, Trigger drove her around Fort Hood. He showed her where his office was and even walked her around one of the motor pools. When she said she'd never seen the inside of a tank, he arranged for a mechanic working on one to let her peek inside. He took pictures of her sitting inside, and Trigger knew he'd never forget how happy she looked.

"That was fun," she told him when they were leaving the base.

"Yeah," he agreed quietly.

"What's wrong?" she asked, easily reading his mood.

Trigger glanced over at her. He could only see flashes of her face when they passed under streetlights as it had gotten dark outside. He'd done all he could to prolong their time on the base but eventually he'd run out of things to show her.

"I'm not ready to bring you home yet," he blurted, then cringed. He was supposed to be moving slow, and keeping her out all night wasn't exactly doing that.

"I'm not ready to *go* home yet," she said, surprising him. "What do you have in mind?"

"I'm sure there's a late movie we could see," Trigger told her. "Or we could find a bar and hang out. Or..." He let his words trail off.

"Or what?"

Glancing over at her again, Trigger felt the familiar twinge in his belly. She was so pretty. The hair in her braids had started to escape their confines and she looked somewhat mussed after crawling around the tank in the motor pool. But she looked completely relaxed, leaning against his car door with one knee bent and her foot tucked up under her thigh.

"I was going to suggest that maybe we could go back to my apartment and watch a movie there or something. It would be quieter, and we could talk easier...but I'm not sure that's a good idea."

"That sounds really nice, actually," Gillian told him. "Honestly, I have a slight headache from being out in the sun all day today."

Trigger fought an internal war with himself. He wanted to take Gillian to his home. Wanted to see her on his couch, relaxed and happy. But he knew if they went back there, it would be extremely difficult to keep his hands—and lips—off of her. He'd never had a problem controlling himself around women before, but something about Gillian pushed all his buttons. "You're safe with me," he told her.

She looked surprised, but said, "I know. I wouldn't have agreed to let you drive me up here to Killeen if I didn't think I was safe."

"We're taking things slow," he added, a little harsher than he'd meant to.

"I know that too," she agreed.

"Me taking you to my apartment isn't a ploy to get you into my bed." Trigger didn't know why he wasn't letting this go. Probably because a part of him hoped she might push back and tell him it was all right. That she didn't want to go slow anymore.

She shifted in her seat and reached over to put her hand on his arm. "If you need to take me home, it's okay," she said quietly.

"No!" he blurted.

After a beat, they both chuckled softly.

"I'm fucking this up—again," Trigger told her, kinda glad he was driving and didn't have to look her in the eyes. "I've enjoyed being with you tonight. There's just something about you that makes me happy. You take such joy in the littlest things, and you don't get all freaked out by a little barbeque sauce on your chin or at having to meet my friends and acquaintances. The more time I spend with you, the more time I *want* to spend with you."

"I feel the same way. I feel comfortable around you, Walker. I don't feel as if I need to pretend to be someone I'm not. And you have no idea how amazing that is. I don't want to go home yet, but if it's going to stress you out to have me come over, then you can take me home."

"How about this," Trigger said. "We go to my place and watch one movie. It'll be after midnight by then, and I'll take you home and we'll figure out when to see each other again."

"Deal," Gillian said immediately. "But I get to pick the movie."

Trigger grinned. "Okay, but you should know I don't have any romantic comedies."

"I'm sure you've got something I'll like."

Trigger wanted to retort that he definitely had something she'd like, but he kept the comment to himself.

Relieved that he didn't have to say goodbye to her just yet, Trigger drove the rest of the way to his apartment with a huge grin on his face.

* * *

Two and a half hours later, Trigger lay on his couch with a comatose Gillian in his arms. She'd discarded her boots and had taken her hair out of its braids. It was extremely wavy and fell around her shoulders in disarray. Trigger had wanted to run his hands through it, but refrained.

Gillian had picked *Die Hard* for them to watch, a movie he'd seen countless times. They'd argued about whether it was a Christmas movie or not and within twenty minutes of the first shot being fired on screen, Gillian was sound asleep.

She'd been sitting next to him on the couch and her neck had been leaning sideways at an awkward angle, and Trigger knew it couldn't be comfortable. So he'd pulled her into him and shifted so his head was resting on the armrest, and she was snuggled between him and the back of the couch.

She'd wiggled a bit, then settled. Her cheek was resting on his chest over his heart, an arm and leg slung over his body. She was holding him as tightly as he was holding her.

Trigger was tired—it had been a long day filled with the anticipation of seeing her again—but he couldn't sleep. He'd turned off the DVD and the only sounds in the apartment were Gillian's deep breaths and the occasional shout or car engine revving from outside.

He knew he should wake her up and get her home, but Trigger couldn't bring himself to move. Holding Gillian felt right. It soothed him in a way he'd never experienced before. He wasn't aroused, didn't feel the need to fuck. He was content to simply hold her while she slept.

Shifting so he could put a hand on the back of Gillian's head, Trigger inhaled deeply. The scent of honeysuckle surrounded him as if he were standing in a field of flowers.

He'd never be able to smell it again and not think of this moment.

Deciding he'd just close his eyes for a second, then he'd get them both up so he could take her home, Trigger relaxed into the cushions even farther.

He fell into a sleep so deep, so content and comfortable with the woman in his arms, he wouldn't wake up until the sun was breaking over the horizon.

CHAPTER NINE

Gillian woke feeling more rested than she had in what seemed like ages. She hadn't had any bad dreams, that she could remember, and actually felt pretty good.

Shifting, she realized immediately that she wasn't alone. Her eyes popped open and she saw she was still on Walker's couch. Was, in fact, sleeping in his arms. Her back was to the cushions and her front was plastered against Walker's side.

When she lifted her head, she found herself staring into Walker's gray eyes. He had a five o'clock shadow, which reminded her of how he'd looked in Venezuela. Except now his guard was down and he seemed somewhat vulnerable.

"Morning," he said softly.

"I didn't mean to fall asleep on you," she said.

"And I didn't mean to fall asleep at all," he returned. "I meant to only close my eyes for a second, then wake you up and take you home."

Gillian gave him a small smile. "I'm glad you didn't. I slept better last night than I have for the last month."

He frowned. "You're not sleeping well?"

Realizing her mistake, Gillian tried to brush off the comment. "I just meant in general."

"No, don't do that. You're not sleeping well?" he repeated.

Gillian pressed her lips together and shook her head slightly.

"Nightmares?"

"Sometimes."

"Flashbacks?"

She nodded.

"You need the lights on?"

Gillian nodded again. "How'd you know?"

"I've been there, Gilly. PTSD isn't fun."

"Oh, this isn't that," she protested. "I'm just having a hard time acclimating back to life from before."

"Which is PTSD," Walker said firmly.

Then he moved so quickly, Gillian didn't have a chance to protest or to do anything except squeak. He was sitting upright and had her straddling his lap before she could think. His hands pushed into her hair on either side of her head and he held her firmly. She should've been concerned over how easily he maneuvered her. How he was holding her and not letting her go...but she wasn't.

"It's nothing to be ashamed of. What you went through was awful, Di. You're strong as hell, but even though I've nicknamed you after Wonder Woman, you *aren't* her. You need to talk to someone, I'll get you some names. It's fine if you need the light on; some of the strongest men I know have nightlights all over their houses. You do what you need to do to cope. Period."

"I didn't dream last night," she told him.

"What?"

"I didn't dream. And didn't even notice the lights weren't on. With you holding me, I think I knew I was safe."

"Fuck," Walker said softly, closing his eyes for a second before opening them again and staring at her with a fire she didn't want to pull away from. "I'm going to kiss you, Gillian," he warned.

"Okay," she whispered.

"But that's all. Just a kiss."

Gillian nodded and licked her lips in anticipation.

One of his hands moved up and over her hair, smoothing it down. Then his fingers went under her chin and tipped her head up gently.

Gillian felt her heart beating out of her chest. She gripped his arms and dug her fingernails into his skin. She wanted him to both hurry up and slow down at the same time. She wanted this moment to last forever, but she also wanted him to kiss her already.

She watched as he licked his own lips, then his head dropped ever so slowly.

Whimpering a little, she leaned forward and met him halfway.

At first the kiss was a bit tentative. Their lips touched once. Twice. Then he growled and the hand at her chin moved to grip the back of her neck. His fingers flexed and his mouth covered hers. He didn't tease, didn't lick her lips to ask for permission to enter.

He plundered.

And Gillian let him. Gladly.

She opened her mouth wider and felt his tongue swipe over hers.

How long they sat there kissing, she had no idea. All she knew was that she'd never felt as excited and treasured as she did in Walker's arms. He held her to him tightly. Pulling a bit on her hair when he wanted to move her head, but it didn't hurt. No, Walker Nelson's kisses didn't hurt in the least.

Gillian sucked on his tongue and felt more than heard the growl he let out. Not too long after that, he pulled back abruptly and forced her forehead to rest on his shoulder. Gillian could feel his chest rising and falling under her and felt some satisfaction that he was breathing as fast as she was.

"Holy hell," he muttered, and Gillian couldn't help it. She giggled.

With his hand still on the back of her neck, Walker pulled her upright. "You laughing at me, woman?"

She tried to stop, but couldn't. By the time she had herself under control and could look Walker in the eyes again, she was surprised to see the gentle way he was staring at her.

Self-conscious, she brought one of her hands to her mouth and wiped at it. "What? Is there something on my face?"

He pushed her hand out of the way tenderly and ran his thumb over her bottom lip. "Your lips are pink and swollen," he told her. "I like knowing that I made them that way."

Gillian licked Walker's thumb, and she saw his pupils dilate.

"No more of that. Or I'll think you're trying to seduce me. I'm not that kind of guy," he teased.

Aware of her position in his lap, how she was straddling him and could feel his erect cock against her, she wiggled and arched a brow. "You're not?"

Without warning, Walker stood, and Gillian was once more made aware of how strong he was and how easily he could move her body around. He put her on her feet, but pulled her into him. They were plastered together from hips to chest and they stood there for a long moment, staring at each other.

"Thank you for the best kiss I've ever had," he told her.

"Thank *you*," she returned.

"And thank you for not freaking when you woke up on my couch this morning. I swear I had good intentions. I was going to take you home and give you that kiss on your doorstep, then leave like a gentleman."

"I liked sleeping in your arms better," she said honestly.

"You have plans for today?" he asked.

Gillian shook her head. "Not really. I need to do some work for a sweet sixteen birthday party I'm planning, but otherwise, Sundays are my lazy day."

"How about I make you some coffee? You can drink it while I shower. Then I'll take you home, you can change, and I'll take you out for breakfast. *Then* I'll leave you in peace to have your lazy day."

"That sounds good," Gillian told him. And it did. She wouldn't mind spending the day with him, but she also kinda felt as if she needed some space. She was falling head over heels for this man, fast, and it scared the hell out of her. Yes, she'd thought he was the one for her from the first time she'd heard his voice, but now that she was in the midst of getting to know him, she was freaking out a bit at how perfect he seemed.

Walker leaned forward and kissed her forehead gently. And somehow that kiss felt as intimate as the one they'd just shared.

"There's a half bath down the hall. There's a bunch of extra toiletries under the sink in there...my mom stocked me up the last time she was here. Apparently it doesn't matter that I'm almost forty, she still feels the need to take care of her son."

Gillian grinned. "And you love it."

"Of course I do. I don't think I've ever bought a toothbrush in my life. I use them until they fall apart then I'm damn glad my mommy had the foresight to make sure I had a replacement on hand."

Laughing, Gillian knew at that moment, she was a goner. One date, and one night sleeping in his arms, and hearing him make fun of himself and how he liked his mom fussing over him...and she was in love. Instead of being scary, it simply felt right.

As if he could tell something had changed, Walker ran the backs of his fingers down her cheek. "Go, Di. Before I do something stupid like throw you over my shoulder and drag you into my lair."

Knowing he was only half kidding, Gillian slowly backed away from him. His shirt was wrinkled and he needed to shave, but he was so beautiful, it almost made her heart hurt.

Finally, she turned and headed for the bathroom... making sure to roll her hips just a little more than usual, knowing he was watching her ass as she left.

* * *

"I'll call you later if that's okay?" Trigger said as he held Gillian in his arms outside her door. He couldn't remember a better morning. He'd showered while she'd gotten some caffeine in her system, then they'd laughed and joked all the way back to Georgetown. It had taken all he had not to burst into her bathroom when he'd heard her shower turn on.

All he could think about was how she'd look naked as water sluiced over her curvy body. Luckily, it had taken her about twenty minutes to get ready, and that had given him a chance to get his libido under control.

She'd directed him to a small diner near her apartment complex and he'd had the best omelet he'd eaten in ages. Now they were back at her apartment, and he was saying goodbye. He wasn't sure when they'd be able to get together again, but he hoped he could make that happen sooner rather than later.

"It's more than okay," she reassured him.

He looked down at her purse when he heard the sound of another text coming through. She'd been getting texts all morning, and other than a quick reply to her friends to tell them she was alive and well, she'd been ignoring them.

"You're a popular person," he noted.

"I'm friendly," she said with a shrug. "And I know a lot of people. Both professionally and personally."

"Be careful," Trigger told her. "I don't want to lose you now that I've found you."

Her face gentled. "I will."

"I had a good time," he told her, prolonging their goodbye.

"Me too."

"Okay, before I get too sappy, I'm gonna go." Then he leaned forward, thrilled with how quickly Gillian went up on her tiptoes to meet his mouth. He kissed her, not as hard or as long as he wanted, but long enough for his toes to curl and his cock to harden.

"I'll talk to you soon."

"Okay. See you later."

"Bye, Di."

Trigger backed away, then turned and strode for the stairwell with a purpose. He needed to go before he forgot about his "going slow" edict.

CHAPTER TEN

Gillian smiled as she hung up the phone. She'd just finished reserving the ballroom at a nearby hotel for a fiftieth anniversary party for a truly wonderful couple. Their daughter wanted to have a huge party for her parents, and Gillian was more than happy to help give the couple an over-the-top celebration.

The last month had been amazing. Even with the hijacking still fresh in her mind two months later, she'd never been happier.

Walker was better than she'd ever imagined a boyfriend could be. Of course she'd dated in the past, but she'd never felt as content with another man as she did with Walker. On the days they didn't see each other, he texted, emailed, and called. She'd communicated more with him in the last month than she did her last boyfriend in all the months they'd been so-called dating.

She knew Walker was very close to his parents, even though they lived up in Maine. They enjoyed their solitude and had no problem with the long, cold winters in the northeastern state they'd made their home. It was funny how different their parents were, since hers moved to Florida because they'd hated the cold. Barbara and Thomas Romano were also very social. They lived on a golf course, and every day her mom drove the golf cart for her dad while he played nine holes. Of course, she did so only so she could see and gossip with the other wives who drove their husbands around.

Gillian had spent every weekend with Walker. Ever since that first night when she'd fallen asleep on his couch, it had been an unspoken agreement that when he took her out, she'd stay overnight with him. He'd been nothing but a gentleman, going no further in their physical relationship than some very intense kisses. She'd wake up in his arms on his couch and couldn't remember ever sleeping better.

Last weekend, Ann, Wendy, and Clarissa had insisted they wanted to spend time with Walker, so, along with their significant others, they'd all gone out to eat. Gillian had been thrilled when Walker had fit in easily with Tom, Wyatt, and Johnathan. By the end of the night, the men had all exchanged numbers, and Walker had somehow gotten the others to all agree to keep their eye on her...just in case.

The seventh hijacker still hadn't been identified, and the next day, she was meeting with a Drug Enforcement Administration employee and someone from the FBI to discuss, in detail, what she could remember about each of the passengers she'd been stranded with.

Gillian wasn't looking forward to the meeting, but Walker had said he'd accompany her, which made her feel ten times better about the whole thing. A part of her felt weak, as if she was no longer the independent business owner she'd spent the majority of her adult life working to make people see her as...but another part didn't care.

She liked being with Walker. And meeting with the two agencies made her nervous as hell. She wasn't a troublemaker. Hadn't even gotten a speeding ticket before. Hell, the first time she'd received a parking ticket she'd nearly had a panic attack because it felt as if she'd broken a major law.

Gillian realized she'd been sitting in her apartment staring off into space as she thought about Walker when her phone vibrated in her hand. Looking down, she saw a text from Andrea.

Over the last few weeks, the other woman had slowly started messaging more frequently, and Gillian was relieved to see that she was starting to heal from her ordeal. Gillian knew she'd gotten off way easier than Andrea had. Luis had taken a liking to the other woman and had forced himself on her. It was hard enough for Gillian to come to terms with what had happened...she wasn't also trying to deal with the aftermath of sexual abuse on top of everything else.

Andrea: Hey. How'd your day go? Did you get the hotel nailed down for that party?

Gillian: Yeah. The Marriott turned out to be too expensive, but The Driskill worked out perfectly.

Andrea: Cool!

Gillian: Any chance you'd want to meet up soon for coffee or something?

. . .

Gillian really wanted to see Andrea in person. So far, every time she'd suggested meeting, the other woman had balked, saying she just wasn't ready. That things were still fresh in her mind and she was afraid seeing any of the other hostages would bring back too many unwelcome memories. While Gillian hated that the sight of her could make Andrea unhappy in any way, she totally understood.

Andrea: Soon.

Gillian: Good. I have a meeting with the DEA and FBI tomorrow. I'm not looking forward to it.

Andrea: Can't blame you. They would intimidate the hell out of me.

Gillian: Exactly!

Andrea: What do they want to know?

Gillian: I guess they're still trying to identify the seventh hijacker and they want me to go over everything I can remember about everyone.

Andrea: Jeez, they're not asking much, are they?

Gillian: Right? I keep telling them that I didn't spend much time with the men since they kept us separated, I can't imagine who the other hijacker is. Honestly, I'm trying to put it all behind me, but when the FBI asks you to meet with them it's kinda hard to say no.

Andrea: True. Anyway, glad you got that party worked out. When is it again?

Gillian: Less than two months away.

Andrea: Isn't it late in the game to be reserving the ballroom?

Gillian: lol. Yes! The daughter had a hard time deciding on a venue. She's just lucky The Driskill had a cancellation. If there hadn't been, the party might've had to be held at the Super 8 motel or something.

Andrea: I'm sure if that happened, you still would've made it awesome.

Gillian: Thanks.

Andrea: I'll give you a shout later about getting together.

Gillian: I'd like that. Take care and be kind to yourself, Andrea. What happened wasn't your fault, and you couldn't have done anything differently without putting yourself in great danger.

Andrea: I'll try. Later.

Gillian: Bye.

Gillian sighed and put down her phone. Everything she'd said to Andrea was the truth. She couldn't have done anything differently. If she'd fought Luis, and refused to do what he wanted, he would've killed her. He'd already proven he had no problem using and hurting people to get what he wanted.

She thought about Janet and her daughter. Luis had threatened to hurt the little girl over and over if Gillian didn't do what he wanted, and she knew without a doubt he would've followed through. He'd even let one of his friends use little Renee as a shield when they'd bolted for the Beechcraft airplane. Using women and kids to make their getaway was low. Really low. But Gillian wasn't surprised. They were drug-dealing terrorists, after all.

Trying to shake off her sudden bad mood, Gillian headed into the kitchen to find something to make for dinner. She wasn't really hungry anymore but knew she needed to eat, otherwise she'd feel sick tomorrow when she had to talk about the hell she'd been through two months ago.

She was staring blankly into her pantry trying to decide on what to make when the buzzer for the downstairs door sounded. Frowning because she wasn't expecting anyone, Gillian went over to the wall and pushed the intercom button to see who was there.

"Hello?"

"Hey, it's me."

Immediately, Gillian's mood shifted. "Walker! What are you doing here?"

He chuckled. "Let me up, and I'll tell you."

Gillian immediately pushed the button to unlock the door to the building. She ran a hand over her hair, wondering what the hell she looked like. Walker had made it very clear he liked her exactly how she was—with mussed hair in the morning, or all made up for one of their dates—but she still couldn't help wanting to look her best for him.

She'd never seen Walker look anything but completely put together. Even down in Venezuela. He was dirty and sweaty, but she'd still thought he looked intimidating and *hot* in his black soldier ensemble. Not only that, he had confidence and manliness oozing from every pore at all times.

Gillian had the door open and was waiting impatiently for him when she saw him exit the stairwell and head her way. He was holding a large bouquet of flowers, and inside, she melted a bit. Seeing such a tall, masculine man holding a delicate bunch of flowers made him even more heart-stoppingly gorgeous.

The smile on his face as he approached made her heart

rate pick up, and she tipped her chin higher as he got near. The feel of his lips on hers made an electric shock shoot from her lips to her toes. As usual, however, he didn't deepen the kiss, but put his hand on her waist and encouraged her to step back inside her apartment.

When the door shut behind them and he'd locked it, she asked, "What are you doing here?"

"Can't I come visit my girl?"

"Of course," she told him with a smile. "But it's Wednesday."

"I can't come visit in the middle of the week?" he asked.

"You can, but you have work tomorrow. PT early. And it's not like you to just pop in on a random Wednesday."

The small smile that had been on his face disappeared and he put the flowers down on her kitchen counter. Then he leaned in and held her face in his hands.

Gillian loved it when he did that. She stared up at him as he spoke.

"Tomorrow's gonna be hard on you. There's no way I wasn't going to be here to support you through that. *You* don't need me here, but I *need* to be here."

Gillian couldn't remember a time when a man's words felt so good.

"And PT?" she asked.

"The guys know I won't be there."

"That's two," she told him.

"Two what?"

"Two times you've missed PT because of me."

His smile was tender. "And I'd miss a hundred more if you needed me."

"Walker," she sighed.

"Come 'ere," he said and pulled her into him.

Gillian went willingly. Without shoes, she was quite a bit shorter than him, and she could easily bury her nose in the crook of his neck and shoulder. She inhaled deeply, loving the way his woodsy scent made her feel safe and cared for.

They stood like that for several minutes before he pulled back. "Your appointment is at nine, right?"

She nodded against him.

"Austin traffic sucks, so we'll leave at seven-thirty and if we're early, we can stop and get some chocolate doughnuts for you."

Smiling, Gillian raised her head. "What'd I do to get so lucky to find you?"

Walker didn't answer, but his smile said it all for him. "How'd your call for the Howard anniversary shindig go today? You find a venue?"

"Yeah, The Driskill Hotel agreed to my terms. The party's less than two months away."

"That's good they agreed," he told her.

"Next weekend, I've got a corporate event I organized. It's a casual family thing the president is throwing to show his appreciation for his employees. He's rented out the Austin Zoo for four hours, and I have four food trucks parking nearby where everyone can get lunch and drinks for free...do you want to come with me?"

"You want me to?"

"Well...yeah. I wouldn't have asked if I didn't."

"I won't get in your way?"

Gillian chuckled. "Well, if you insist on following me so closely I bump into you every time I turn around, and if you don't let me do my thing, making sure everything is set up and good to go, then yes you will. But I think I know you well enough to know that you'll stand back and watch me from a distance, so no, you won't get in my way."

He smiled. "Then I'd love to come and watch you work."

"Have you been to the zoo before?"

"Di, do I look like a man who spends his time at zoos?"

"No."

"Right."

"So you haven't been before?"

He grinned. "No, Gilly, I haven't been to the zoo before."

"You'll like it."

"No offense, but I don't normally like zoos. Or circuses. I don't like seeing animals penned up for the amusement of humans. But that aside, I can't fucking wait to go to the zoo next weekend, for the simple fact it means that I'll get to hang out with you and see you kick ass at your job. I can't wait to see that. And after you're done corralling food trucks and making sure every man, woman, and child has had an amazing time, I get to stroll around with you, hand in hand, and feel proud and honored that you've chosen *me*, not any of the other men chomping at the bit to have their shot with you."

Gillian rolled her eyes. "No one's 'chomping at the bit' to go out with me, Walker. You seem to have a warped idea of my appeal."

Walker leaned in. One arm went around her waist, pulling her against him, and the other snaked behind her head and gripped her nape. "No, I don't. You're just clueless. You don't see the way the stock boys check out your ass in the grocery store. You ignore the guys who live in this apartment complex who practically drool as you walk by, and you've taken no notice of the scores of soldiers on base who can't keep their eyes off you. I don't give a shit if they look, but as long as you're with me, I'll make sure they know you're off limits."

"Walker," Gillian whispered, overcome with feelings she had no idea how to process. She still thought he was seeing things that just weren't there. She wasn't popular in high school. She didn't get asked out a lot in college. And since she'd graduated, she'd struggled to find men she was attracted to. But the fact that Walker thought she was the kind of woman men couldn't help but stare at felt pretty damn good.

He leaned his forehead against hers as he held her to him, and Gillian lifted his shirt slightly and put her hands on the bare skin of his waist. She felt him shudder, but he didn't move for several minutes.

She knew the second he was going to pull back, and for just a moment, she resisted. She'd been all right with him wanting to take things slow. She'd encouraged it, in fact. But the more time Gillian spent with Walker, the more she wanted him to go a little faster.

She wanted his hands on her. Wanted to know what all the intensity she felt in his gaze and his brief kisses felt like when he let himself go.

She knew he'd be a bit rough and overwhelming, but she *wanted* that. She wanted to get lost in passion for once in her life. Every other time she'd been with a man, she couldn't stop thinking about where she should put her hands. Or if the sounds she was making were weird or not. But Gillian had a feeling when Walker finally lost his restraint, she wouldn't be thinking about anything other than how he was making her feel.

Letting go of her neck and waist, Walker did indeed step back. "You had dinner yet?"

Gillian shook her head.

"What are you hungry for?"

"I don't know. I'm not really all that hungry, to tell you the truth."

"You need to eat," he said.

"I know."

"How about we order something from Uber Eats?"

"Let me get this straight, it's okay to use Uber to deliver dinner, but not for a ride, right?"

"Right," he said with a grin.

"But they could spit in my food. Or contaminate it with rat poison. Or put a roofie in it or something."

She could see Walker digesting her words. Then he said, "You're right. If you want something, we'll call to order it directly and I'll go pick it up."

"I was kidding."

"No, you're exactly right."

"I don't want to order anything," Gillian told him, more because she didn't really want him to leave now that he was there, even if it was just for twenty or thirty minutes to go pick up dinner. "I'm sure I've got something we can make here. There's some chicken in the fridge that I probably need to cook. We can bake it, if that's okay."

"Sounds perfect. I'll help," Walker said.

It took only about fifteen minutes to heat up the oven and prepare the chicken. They watched a cooking show on TV until the chicken was done, then they sat at the table and ate together.

Gillian had lived by herself for almost a decade, and she'd gotten used to eating alone, watching her favorites on the television, and pretty much doing whatever she wanted. But she'd been lonely. Seeing Walker on the weekends had spoiled her. She thought about him all week long and counted down the days until she could see him again.

Yes, she was busy with her work, but that didn't mean she didn't enjoy talking to him and spending time with him. Having him show up on a Wednesday was a surprise. A happy one. And Gillian could feel how much more content she was just having him near.

"You...you're staying the night, right?" she asked after they'd eaten and had gotten the dishes put away.

"I'd planned on it...unless you don't want me to," he told her.

"No! I do. But you don't have a bag or anything with you."

"It's in the car. I didn't want to presume."

Gillian decided to take a chance. She scooted over until her thigh was touching his and put her hand on his knee. "Walker, I don't think it's a secret that I like you. I live for the weekends. You're funny and sweet, and the more I get to know you, the more I enjoy spending time with you. I can't wait to officially meet your friends, and I hope like hell they like me. I know *my* friends have wholeheartedly approved of you, and I'd like to think we're moving forward with our relationship. It's not presumptuous of you to think that you'll be spending the night. I'd probably be offended, or at least really confused, if you didn't. Hell, we don't even talk about me staying over at your place on the weekends anymore. Is *that* presumptuous? Should I feel bad about not even thinking twice about bringing an overnight bag when you pick me up on Fridays?"

"No," he growled, as he leaned over Gillian so abruptly, she fell onto her back on the couch. He braced himself on his hands as he hovered over her. "My friends are going to love you. In fact, this weekend we're going to an event on base with them. It's an event for kids, and one of our friends' little girls is competing. Everyone'll be there, and we'll cheer her on and you can get to know the guys.

"I'm trying really hard not to overwhelm you, Gillian, but it's hard. I think the only thing that's kept me from moving too fast is the fact that you live forty miles away. I'm not a texting kind of guy. Or someone who likes to talk on the phone much, but with you, I find that I can't wait to share the shit that amuses me during the day. I've had to call my cell phone company and get the unlimited texting package for the first time in my life, just so I didn't spend eight hundred dollars on overage fees. It somehow feels different for you to stay with me...as if it's just a given. But I would never want to overstay my welcome or do something that makes you uncomfortable...like invite myself to stay without your permission."

"Permission granted," Gillian told him, running her hands up under his T-shirt to his chest. He couldn't grab her hands and stop her since he was using his arms to hold himself up.

She felt his nipples harden immediately at her touch, but before she could even enjoy the fact that she could turn him on, he was standing next to the couch.

"I'll go get my bag. Lock the door behind me."

Then before Gillian could say anything, he was gone.

There was no doubt Walker was intense and all man.

But he was holding back a lot, and it was beginning to concern her.

Taking a deep breath, she tried to get a grip on her out-of-control hormones. She was wet between the legs, as she was most of the time when Walker went all alpha male on her. As much as she wanted his hands on her, she had a feeling if she could just wait until *he* was ready, he'd make it more than worth her while.

CHAPTER ELEVEN

As much as Trigger had enjoyed waking up with Gillian in his arms—she'd refused to go to her bed, opting to stay with him on the couch the night before—he knew they had shit they needed to get done. He had to get her up, get some coffee in her, and get her to the courthouse downtown to meet with the DEA and FBI.

They'd talked about it a little last night, and he knew Gillian still had no idea in her own mind who the seventh hijacker might be. She was leaning toward it being Leyton, but his actions could be explained away by shock over what was happening. She was nervous about the interrogation she was sure she was going to be put through, even though Trigger had tried to tell her it was just a meeting, not an interrogation.

He wouldn't be allowed in the room, even with his level of security clearance; this wasn't his investigation. It was frustrating, but he hadn't expected anything different. The only thing he could do was try to take as much of the stress off Gillian as possible.

She was quiet that morning, and it wasn't normal. He'd spent enough mornings with her now to know that she was naturally chatty and didn't shy away from talking about whatever came to mind after they woke up. But this morning, she wasn't her usual lively self.

Hating that she was worrying about the meeting, but not able to do much about it, Trigger simply held her hand as he drove them into downtown Austin. Traffic sucked, as usual, but because they'd left plenty early, neither of them were stressing about it.

After he'd parked in a garage near the courthouse, he turned to Gillian. "You holding up okay?"

She took a deep breath. "Yeah. I just...I keep trying to figure out who could've been in on it. And it seems impossible that *anyone* could've been in cahoots with those killers. Everyone I saw was crying or acting like zombies because of shock over what was happening. Even the men. Okay, they weren't crying, but it was obvious they weren't happy. They were the ones who had to throw the first-class passengers' bodies out the hatch when we first landed in Venezuela, and it was just awful. It's hard to believe that anyone was that good of an actor. Maybe Brain and the other officials translated the conversation between the other hijackers wrong? Maybe there isn't someone else involved?"

Trigger wanted to agree with her, but he couldn't. He shook his head sadly. "There was no mistaking what they said, Gilly."

"I hate this," she whispered.

Without a word, Trigger let go of her hand and climbed out of his car. He quickly walked around to her door, opened it, and, instead of helping her out, he wrapped his arms around her and pulled her close. She melted into his chest, holding on to him with more desperation than he'd felt in her since he'd first taken her in his arms on the tarmac in Venezuela.

"It's gonna be okay," he murmured.

"I know," she replied.

Trigger gave her another few moments, then pulled back and put his hands on her shoulders. "Your job is not to figure out who the bad guy is here. All you need to do is tell the investigators everything you can remember. Don't analyze anyone's actions. They'll take your information and compare it to the data they've dug up from the other hostage interviews, and hopefully come to a conclusion. It is *not* your responsibility to tell them who you think the seventh hijacker is. They're the experts, not you. Understand?"

Gillian took a deep breath, then nodded. "Thank you. I needed to hear that."

Trigger leaned forward and kissed her gently, then said, "Good. Ready?"

"Ready," she said in a stronger voice.

He couldn't *not* be proud of her. She hopped out of his Blazer and he locked it as they walked hand in hand out of the garage toward the courthouse.

Gillian sat in the chair the DEA investigator gestured to and wiped her sweaty palms on her khaki slacks. She tried not to live her life being intimidated by anyone; she'd met with CEOs, presidents, managers of some of the best-ranked hotels in the world, and politicians without blinking.

But for some reason, sitting down with FBI Special Agent Tucker and Calum Branch, the DEA investigator, was freaking her out.

"Thank you for coming to meet with us today," Gary Tucker said. He was a middle-aged man with a receding hairline and a slight paunch. He was dressed in what she thought a typical FBI agent would wear...black slacks, dark shirt, and a blue tie that didn't match his pants.

"Yes. We're both very glad that you're alive and well," Calum added. He was a bit younger than Gary, and had on a pair of jeans, cowboy boots, and a button-down gray long-sleeve shirt. He even had a cowboy hat sitting on the table next to him. But instead of looking like a Texas cowboy, he looked like a tourist who was trying too hard to emulate a native rancher.

"That makes three of us," Gillian said nervously. She wished Walker was with her, but she understood why he couldn't be. He was sitting right outside the small conference room, looking way too big for the uncomfortable little office chair he'd parked himself in. He'd promised that he wouldn't budge and he'd be right there when she was done, no matter how long the interview took.

"If it's all right with you, I think we should just get right to it," Gary said. "How about you tell us what happened from the moment you realized something was wrong until you were rescued."

Gillian wanted to laugh. They weren't messing around. She took a deep breath and told them everything she could remember. How scared she'd been when she realized what was happening and that the hijackers had actually killed some of the passengers. How terrified she'd been when Luis told her she was going to be the one to talk to the negotiator. She even told the two men how much she'd hated the first negotiator, how he hadn't listened and that she thought it was *his* fault another passenger had been killed.

She praised Walker and said he'd done an amazing job of keeping her calm, decoding her lame clues, and making sure they'd received food and water. He also hadn't gotten anyone else murdered, which was a huge plus in Gillian's mind.

She thought she'd been matter-of-fact in her retelling of what she'd felt, but obviously the men had caught on to her feelings for Walker.

"Did you and Mr. Nelson have a relationship before the hijacking?" Calum asked.

Appalled, Gillian shook her head. "No! I hadn't ever met him before. We don't exactly run in the same circles."

"What do you mean by that?" Gary asked.

"Just what I said. He's in the Army. He lives forty miles away from me. I'm busy with my life and job, just as he is. He was in Venezuela doing his job and I was there...well, being held captive."

"But you and he are dating now," Gary insisted.

"Yes," Gillian said firmly. She wasn't going to be ashamed of Walker.

"Don't you think that's odd?" Calum probed.

She frowned. "What's odd?"

"That the two of you just happen to live near each other and he's the one who was sent to free the hostages from that plane?"

Gillian stared at the DEA agent in disbelief. "Are you

insinuating that I somehow arranged for us to meet? That
we planned this?"

"Well, no," Calum backpedaled a bit. "But you have to
admit it's a bit too coincidental."

"No, I don't," she fired back. "No more coincidental
for anyone else on that plane who was headed to Texas.
Most of them live here, like I do. And I can't believe
you're sitting there accusing me of...what *are* you accusing
me of?"

Calum held up his hands in a conciliatory gesture, but
Gillian could tell it was a bit condescending. "I'm not
accusing you of anything. I'm just thinking out loud."

"Then maybe you can stop, because it's annoying me."

She thought she heard Gary chuckle, but he deftly
covered it up with a cough. "We're just doing our jobs,
ma'am," he told her. "I know this is hard, but put yourself
in our seats. We can't dismiss anything that might lead us
to the seventh hijacker. Do you want this person to
continue to be free? To possibly participate in other
terrorist activities that might result in the deaths of more
people next time?"

"Of course not," Gillian said, "but—"

"Right, so we have to ask some uncomfortable questions sometimes," Gary went on deftly. "Not that we think
you're the unknown hijacker...but you could be. I mean, it
would be pretty smart of Luis to put someone he's in
cahoots with on the phone to talk with the negotiators."

Gillian could only stare at the other man in astonishment. "I'm not a terrorist," she insisted.

"Isn't that what the seventh hijacker would say?" Gary
asked reasonably.

A headache was beginning to form behind her eyes.

"For the record, we don't think you're who we're looking for," Gary said, obviously expecting her to blow off the fact that he'd pretty much accused her of partnering with murderers. "But you can understand where we're coming from, I'm sure."

"We need to go over the passenger manifesto person by person. We'd like for you to tell us everything you can remember about each person. What they were wearing, any conversation you might've had with them, and your personal thoughts about them. The smallest thing you recall could be the difference between catching this person and them going free. Understand?"

Yeah, Gillian understood. She understood that this was going to be a hell of a long day. Much longer than she'd anticipated. She had a quick thought about Walker sitting outside the door in that tiny, uncomfortable chair, and she felt bad. Then she had no time to think about anything other than her fellow hostages.

Gary and Calum started off by showing her pictures of the first-class passengers. They wanted to know what she remembered about them during the first part of the flight. Did they ask for a lot of drinks? Did they get up to use the restroom?

Gillian tried to tell the investigators that she hadn't paid any attention to anyone beyond her row, but they kept pressing. They wanted to know about the flight attendants; did any of them look suspicious, had she noticed anything odd with them, were they extra friendly with any of the passengers?

The questions went on and on, and for the most part, Gillian's answers were "I don't know" or "not that I noticed."

Then the interview got harder.

They showed her picture after picture of her fellow coach passengers, and wanted to know her thoughts on each person. They wanted her to talk about their personalities, how they dealt with captivity, and anything she could remember them saying. In detail.

"How about Janet Cagle?" Gary asked, showing Gillian a picture of the young mother.

"She was scared out of her mind," Gillian told them. "The hijackers kept threatening her and her daughter, Renee. Most of the time they sat on the floor between the seats and tried to be invisible."

"Which one of the hijackers used the girl as a shield when they were trying to escape to the Beechcraft?" Calum asked.

"I'm not sure...Isaac? Carlos? In the chaos, I wasn't paying attention. They were forcing pairs of men and women out onto the slide and until Alberto grabbed me, I didn't realize what they were doing."

"What *were* they doing?" Gary asked.

Gillian sighed. She had a feeling he knew the answer to his own question, but wanted to hear what she was going to say. "They were trying to create uncertainty for our rescuers. With one woman and one man paired up, and everyone running toward the smaller plane, it would be hard at first glance to know who was a hijacker and who was a hostage."

Both men nodded. "What about Maria Gomez?" Gary put another picture in front of her.

And so it went. The pictures kept coming, one after another. Camile Millan, Rebecca Crawford, Reed Stonegate, Charles Wayman. Their faces swam as Gillian did her best to recall every little detail about each person. It was hard because most of the men she'd just seen at a distance and hadn't had any real contact with. But of course, Gary and Calum weren't satisfied with that. They pressed for more.

"Leyton Morales," Gary said, putting another picture in front of her.

Taking a sip of water, Gillian stalled a bit. She didn't want to say anything bad about anyone. Didn't want to finger anyone as the hijacker if they weren't. She'd feel terrible if they were unfairly accused. "He...um...I thought he was a bit weird," she said at last.

"Weird how?" Calum asked.

"Just...weird. He stared at the women intently. He also paid a lot of attention to the hijackers. Maybe he was in shock though. I know I was having a hard time processing everything that was happening. He didn't *seem* to be quite as scared as the rest of us. I mean, I don't know him at all, so maybe he had a horrible life and being held at gunpoint and threatened wasn't a big deal for him, and that's why he wasn't as scared." Gillian knew she was talking really fast and making excuses for Leyton, but she couldn't help it.

"Give us an example," Gary ordered.

Sighing, Gillian nodded. "When the hijackers inflated the slide and started pushing people out, he kinda just stood there watching. When Alberto grabbed me, Leyton told him that *he'd* go out the slide with me. But, to be fair, Wade also volunteered to go with me. I think they were both trying to get me away from Alberto, which was really brave of them. Alberto refused, and then Leyton actually reached out and grabbed my free arm. He and Alberto kinda had a tug-of-war with me for a second. Eventually,

Alberto shoved him away from me with a hand to his chest, but Leyton didn't back off very far. He just kept staring at us. Then I noticed, when I was struggling and trying not to be pushed inside the smaller plane, that Leyton was once again standing nearby, just watching. Or maybe he was staring off into space."

"Did you see Wade?" Gary asked.

"No."

"Hmmm," Gary said.

He didn't say anything more than that. Just *Hmmm*. It was maddening.

"How about Andrea Vilmer? We understand she had a hard time of it on the plane."

That was the understatement of the century. Gillian nodded.

"What can you tell us about that?"

"What do you want to know?"

"Everything you can remember," Gary said without any emotion.

Her frustration piqued again. "You want to know about her expression of revulsion when Luis licked her neck obscenely? How scared she was when he decided to assault her? How she whimpered in fright when he dragged her down the aisle of the plane? Maybe you want to know how long it took for him to get off as he forced her to suck his dick right there in the exit row? What *exactly* do you want to know?"

She was breathing fast when she was done, but she took a deep breath and continued in a more even tone. "I don't know why Luis decided to single her out. Probably just because she's pretty. I'm ashamed to admit that at the time, I was just relieved it wasn't me...but that didn't mean

I wasn't horrified on her behalf. There was nothing anyone could do, and we knew it. If we tried to interfere, he would've killed us without blinking. He was that cold-hearted. I think Luis was the first one to say he was taking her with him, and that's probably why Alberto tried to drag me onto that plane too."

"You've been in touch with Andrea," Gary said. It wasn't a question.

"Yeah. Texts. She's not dealing very well with what happened. She's been in therapy but I'm not sure it's helping yet."

"You've talked to others too, right?" Calum asked.

Gillian nodded again. "Yes, a bunch of us exchange texts and emails regularly. We feel as if we've bonded. We've been through hell and somehow survived."

"How often do you talk to them?"

Gillian shrugged. "I don't know. I talk with some more than others. I text Andrea pretty regularly. And Janet sends me texts and pictures of Renee. We've talked about how best to deal with the angry feelings that we all still seem to have. About how unfair it was that it happened to *us*."

"What about Alice Hicks and her husband Wade?" Calum asked. "You were seated next to them before the plane was taken over. Right?"

"Yes."

"Do you talk to them?"

"I've gotten an email or two. The situation was really hard on Alice. She and Wade are newlyweds. They were asleep when it all started and they were separated. Alice seems to be the kind of woman who doesn't do well at all in stressful situations. She cried a lot, and I saw Wade doing his best to make eye contact with her throughout the entire ordeal."

"What about Muhammad Nassar? He's Muslim. Did you see him have any one-on-one contact with the hijackers?"

"No," Gillian told them. "As I've said over and over, I didn't have much contact with the men at all. I didn't even see most of them. I couldn't tell you what Muhammad did, although I don't think it's fair to think he might be the seventh hijacker simply because of his religious beliefs."

"We weren't accusing him of anything," Calum said smoothly. "We're just trying to find out as much information about everyone as possible."

And so the questioning continued. Alejandro Chavez, Mateo Herrera ...they went through every single person, including the passengers from Canada, Japan, Colombia, Panama, India, Nicaragua...

By the time they were done, Gillian could hardly function.

She felt as if she'd taken the world's hardest test...and failed. She didn't think she'd given them anything useful. If she had any suspicions about who the wolf in sheep's clothing might be, she would've told someone before now. The entire interview just seemed so pointless. Did they really care who had stomach problems because of lack of food and water, and who didn't?

"If you think of anything else you didn't tell us today, please contact us as soon as possible," Gary told her. "Anything, no matter how small, could be the difference in taking one more terrorist off the street or letting them continue to ruin lives in the future."

Well, gee, no pressure, Gillian thought. She nodded.

"And you need to be extremely cautious," Calum added. "You were handpicked by Luis to be their voice for some reason. It could be the seventh hijacker was really the one calling the shots, and *he* chose you. Until this person is behind bars, your life could be in danger."

Gillian shivered. Wasn't *that* a fun thought? "Do you really think whoever it is will come after me?"

"That's the thing, we just don't know," Gary told her. "But killing you could be a way to get back at the fact that six of his friends didn't survive their mission."

"They had to know there was a pretty big chance they weren't going to live," Gillian insisted.

Both investigators shrugged.

Great. Just great. "Can I go?" she asked, hating how weak her voice sounded.

Gary and Calum stood, their chairs making obnoxious and ear-splitting screeches as they moved back.

Moving stiffly, Gillian nodded at them, not bothering to shake their hands, and made her way to the door. She knew the men were just doing their jobs, but she needed out of that room.

The second she opened the door, Walker was there. He stood in front of her saying something, but she didn't hear it. She walked to him, then leaned her head against his chest. His arms went around her and held her close.

Gillian didn't even have the energy to put her arms around him in return. She just stood in his embrace with her arms hanging limply by her sides and closed her eyes.

Walker had her. He'd make sure she got home. She didn't have to think about anything but how good he smelled and how thankful she was that he was there.

* * *

Trigger wanted to know what the fuck happened behind that closed conference room door more than he wanted his next breath. His woman was fucking exhausted and almost catatonic. He should've tried harder to be allowed in there with her. He would've made sure the two investigators didn't push her too hard.

"What'd you do?" he growled as Gary and Calum exited the room.

They both looked surprised at the venom in his tone. They looked from him to Gillian then back.

"She did good," Gary said quietly. "Much better than we'd expected."

"We might've gone on a little longer than we did with the others, but she had a lot of really useful information," Calum told him.

Again, Trigger mentally kicked himself for not at least forcing them to take a break. Gillian had been in with them for over five hours. She'd missed lunch and had obviously been pushed too far.

Wanting to lambast the investigators, but knowing that would delay getting Gillian home, he turned his back on the two men and leaned down to the exhausted woman in his arms. She was strong as fuck, but even superheroes had their breaking points.

"Ready to go home?" he asked gently.

She nodded against his chest.

"You want me to carry you?"

She shook her head but didn't move.

Trigger couldn't help but smile. He didn't rush her, simply waited for her to gather enough strength to walk out of the building by his side. Within a minute, he felt her take a big breath and pull away from him.

He didn't let her go far, keeping his arm around her waist. She leaned heavily on him and he felt her finger hook into one of the belt loops of his jeans. He wanted to ask her what happened, what was said, but knew that was the last thing she needed. Right now she needed food, and to feel safe.

Gillian didn't need his protection because she was weak. She was far from it. But he needed to give it to her because she was important to him. Over the last month, he'd found himself thinking about her almost every minute of the day. She'd quickly become one of the most important people in his life. And he'd be damned if he did anything to harm her in any way.

He got her to his Blazer and helped her get buckled in. She closed her eyes and rested her head on the back of the seat, exhaustion easy to read in her body language. Before starting the car, Trigger took the time to order food for them from a diner near her apartment. He stopped to pick it up before heading to her place. She didn't even ask what he'd ordered or what he was doing, she was that tired.

The second they entered her apartment, she turned to him. "I'm going to go lie down...is that all right?"

He hated seeing her like this. "You don't have to ask my permission to lie down in your own apartment, Gilly. Go on. I'll be in soon with some lunch."

"I'm not hungry."

"I know, but you need to eat."

For a second, she looked like she was going to argue with him, but in the end, she just nodded and headed down the hall. He hated how her shoulders were slumped and she looked as if she'd just gone ten rounds in a boxing ring.

He gave her twenty minutes—the longest twenty minutes of his life—before following her. He had a bowl of her favorite chicken fajita soup and two of the breadsticks she always raved about. They were soft and buttery, and would give her a needed boost of energy.

She was lying on her side on her bed with her back to the door. Trigger put the food down and sat on the edge of the mattress. He put one hand on her thigh and waited for her to acknowledge him. He knew she was awake because she'd stiffened when he'd sat down so she wouldn't roll into him.

With the patience he'd learned in his Delta training, Trigger waited. Finally, she rolled over and stared up at him.

"You all right?" he asked softly.

She nodded. "Yeah. I just...it was a lot."

"I'm sorry, Di. I should've been there with you."

"You weren't allowed. It's okay."

Trigger shook his head. "It's not okay. If I was there, I could've made them let you take some breaks. Warned them when they were pushing too hard—and don't deny it. They pushed you *hard*."

She gave him a small nod. "But they needed to. If they're going to catch this guy, they need to know—"

"Uh-uh," he said with a shake of his head. "If they're going to catch this guy, then they need to investigate...not push innocent women past their breaking points for information that won't make a lick of difference."

Gillian stared up at him. "So you're saying you think what I told them was pointless?"

"No, not at all," Trigger said firmly. "I know your interview gave them a more well-rounded idea of each and every passenger. You're observant and smart; whatever you told them was absolutely useful. But there was no point in pushing you until you were practically comatose to get it. I'm sure they already have their suspicions about who the seventh hijacker is. They were just using interrogation tricks to see what they could get out of you."

Gillian closed her eyes. "I wish you were there too," she said. Her eyes opened. "But it's done."

"If you want to talk about it, I'm here," Trigger told her.

"Thanks," she whispered. "I mean, I've already told you most of what I told them. I just don't like thinking that someone I thought I'd shared this awful experience with might be in on the whole thing. It makes me sick."

"Come on. Sit up and eat something. It'll make you feel better. Then we can watch TV together the rest of the afternoon. I'll run you a bath tonight and by morning, you'll feel like yourself again."

Gillian smiled at him and scooted up until her back was against the headboard. While she started in on her lunch, Trigger went back out to the other room to get her the present he'd found for her that week.

He held the small box in his hand as he sat back down.

"What's that?"

"Open it and see," he said. "I saw it and thought of you."

Trigger loved seeing the spark of life in her eyes. He hated seeing her so beaten down, and if a little gift was enough to make her smile, he'd make it his goal in life to buy her a million tchotchkes to make that smile permanent.

She opened the box and pulled out the mug that was inside. Grinning, she said, "I like it."

"Told you it reminded me of you," Trigger said. The blue mug had pictures of a cartoon Wonder Woman all over it. She was leaping, running, using her bracelets to deflect bullets, and generally being kick-ass.

"I'm not feeling very Wonder-Woman-like at the moment," she admitted.

"You'll get there," Trigger said without hesitation. "You're human. You're allowed to feel how you feel. You're still one of the strongest people I know."

"Thanks."

"You're welcome. Now, hurry up and finish so we can go out and watch *Luther*."

"You're addicted to that show," she said while chuckling.

"And you aren't?" he asked.

She merely grinned.

* * *

Hours later, Gillian already felt more like herself. Lunch had done wonders to elevate her mood, then sitting on the couch being lazy with Walker for the rest of the day had finished the job. Yeah, she'd had a hard morning, mentally, but it was over and done with, and she needed to pull her head out of her ass and get on with her life.

It was Thursday, and Walker was spending the night, and Gillian was determined to have him sleep in the bed with her. In all the nights they'd slept together—*slept*-slept, nothing more—they'd always done it on a couch, his or hers. He'd never moved them to a bedroom. And while Gillian loved waking up in his arms, she wanted to do so in her bed.

After they'd made spaghetti for dinner, laughing throughout the preparation, and before watching more episodes of *Luther*, she'd changed into her sleep shorts and top. It was the first time she'd actually put on a pair of pajamas before snuggling with Walker on the couch. Oh, she'd worn leggings, and a T-shirt without a bra, but this was different. The sleep shorts were *short*, and the top was sleeveless. She felt sexy in the outfit and wanted nothing more than to entice Walker into giving her a few kisses and hold her all night.

He looked like he'd swallowed something sour when she'd come back into the living area after changing, which wasn't exactly encouraging. And when he hadn't immediately pulled her into his side after she sat down, Gillian began to worry that she'd messed up somehow. After he'd been so attentive and concerned about her earlier, she'd thought for sure this was the perfect time to move their relationship forward.

But now Walker sat stiffly on the other end of the couch watching the television screen as if it was the most fascinating thing in the world. It was disheartening.

Wanting to be the brave, kick-ass woman he'd nick-named her after, Gillian decided to go for what she wanted.

"Walker?"

"Hmmm?" he asked, not looking at her.

"Are you all right?"

"Yeah, why?"

At least he'd turned to look at her. "Because ever since I changed, you've been avoiding looking at me as if you'll get the plague if you even glance over here."

He sighed. "It's not you."

Oh, shit, she didn't like the sound of that. "What do you mean?"

"You've had a hard day...maybe you should turn in early."

Gillian could only stare at Walker in disbelief. Had he really said that?

Yeah, he had.

So much for her feeling good about herself and confident in the relationship they'd been building.

She'd never felt so confused. Walker had pampered her and treated her as if she was the most precious thing in his life all day. And the second she'd changed into something a little more revealing—it wasn't as if she'd put on a sexy teddy or anything; she was wearing shorts and a tank top—he'd frozen solid and was desperately trying to pretend she wasn't even there.

Without another word—what was she going to say? Beg him to look at her? To tell her why he'd suddenly turned into the ice man?—Gillian got up off the couch and headed to her room. She pulled off her cute little sleep set and put on a pair of leggings and a long-sleeve shirt. She had the urge to completely cover up before she went to bed.

Climbing under the covers, she did her best not to cry...but it was no use. The tears fell from her eyes, and she tried to be quiet as she sobbed and wondered what the hell was wrong with her.

* * *

Trigger's fists clenched and it took everything he had to stay where he was. He could hear Gillian crying, and it tore at him. When she'd come out of her room wearing that sexy-as-hell sleep set, he'd immediately gotten hard.

He respected Gillian more than she'd ever know, and he'd been doing his best to take things slow. The only way he knew to do that was to keep his dick in his pants. Women didn't like being used for sex, and although that was far from what he'd be doing if he slept with her, he didn't want her to get the wrong idea.

He wanted Gillian. Permanently. But he didn't want to do anything that might make her think this was a short-term relationship. Seeing her silky skin on display and knowing the shorts would give him easy access to the part of her he was getting more and more desperate to touch, to taste, he'd had to distance himself.

He was weak. If he'd pulled her into his side, he wouldn't have been able to keep his hands off her. After the day she'd had, he wanted nothing more than to show her how proud he was. To worship her from the top of her head to the tips of her toes. But it still felt too early. They'd only been dating a month. He had no idea what the rules were for sex in today's world, but he respected Gillian too much to push her into a physical relationship before she was ready. She was vulnerable, and he'd be damned if he did anything to take advantage.

But now she was in her room crying. And *he'd* done that.

He'd fucked up. Instead of respecting her, she'd thought he was *rejecting* her.

Before he registered what he was doing, Trigger was on his feet and headed for her bedroom. It was obvious she was trying to be quiet, but he could still hear her sobs through her closed door. Without knocking, he opened the door and entered.

The entire room smelled like honeysuckle, making his dick once again rise. He ignored his body and walked over to where she was huddled under her covers on the bed. He cringed when he saw she was now wearing a long-sleeve shirt. Seeing the sexy pajamas lying on the floor by the bathroom, he knew she'd probably put on a pair of leggings as well.

He didn't hesitate to climb into her queen-size bed and snuggle up behind her. His arm wrapped around her waist, and he pushed his other arm under her head, so she was now using it as a pillow.

"Go away, Walker," she said quietly.

"Nope."

"I get it. You aren't ready for a relationship. It's fine. I just need some space from you right now."

"And you aren't getting it," Trigger said firmly. "I need you to listen to me."

"I can't," she said, shaking her head. "Don't you get it? You've already said enough tonight."

"When you walked out of this room earlier, it was all I could do not to pull you to the floor, strip you naked, and fuck you until neither of us could walk."

The words came out without thought. They were pure, naked emotion.

Gillian froze in his arms. She hadn't pushed him away in disgust, so Trigger kept going.

"We've only been dating a month. I don't want to rush

you into a physical relationship with me. I'm trying to be a gentleman. You had a hard day, and I didn't want to take advantage of that. I knew if I touched you while you were wearing that shorty sleep thing, I wouldn't be able to stop with a little cuddling."

"What if I don't want you to stop?" she asked.

Knowing there was no way she could miss the erection against her ass, since her back was plastered against his front, Trigger didn't even bother trying to hide it from her. "I need to wait," he said simply. "I can't tell you exactly why. I just feel the need to treat you with respect, like the amazing woman you are. To not rush into sex simply because I want you so bad. I want this relationship between us to last. Forever, hopefully...and a part of me feels as if I'm cheapening my feelings for you if I rush us into bed."

Trigger felt stupid voicing his thoughts out loud, but he wouldn't keep them to himself if his silence hurt her. He wanted no misunderstandings between them.

"Make no mistake, I want you, Gilly. But I want to do things right. The last thing I ever want you to think is that I'm using you in any way. I've got good control, but you make me feel as if I'm fifteen again and trying to hide my erection in Miss Noonbreaker's class."

He felt her chuckle against him and relax a fraction.

"I thought you didn't want me."

"I want you," he said immediately. "Don't ever doubt that."

"Will you stay the night with me? Here?"

Trigger winced. "I can't," he whispered.

Gillian turned in his embrace, and Trigger found

himself staring into her puffy, red-rimmed eyes, and he wanted to kick himself all over again for hurting her.

"I trust you," she whispered.

"I appreciate that, more than you know, but I can't," he said, praying she'd take his word for it and let it go.

"Why?" she asked.

Closing his eyes, Trigger had known she'd want to know why. He opened his eyes and stared into hers. "Because you feel too good. Being in your bed is too close to what I want for the rest of my life. Everything in here smells like honeysuckle, and there's no way I'd get any sleep. I know I'm not making sense...I can hold you in my arms on the couch and sleep all night because a part of me knows we're not in a bed. The first time we make love, it's not going to be on a fucking sofa. So I can control myself. But if I fall asleep in a bed with you, I don't trust myself not to touch you. To take what my subconscious is screaming is mine."

She stared up at him for a long moment before nodding. "Okay."

"Okay?" Trigger asked. "Are you saying that because you think it's what I want to hear, or because you understand?"

"I get it. I want you too, Walker. I've thought you were mine from the get-go. At least I wanted you to be. I can wait until you're ready."

Trigger chuckled, but it wasn't a humorous sound. "How did I get to be the insecure one in our relationship?"

"I think it's cute. Frustrating, but cute," Gillian told him. Then she got serious. "I'm flattered that you want to respect me. I've never had a man treat me like you do.

They were all about themselves and getting what they wanted."

"I'll always put you first, Gillian. Even when it goes against what I want. Understand?"

"I'm beginning to."

"Tell me you understand why I can't sleep in this bed with you. And mean it."

"I understand. Would it be okay if I came out to the living room and slept on the couch with you?"

Trigger stared down at her. He used his thumb to brush away the lingering wetness on her cheeks. "I hate that I made you cry."

Gillian shrugged. "I overreacted."

"No, you didn't. I was an ass and didn't explain myself. I'll try not to let it happen again but...I'm a guy, so it probably will. But in the future, don't let me get away with being all closemouthed and shit. Get in my face and force me to talk to you. Don't slink away and cry because I made you feel bad, okay?"

"I...I'll try."

"Okay. And yes, if you think you'll be comfortable, I'd love to have you sleep in my arms—on the couch."

"I'm comfortable anywhere you are," she reassured him.

Running his hand over her hair gently, he couldn't help but wonder how the hell he'd gotten so lucky. Going down to Venezuela should have been just another mission. Just another opportunity to take out some of the bad guys in the world. Instead, it had changed his life forever. It had brought him Gillian.

He pulled himself from her hold and helped her stand, guilt swamping him once again when he saw she was indeed wearing leggings. That she'd covered herself from head to toe in fabric. Wishing he was strong enough to tell her to put her shorts and tank top back on, Trigger pulled her out of the room toward the couch, and their bed for the night.

He sat and immediately pulled her into his embrace. He swung his feet up onto the soft leather and lay back with her in front of him. They were cramped, and the sofa wasn't overly comfortable, but it was what Trigger needed to keep himself under control. He felt bad that he was putting his own needs above Gillian's, but he didn't change his mind on their sleeping arrangements.

"I'm sorry you had a hard day," he said softly.

"You made it better in the end," she told him.

Trigger kissed the back of her head and inhaled her sweet scent, filling every cell of his body with her honeysuckle smell.

"Sleep well."

"I will now that you're here," she said sleepily.

Trigger stayed awake a long time, thankful that he hadn't fucked things up between them so badly she'd kicked him to the curb. Gillian was always so competent, so take-charge and confident, that he needed to be extra careful not to say or do anything that would take a chunk out of her armor. He loved her just the way she was.

CHAPTER TWELVE

Friday, Gillian had to work, and to her surprise, Walker was completely all right with just hanging around her apartment. He did some work of his own on his laptop, but otherwise spoiled her rotten. He brought her coffee in her new Wonder Woman mug and made her an amazing breakfast of eggs and bacon with homemade biscuits to top it off. For lunch, he went out and grabbed them some sushi. After she'd called a few new clients and got some research done on the events they wanted her to plan, she and Walker had talked more about where he was taking her the next day.

Apparently, the daughter of one of his Army buddies was a tomboy and loved participating in the obstacle course events the base had for kids. She was twelve years old and, according to Walker, one of the cutest kids he'd ever met.

Gillian hadn't spent a lot of time around children, but was looking forward to meeting Annie and spending time with the guys on Walker's team. She'd met them, of course, in Venezuela, but hadn't spent any quality time with them. She was nervous, but looking forward to getting to know everyone.

For dinner, Walker grilled steaks on her cheap outdoor grill—complaining the entire time about how crappy it was, and how he was going to need to get her a new one since he'd be spending a lot of time at her place.

Gillian liked that thought.

That night, they once again fell asleep on her couch, but this time Gillian didn't overthink it. She wanted to move her relationship with Walker forward, but she wanted *him* to want that too. It felt a little weird to be the one pushing for more, but even that made Walker more attractive to her.

Saturday morning, they woke up early and, while Gillian showered, Walker once more got her coffee and breakfast ready.

"You're totally spoiling me," she mock complained when she emerged from her room dressed and ready to head to Fort Hood.

"Good," he said with a smile. "Just buttering you up so when I screw up, you'll find it easier to forgive me."

Gillian knew he was joking but frowned anyway. "Walker, I don't expect you to be perfect all the time. You're going to mess up, just as I am. I'd like to think that, while I might be irritated, I can put it behind me. I like you for who you are."

"Good," he said, pulling her into a hug. "Because I like you just the way you are too. And if you drive me crazy by leaving dirty clothes on the floor, I can look past that too."

She chuckled and playfully hit him in the arm. "I'm guessing that's your way of telling me you're a neat freak?"

He smiled. "Yup. The Army trained me well."

"As long as you don't leave beard trimmings in the sink, I'm okay with that."

He looked horrified. "I don't."

"Good. Can I use your razor in the shower?"

"Nope. I have to draw the line somewhere," he said with a smile. "I'll get you your own razors."

"Deal."

Gillian sighed in contentment. She was enjoying spending time with Walker. She knew next week he'd be back at work and she'd be busy with her own business, but she'd hate not being able to wake up with him and banter like they were right now.

"What's that look for?" he asked with a tilt of his head.

"I like this," she said.

"What?"

"This. Teasing. Chatting. Having you make my coffee and eating breakfast with you. I was just thinking about how I was going to miss it...you...next week, when we went back to our regular lives. Forty miles isn't that far, but when I wake up alone on Monday morning, I have a feeling it'll feel like a thousand."

"I know, Di. I feel the same way. We just have to make the most of the time we do get to spend together," Walker said softly.

She nodded. "I'm looking forward to today."

"Me too. Come on, enough melancholy. Let's concentrate on one day at a time."

"Agreed."

An hour later they were on their way to the Army base and Gillian couldn't wait. They pulled onto the base and, after having their IDs checked, continued to the parking area for the competition. It was packed, and Walker had trouble finding a place to park, which surprised Gillian. She had no idea something like this would be as well attended as it was.

Taking hold of her hand, Walker headed around a building to the field where the obstacle course was located. Gillian had a hard time believing *kids* would be going through the course laid out in front of her.

It had tires and ropes, but there were also wooden boards set up so high, she didn't think any kid would be able to get over them. "Holy cow," she said under her breath.

"Impressive, isn't it?" Walker said with a chuckle.

"Yeah."

"The first time I went to one of these, I didn't think there was any way a kid would be able to complete it, but I was pretty quickly shown the error of my thinking. Over there," he said, pointing off to the side, "is the obstacle course for the kids under six, but everyone from seven and up uses the main one."

"I'm having a hard time imagining anyone being able to complete this...especially a kid."

"Just wait. They're pretty impressive."

"I'm *already* impressed, and I haven't even seen anyone do it yet," Gillian told him.

As if he knew exactly where his friends would be, Walker headed up the bleachers to a section in the top right. There were six men already sitting there when they arrived.

"Hey," Walker said to the group.

A couple of the men gave him a chin lift and the others verbally said hello.

"About time you got here," one of the men ribbed.

"Whatever," Walker said. "We're right on time. Guys, I know you met her before, but this is Gillian Romano. Gillian, this is Lefty, Grover, Brain, Oz, Doc, and Lucky."

She shook each of their hands as they were introduced, and Gillian couldn't stop herself from saying, "I can't wait to find out what your nicknames mean."

Everyone chuckled.

"I think we'll wait another day for that," Walker said with a wink, gesturing to a seat. "I wouldn't want you to think we're all completely nuts."

"Glad to see you looking so good after everything that happened," Doc said.

Gillian smiled. "Thanks. Every day I get better. I still have a bit of trouble at night sometimes, but otherwise I'm good."

"It can take a while for the dreams to stop," Oz told her sympathetically.

"How'd the interview go on Thursday?" Lefty asked.

Gillian shrugged. "As good as it could've, I guess. I told them everything I could remember, they warned me that the seventh hijacker could still come after me, and that I should be careful, and that was that."

Walker frowned at his teammate, and Gillian put her hand on his knee. "It's okay, Walker. I don't mind talking about it."

"*I* mind," he replied. He turned to Lefty. "Can we not talk about that now?"

"Sorry," Lefty said.

"It's fine," Gillian stated firmly. "Walker, I don't want your friends walking on eggshells around me. I want them to feel free to say what they want. It's no secret what happened, duh, you guys were there. It's kinda nice that they're concerned. So back off, okay?"

Brain smirked. "I like her," he said.

"Me too," Grover agreed. "If you decide to dump this asshole, I'll give you my number."

"Shut the fuck up," Walker mumbled, kicking Grover's leg. "She's not dumping me, and even if she was, she wouldn't call you."

Gillian giggled. It was funny how disgruntled Walker sounded. "I appreciate it," she told Grover. "But I'm pretty happy with Walker. But seriously, yeah, the interview wasn't exactly fun. I had to look at every single passenger's photo and tell the investigators what I knew about them. In most cases, it wasn't much, which made them frown a lot and stressed me out. But I told them what I could and that's that. I bought a bunch of those video camera things and I'm being as careful as I can. There's no reason for me to be targeted, and I can't live my life shut up inside my apartment."

"Sounds like you're taking this seriously, which is good," Lucky told her. "We've seen way too many people be stupid when it comes to security or their own well-being."

"Tell me about it," Lefty muttered. "Sometimes we're tasked to be security for dignitaries and other bigwigs. We were in charge of this one guy once who didn't listen to a damn thing we said. It wasn't until he found himself on the wrong side of a picket line, and got caught in a tear gas attack and was almost trampled to death, that he decided to do what we told him."

"Lefty," Walker warned.

Gillian was fascinated. Walker didn't talk about what

he and his team did, but she knew he wasn't an ordinary soldier. She put her hand on Walker's knee and squeezed.

"The last thing I want is to end up a sad story on the evening news. While the investigators told me they thought the risk was minimal, they couldn't reassure me that I wasn't in any danger. So, I'm keeping a low profile and going about my business...cautiously."

"Good," Lefty said, nodding. "If you're ever uncomfortable for any reason, get yourself out of the situation, even if you think it makes you look rude. You'd rather be alive than be hurt or killed because you were trying to be polite."

"Has that happened to you before? I mean, to someone you were trying to keep safe?" Gillian asked.

She saw some extreme emotion in Lefty's eyes before he blanked them.

"Sort of," he said with a shrug. "She was an assistant to the bigwig I mentioned earlier. She did everything in her power to get her employer to listen to us, but of course when he didn't, this person was caught up in the danger right along with him. It sucked to realize she understood she was putting her life in danger, but couldn't do anything about it because she had to do what her employer wanted or end up without a job."

"That does suck," Gillian agreed. "Did she quit after that? Find someone else to be an aide to?"

"No," Lefty said flatly. "Not as far as I know."

Gillian wasn't sure what to say to that. It sounded as if Lefty was emotionally tied to this assistant, whoever she was, and she was a bit sad for both the woman *and* Lefty.

"Anyway," Grover said, obviously trying to lighten the mood, "I've got it on good authority that if you want to try out the obstacle course after the competition, you're welcome to."

"Ha. Seriously?" Gillian asked. "That's not happening. Although if you guys want to, be my guest. I mean, you're obviously all in shape, I wouldn't mind ogling if you wanted to strip down to your shorts and have a go."

Walker growled next to her, and Gillian couldn't do anything but laugh.

"The only ogling you're gonna do is of *me*, woman," he said into her ear as his friends all chuckled around them.

A man's voice sounded over a loudspeaker just then, saving Gillian from having to respond to her jealous boyfriend.

"Welcome to another fun-filled day at the races! First up will be our seven-to-ten age group. If heat one could line up behind the starting line, we'll get started soon!"

Gillian eagerly watched as six children, both boys and girls, lined up at the far left side of the field in front of them.

"Man, I can't believe how nervous I am for them," Gillian said with a small laugh. "I don't even know them and my palms are sweaty."

Walker grabbed hold of one of her hands and stroked it. "Not sweaty at all," he declared with a grin.

Gillian rolled her eyes and focused on the field.

Within minutes, the first heat of competitors was off.

Gillian watched in awe as the children raced toward a set of tires. They had to run through them with one foot in the middle of each and get through the entire row without tripping. Then they ran toward low-hanging ropes and fell to their bellies and crawled under them. The next obstacle was a series of stumps at different heights. They had to jump from one to the next, and if they fell off, they had to go back and start from the beginning.

There was obstacle after obstacle, and it seemed with each one, the course got more and more difficult.

By the time the kids got to the end, they had to climb up a rope about fifteen feet to a platform, where they then went hand over hand from one ring to the next, across to a second platform. There, they had to jump up and grab a handhold, using their upper-body strength to pull themselves up and over an eight-foot wall. To get down, they traversed a spider web of ropes to the ground, then leaped over three obstacles before once again getting down on their bellies and crawling in a pit of water and mud under a series of logs, before finally racing to the finish line.

Gillian was exhausted just watching, but every single kid in the first heat finished...and they had huge smiles on their faces to boot.

"They love this, don't they?" Gillian asked Walker.

But it was Brain who answered. "Yup. A lot of the kids practice for months for these kinds of competitions."

"What do they get if they win?" Gillian asked.

"Well, everyone who participates gets a small medal," Brain said. "Usually I'm against any kind of participation trophy, but in this case, it's totally warranted. This isn't some summer club sport where they stand around in an empty field for a few weeks and get a prize for it. They work their butts off. But the winner of each of the six heats goes on to the final round, and the winner of *that* heat gets a hundred-dollar gift certificate to the PX...the post exchange, where they can buy whatever they want."

"Cool," Gillian breathed. "What heat is your friend's kid in?"

"Three," Oz said. "Annie's last year's winner. She beat the time of a bunch of fifteen year olds, and she was only eleven. She wasn't in their competition group, but she would've smoked them if she had been. She's totally gonna win this year too."

"And her dad's okay with her doing this?"

"Fletch? Oh, yeah, he's more than okay with it," Walker answered. "He brings Annie with him when he and his friends practice the adult obstacle course. I've heard her say more than once that the kids' one is too easy."

"Jeez, she must be crazy," Gillian murmured.

"Nope," Walker said. "Only crazy about being just like her dad. Her mom learned pretty early on that the best way to keep her in line was to threaten to take away her obstacle course privileges if she disobeyed. Worked like a charm."

"Are you close with Annie?" Gillian asked.

"Not as close as I'd like. Fletch and his team have been around a bit longer than we have, and they've cut back on missions in the last few years. But mark my words, that kid's gonna be someone special when she grows up. I don't know what she's gonna do, but it's gonna be something pretty damn amazing."

"I'd like to meet her," Gillian said.

"I'll make it happen," Walker told her.

Then their attention was turned back to the field as they watched the second heat of kids run through the obstacle course. It was just as impressive the second time as it was the first.

"Come on, Annie!" Lefty yelled as the third heat got lined up behind the starting line.

"You got this!" Oz called out.

Gillian saw another group of men closer to the field, standing and yelling for Annie as well.

"That's her dad and his team," Walker said into her ear.

Not able to stand the suspense, Gillian stood, as did the rest of the guys around her. Since they were in the back of the stands, they weren't blocking anyone else's view.

"I don't even know her, and I wanna throw up, I'm so nervous," Gillian muttered.

"She's gonna kill it. Don't worry," Walker said.

Then the announcer counted down, and the kids were off and running.

Not only was Annie fast, she was extremely nimble too. She was the first one through the tires, and she practically threw herself on the ground before using her arms and legs like a piston to propel her under the ropes. She almost seemed as if she were soaring through the air as she leapt over the stumps. Her long hair was in braids so it didn't get in her eyes and they flew up and down in the air as she moved.

Every so often, she'd look behind her at the kids following in her wake. Gillian figured she was checking to see if anyone else was coming up behind her.

Some of the other kids caught up to her as she made her way through the obstacles, and when she got toward the end, where she had to climb to the first high platform, she shimmied up the rope as if she were a little monkey and had done it every day of her life.

"She's gonna win for sure," Doc muttered.

Gillian thought so too—but then the little girl did something surprising.

She was about to start across the rings when she looked

behind her again. There was a boy in her heat who was obviously struggling at the rope climb. He'd been behind the older kids the entire course, but was still hanging in there.

But no matter how hard he tried, he couldn't make it all the way to the top of the rope. He'd make it halfway up then slide back down.

Instead of continuing on through the course, and winning and heading to the final round, Annie let go of the first ring and dropped to her knees at the top of the platform above the ropes.

Gillian was too far away to hear what she was saying, but it was obvious she was encouraging the boy. She ignored the fact that the other kids in the heat had passed her and were well on their way across the rings. All of Annie's attention was on the boy trying to climb the rope.

At one point, the boy stopped about halfway up once again, and Annie yelled something to him and reached down to grab the rope herself—then she started pulling it upward. The boy was just hanging on with all his strength, and Annie was bringing him, rope and all, up to the platform. She turned and looped the rope around one of the poles at the top used for safety, which gave her more leverage and allowed her to pull faster.

Gillian turned to Walker. "Is that legal?"

Walker and the other men were all smiling. Huge toothy smiles that went from ear to ear. "No clue. But it's not like she's gonna win the heat, so what does it matter?"

It didn't matter. Not really. Gillian watched with pride as a girl she didn't even know went out of her way to help a fellow competitor. She grabbed hold of his hand when she'd pulled the rope up high enough so she could reach him, and then put her arm around his shoulders when they stood side-by-side on the platform.

They both had some pretty serious obstacles to get through still, and Gillian wasn't sure the boy could make it. But after a short rest, she saw him nod, and both he and little Annie moved to the rings. Annie made it seem so easy to swing to the other platform, but Gillian held her breath as the boy struggled his way across. But he too made it, with Annie cheering on from the other side.

Annie jumped up and grabbed the handhold and pulled herself up to the top of the wall. Then she balanced herself and leaned over, holding an arm downward. The boy was able to jump up and grab the handhold, but Annie was the one who made it possible for him to get up and over the board.

Gillian figured the boy's arms had to be Jell-O by then, but he gamely started down the spider web of ropes, Annie right by his side. They ran together to the mud pit, and Gillian could clearly see the whites of Annie's teeth shining bright as she laughed and smiled at the boy as they shimmied under the last obstacle.

Then, Annie grabbed hold of the boy's hand and they jogged together to the finish line, hand in hand. Dead last in their heat.

But neither kid seemed upset in the least.

A man had run out to the end of the field to meet Annie and the boy, and he pulled her into a huge muddy hug.

"That's her dad," Walker told her. "He's got to be the proudest dad out here today."

"That was amazing," Gillian said in awe. "I mean, it's

obvious Annie's competitive, but she didn't even hesitate to stop and help that other kid."

"Told you, she's gonna make a difference in this world," Walker said with pride.

By now, there was an entire group of adults around little Annie. They'd moved off to the side of the field a bit so the next heat could start.

"Come on," Walker said as the others started down the bleachers. "Let's go congratulate her."

Gillian followed Walker and his friends to the field, and she couldn't believe how excited she was to meet a twelve-year-old girl. It had been a long time since she'd been as impressed with someone as she was with Annie. She had a feeling Walker was right. This girl was definitely something special. And no matter what she decided to do with her life, she was going to make a difference in a big way.

They joined the group of men and women surrounding Annie.

"Pretty damn impressive, Fletch," Walker told one of the men, slapping him on the back.

"Thanks. We think so too," Annie's dad said. He had his arm around a woman, and they both looked proud enough to burst.

Gillian waited patiently as Annie's fans congratulated her before she and Walker got to the front of the line.

"Hey, Annie. Pretty impressive out there!" Walker told her.

"Thanks, Trigger," Annie chirped happily.

If she was upset she didn't win the heat and wasn't going to the finals, she sure didn't show it in any way.

"Did you see Rob? That was the first time he finished

the obstacle course! He was really nervous before he started, but I told him I'd help him if he needed it. But he didn't *really* need me. He just needed a little hand up on the ropes."

"I saw," Walker said.

"And it's like Dad always says...by lifting someone else up, you're lifting yourself even higher. I pretended I was in the Army and we were on a mission. No one gets left behind."

"That's very true. Are you upset that you don't get to compete in the finals?" Walker asked.

Annie scoffed. "Naw. There's always the next time. Besides, it was better to see Rob's smile when he crossed the finish line."

"Annie, this is my friend, Gillian. She came today just to see you race."

"Hi!" Annie said. "You're really pretty. Are you Trigger's girlfriend? He needs one. He doesn't smile enough."

Gillian did her best not to laugh, but couldn't help it. "I am, and I'm doing my best to make him not be so serious all the time."

"Good." Then Annie turned to her dad. "Dad, did you film that so I can send it to Frankie?"

"Of course, squirt."

"Have you sent it yet?"

"No, jeez. It's only been two seconds since you finished."

"I know, but he's been as excited as I have for the race."

"Frankie's her boyfriend." Walker leaned in to explain. "He's her age and lives in California. He's deaf, and Annie learned sign language just so she can talk to him. They met several years ago and both decided then and there they were going to get married someday."

"Sounds kinda familiar," Gillian said with a smile.

"It was good to meet you," Annie said to Gillian distractedly.

It was obvious she wanted to get on the phone with her friend Frankie and show him her race.

"If you need a flower girl for your wedding to Trigger, I'm available. I've already had a lot of practice and stuff, so you wouldn't have to teach me how to do it," Annie said matter-of-factly.

Gillian almost choked. "Um...I'll keep that in mind."

"Annie Elizabeth!" her mom scolded.

"What?" Annie asked, walking over to her parents.

"Just because someone's dating it doesn't mean they're going to get married."

"But you dated Dad and then got married," Annie said reasonably. "And I'm dating Frankie and I'm going to marry him. And Mary dated Truck and *they* got married."

Fletch's wife rolled her eyes and shook her head. "You're going to have to take my word for it. A man and woman can date and not get married."

"Then what's the point?" Annie grumbled, then was caught up in a hug by Lefty and obviously forgot to be upset at her mom's words.

Gillian hadn't been around Walker when he was with his friends, and was pleasantly surprised when he pulled her back against his chest and put his arm diagonally across her body. He leaned down and spoke directly into her ear, so only she could hear him. "No offense to Annie, but I've heard stories about her mom and dad's wedding. Suffice to say, it involves armed robbers and prosthetic limbs being used as weapons. It's probably safer for us to elope."

Gillian's heart was racing. She liked thinking about running off into the sunset with Walker, but she kept her tone light when she twisted her head around to look up at him. "With my parents hating the cold and yours hating the heat, yeah, it's probably better if we just informed them after the fact."

The smile on Walker's face was something Gillian wanted to preserve for all time.

She heard a click, and she turned around to see Annie's mom smiling down at her phone. "Perfect." Then looking at Walker, she said, "I'll text it to you, Trigger."

"Thanks, Emily," Walker told her, then turned Gillian so she was next to him and started walking off the field. "We're headed out," he informed Doc nonchalantly.

"You're not going to stay for the finals?" he asked.

Walker shrugged. "Now that Annie's out...no. I'll see you Monday morning at PT."

With a smirk, Doc simply nodded.

"That was kind of rude," Gillian informed Walker as they headed off the field toward the parking lot.

"Did you want to stay?" he asked, but didn't slow down.

"What if I said yes?" Gillian asked, curious.

Walker stopped and looked down at her. "Then we'll go back."

"Just like that?" she asked.

"Just like that," Walker said without a trace of annoyance.

"What do *you* want to do?"

"I want to take you back to my apartment and hang out. Talk about the upcoming week, what you have planned. I want to kiss you, but only when we're upright and both fully dressed. I want to know more about the event we're going to next weekend at the zoo, and I want to spend every minute of our time together before I have to take you back to Georgetown. I love my friends, but I see them all the time. I already know them. I'm being selfish, but I want to spend time with *you*, not them. But if you want to stay and watch more heats, I'm okay with that because I'll still be by your side."

Walker didn't look away from her as he spoke, and Gillian couldn't help but fall for him even more.

"I don't care if you leave beard shavings in the sink," she informed him. "You can be as neat as you want and it won't faze me. I'll probably worry that you're doing *too* much for me, that you aren't doing what *you* want, so you're going to have to make sure not to go overboard and spoil me too much, okay?"

"Nope. Now, do you want to stay or go back to my apartment?"

"Your apartment," Gillian said immediately. It wasn't a hard decision.

Walker started walking again, taking her with him. All the way to his apartment, Gillian tried to think what she'd done to be lucky enough to have this man by her side. She couldn't come up with a single thing by the time they'd arrived, so she decided to just go with it. If Walker wasn't freaking out by how well they fit, why should she?

CHAPTER THIRTEEN

The next week went by way too slowly for Trigger's comfort. Ever since he'd joined the Delta teams, he'd been single-mindedly focused on his job. He never got distracted, and he spent every day looking forward to training and the possibility of being called for a mission.

But since meeting Gillian, he no longer lived and breathed Delta. He could still focus when he needed to, but in his down time now, he thought about *her*. Wondered what she was doing and if she was having a good day. He was constantly on his phone, texting her just to connect.

It was Friday afternoon, and he and the rest of his team were taking a break from an intense informational meeting they'd been in since nine that morning. It looked like a mission was forthcoming very soon, if the intel they'd been getting was any indication.

"Things seem to be going well with Gillian," Lefty said a little too nonchalantly as he and Trigger stood alone in the Texas heat, trying to thaw out from the frigid air-conditioned room they'd been trapped in all day.

"They are," Trigger agreed.

"She seemed to have a good time last weekend."

Trigger turned to his friend. "What?"

"What, what?"

"Just say what you're thinking before you explode," Trigger said in exasperation.

"I like her," Lefty told his friend. "So before you fly off the handle at what I'm going to say, you have to know that right off the bat."

Trigger nodded, but braced for whatever his friend wanted to tell him.

"I just want to make sure you're not moving too fast with her," Lefty said. "I mean, you met her on an op...that can screw with both your heads."

Trigger waited, knowing Lefty wasn't done. He was right.

"Gillian's pretty, man, so I don't blame you. She's got a good job, she's funny, and all of us like her. She kept her head in Venezuela and seems mature beyond her years. But she also seems like a forever kind of girl. If you're dating her simply to get laid, you're gonna hurt her. Bad. Just be careful, that's all I'm sayin'."

"You've never stepped into my personal life before. Why now?" Trigger asked, genuinely curious.

"Because it's more than obvious she's in love with you. Or at least she thinks she is. It's obvious by the way she looks at you."

Trigger couldn't help but grin at his friend's words.

"And you like that," Lefty said.

Trigger shrugged. He couldn't deny it. "I haven't slept with her," he said.

Lefty gaped at him. "What?"

"I mean, I've slept with her in my arms, but we haven't had sex," Trigger clarified. "I'm already well aware that we met on an op and that it could be skewing my thinking. I'm extremely protective of her. I'm worried about this seventh hijacker and the fact that no one can figure out which one of the passengers it is. So I'm proceeding with caution. But, Lefty, I've never felt like this about a woman before, and you know I've rescued more than my fair share of damsels in distress over the years."

Lefty nodded. "That's why I can't understand what it is about Gillian that's got you so obsessed."

Trigger couldn't even deny that he was obsessed. He was. "I don't know what it is about her, all I know is that she's gotten under my skin...and I'm perfectly okay with that."

"I hope you're not upset I said something," Lefty said.

"Of course not. I'd be pissed if you didn't. You pick the short straw to talk to me about it?" Trigger asked with a smile.

"Something like that," Lefty admitted. "But seriously, she's cool. We all like her. And you *really* haven't fucked her?"

Trigger had been okay with Lefty's questions, and he knew he'd been the one to bring up the fact that they hadn't slept together, but using the word "fucked" seemed to make the topic ugly. "Careful," Trigger warned. "I'm all right with you questioning my intentions because you're my friend, but I'm not okay with you disrespecting Gillian in the process."

Lefty grinned, not at all intimidated by Trigger. "Sorry."

"And no, I haven't made love with her yet. It's the hardest thing I've ever done in my life."

"I bet it's hard," Lefty said with a sly grin.

Trigger couldn't help it, he laughed. "Shut up, asshole."

Sobering, Lefty said, "I'm happy for you. Seriously. Since seeing Ghost and his entire crew settle down, I think we've all been feeling a bit lonely. I was just worried you'd taken that a step too far and settled for someone."

"I'm not settling," Trigger told him. "Not even fucking close."

"Good."

"You heard anything from Kinley?" Trigger asked.

Lefty frowned and shook his head. "No. She hasn't answered any of my emails or texts, so I stopped trying. I've tried to keep track of the Assistant Secretary for Insular and International Affairs, to see where he's dragging his poor aides, but I stopped after I saw he'd gone to visit Afghanistan to talk about international relations over there."

Trigger shook his head. "He has no clue how much danger he's putting himself in, and everyone who works for him, does he?"

"No," Lefty said with a scowl. "And I doubt he'd care even if he did. I told Kinley when I got her out of that fucked-up situation down in Africa that she needed to find a new job, but she told me it was fine, that *she* was fine. It's infuriating."

"You two clicked," Trigger told his friend. He didn't like the look of frustration and sorrow that passed over Lefty's face before he wiped it clean.

"Wasn't meant to be," he said with a shrug. "You're heading down to Georgetown tonight, right?"

Wanting to press him about Kinley, the first woman he'd seen his friend truly care about since he'd known him, Trigger reluctantly let it go. "Yeah. She's planned a corporate event at the Austin Zoo and invited me to go. I'm looking forward to seeing Gillian in action. She's super organized, and I have a feeling she's like a drill sergeant when it comes to the actual execution of the events she puts together."

"Cool. Tell her we all said hello."

"Will do."

They both saw Doc gesturing to them from the doorway.

"Looks like break time's up," Lefty said. Both men walked back toward the building, and Trigger pulled out his phone to send Gillian a quick text.

Trigger: Just thought I'd say hi and that I might be getting a late start in heading your way tonight.

She responded right away, which she usually did. It was one more thing that he liked about her.

Gillian: Hi. :) And no problem. Take your time and drive safe. I've been putting fires out all day for the event tomorrow. One of the food trucks canceled at the last minute and I've been trying to find a replacement. Can't wait to see you.

Trigger: I'm sure you'll find an even better truck to take its place. Miss you too. Gotta go.

Gillian: Let me know when you're on your way so I don't worry?

Trigger: Of course. Later.

Gillian: Later.

Gillian might not realize it, but the way she always worried about him was pretty special to Trigger. Most women he'd dated seemed to think since he was an alpha soldier, he was invincible. But Gillian was always telling him to be careful and warning him about accidents on the road. She'd even told him about a restaurant in the Killeen area that had been shut down for sanitary reasons and wanted to make sure he hadn't eaten there recently.

Yeah, he had no problem with her worrying about him. It was cute as fuck, and he couldn't deny it felt good.

Taking a breath and putting his phone back in his pocket, Trigger did his best to turn his mind back to the top-secret intel they'd been analyzing before the break. He could think about Gillian all day long, but for now, he needed to be one hundred percent focused because it was very likely they'd be shipped out. Soon.

Later that night, after he'd driven to Georgetown, after he'd kissed the hell out of Gillian when she'd opened her door to him, after they'd eaten the dinner she'd made in anticipation of his arrival, after they'd snuggled on her couch as they watched some random show on TV, and after she'd fallen asleep in his arms, Trigger took the time to deeply analyze his relationship with the woman lightly snoring two inches from his face.

He tried to be objective, to really give Lefty's—and thus, his team's—concerns some thought. But after only a short time, he knew for certain what he felt for Gillian wasn't just because of some hero complex. Wasn't a result of him saving her down in Venezuela. From the first time he'd heard her voice over the phone, he'd been hooked.

Trigger wasn't a particularly religious man. But he'd once read a book about reincarnation, and it had struck a chord within him.

The author explained how souls typically reincarnate together. So those you knew in one life would reappear close to you in another. Your brother in one life might be your mother in another. Or your wife in one life, might end up being your best friend in the next. The author also suggested that in each life, a person had something to learn. Like love, friendship, humility. And if the lesson was learned, then the soul would move on and learn something else in its next life.

Everything about that appealed to Trigger. It made it easy to understanding how he and his team were so close. It also explained his instant connection to Gillian.

He knew some people would think he was crazy, that the whole soul thing was a crock of shit, but because of the things he'd experienced and seen in his lifetime, Trigger couldn't dismiss the theory.

Gillian sighed, and the arm around his belly tightened and she nuzzled his chest a bit before settling once more. He knew she was stressed about the next day because she wanted everything to go off smoothly. She'd had one glass of wine and had fallen asleep almost the second he'd settled her against him.

Turning his head, Trigger kissed her forehead gently

and stared back up at the ceiling. He wasn't sure what he needed to learn in this lifetime, but he hoped it involved loving unconditionally, and wasn't something about dealing with loss or something equally depressing.

The last thought he had before he fell asleep was that he hoped Gillian was as strong as she seemed. It was inevitable that he and his team would be deployed again. Very soon. In the past, women couldn't deal with not knowing where he was going or how long he'd be gone, and their relationship had ended as a result. He didn't want that to happen with him and Gillian.

* * *

Gillian felt as if she were being pulled in a thousand directions at once...but she loved the adrenaline rush she got from seeing all her hard work come together. She'd woken up that morning in Walker's arms and the day had just gotten better from there.

Seeing her man in a pair of jeans and a T-shirt did something to her insides. He was good-looking no matter what he wore, but seeing him dressed so casually was a huge turn-on. He seemed to know; it felt as if he touched her way more often that morning. A brush of his fingertips against her waist as he passed her in the kitchen, a light kiss before she headed to get ready for the day, his arm touching hers as they drove into Austin. He was driving her crazy, but she liked the anticipation.

"Ms. Romano," a man called out as he fast-walked toward her.

She turned away from admiring Walker standing near a

group of men, women, and children waiting for the zoo to open its doors to the man coming toward her.

"We need to change the time the food trucks will arrive because I was just informed the monkey demonstration will be starting at eleven."

"It's fine," Gillian informed the harried man who'd been assigned to help her. She thought he was the company president's assistant, but wasn't sure. "Not everyone will want to see the monkeys, and there will be plenty of food for those who do."

"If you're sure..." the man said, his tone indicating that she was wrong.

"I'm sure," Gillian said firmly. "If you can please go tell the employees at the ticket counter that we're all ready out here and it's two minutes past nine. It's time for the doors to open."

"Yes, ma'am," the man told her, then hurried toward the main gate.

Taking a deep breath, Gillian tried to tell herself that she'd done all she could to make sure everything would go off without a hitch.

She felt an arm go around her waist and with one quick inhale, she knew it was Walker.

"Breathe, Di. It's gonna be perfect."

She chuckled. "You're just saying that to calm me down."

"Nope. You've done the work for weeks. Little things might go wrong, but no one's going to care. They're excited about seeing the animals and having a good time. They won't even notice the little shit."

"Thanks," Gillian said, leaning into him for a brief

moment. She was used to being on her own at these things. She occasionally might have assistants and people helping her, but ultimately, everything fell on her own shoulders, as it should since it was her business. But still, having Walker there supporting her made everything seem so much easier.

As the day progressed, and Gillian dealt with putting out small issues that kept popping up, she knew that no matter where she was, if she looked around, she'd see Walker. He was giving her space to work, but staying close. He'd brought her water several times, and around twelve-thirty, he'd made her take a short ten-minute break to wolf down one of the tacos he'd gotten from a food truck. Gillian usually skipped eating altogether at events like this, but couldn't deny she felt a hell of a lot better after getting some calories in her.

Around two, when she was standing at the back of one of the auditoriums watching the president of the company give a short speech to his employees about how thankful and proud he was of his work family, Walker came up and bent down to whisper in her ear.

"Can we talk for a second?"

Surprised, she looked up at him. He looked somber and serious, and she knew immediately something was wrong. Nodding, she let him lead her out of the auditorium to a relatively quiet spot nearby. "What's wrong?" she asked anxiously.

"I need to leave," he said.

"Now?"

"Unfortunately, yes."

"Is everything okay? Your friends? They're all right?"

"They're fine. It's a mission. I need to go."

A mission. They hadn't talked much about his job,

more because Gillian wasn't sure what she was allowed to ask and what he was allowed to tell her, but now she was kicking herself. "Okay. When will you be back?"

A pained expression crossed his face. "I don't know."

"Can I ask where you're going?"

Walker pressed his lips together and shook his head.

Well, shit. She'd known this time would come, and Gillian did her best to keep everything she was feeling off her face. She had to be strong about this. It wasn't as if she didn't know that Walker and his teammates did some pretty serious shit...look how she'd met him. And she'd known all along that he most likely wouldn't be able to tell her where they were going. She just needed to suck it up.

Giving herself some time, Gillian went up on her tiptoes and hugged him, hiding her face in his shoulder.

His arms banded around her, and she thought he held onto her just a little tighter than usual.

She forced herself to relax her arms, but she kept hold of his shirt at his sides. "Be careful," she whispered.

Walker looked down at her for a long time, his expression inscrutable.

"What?" she asked. "Say something."

"You don't want to ask me anything else?"

"I want to ask you a million questions," Gillian admitted. "But now isn't the time, and you probably couldn't answer them anyway. Just please...come back to me. I can't have found you now, only to lose you."

"You're not losing me," Walker said confidently. "I wish I could tell you everything about where I'm going and what I'm doing, but I can't. I can't *ever* tell you. Even when I get back. You understand that, right?"

She thought she had, but now, faced with his first

mission since they'd started dating, it was hitting home exactly how secret Walker's work life was. She nodded. "I admit that this isn't easy for me, but it's harder for someone else out there. Someone who needs a champion. And maybe where you're going isn't a rescue. Maybe you have to go and take out a terrorist or something, but eventually, you'll head to some foreign country to rescue a woman who thinks she's gonna die. And then you and your teammates will be there, giving her another chance at life. I can deal with not knowing because I know what you're doing is important. Maybe not to me, but to someone who might feel just like I did back in Venezuela."

"Fuck," Walker muttered, before leaning down and kissing her as if his life depended on it.

Gillian held on to his shirt and let him take what he needed. She'd give anything to this man; anything he needed from her was his. No questions asked.

The kiss gentled, and Gillian couldn't help the small moan that escaped from deep within her as he nipped her lower lip then pulled back. "Give me your phone," he ordered gently.

Feeling off-kilter from his kiss and the thought that he was leaving, Gillian did as he asked, unlocking it with her thumbprint before handing it over.

He clicked the buttons for a short moment before handing it back to her. "I put Fletch's number in there. He's Annie's dad. He won't tell you where I am or when I'll be back, but he can reassure you if you need it. If too much time goes by and you panic, call him. He'll make some inquiries and let you know what he can. Okay?"

She knew what he was saying. They weren't married. The Army didn't know anything about her. If Walker was hurt or killed on his mission, she'd never know. But his friend Fletch would.

Feeling thankful he'd given her some way to check on him, Gillian could only nod. The lump in her throat threatened to cut off her air along with her words.

Walker took her head in his hands and gently tilted it so she had no choice but to look at him. She loved how he did that all the time. Even more so because it was a very real possibility this might be the last time she'd experience it. She knew more than most how dangerous his job could be.

"I've never regretted anything more in my life than not knowing how it feels to be inside you."

Gillian huffed out a small chuckle. "Then I guess you'd better make sure you come back in one piece so we can get on that, huh?"

He grinned, and Gillian's knees got weak.

"Yeah, I guess so. I'm coming back, Gilly," he said seriously. "I need you to believe that."

"I do."

He stared at her for a long moment before nodding. "Okay. I'm proud of you, you know. Watching you today has given me a new appreciation for what it is you do. You're a jack of all trades and you've handled every crisis that's been brought to your attention with ease. You've come up with creative solutions to issues that would've broken some other people when faced with the same thing. You're able to pivot when needed, and you do it with a smile on your face. I'm fucking impressed, Di. You *are* Wonder Woman."

"Thanks," she whispered.

Walker leaned down and pressed his lips against hers

once more. It was a chaste kiss, no tongue involved, but it was just as intimate as if he'd plundered her mouth once more. "Be safe," he warned. "The seventh hijacker is still out there somewhere. I'm not happy that they haven't figured out who it is or what his next move might be. Same rules apply when I'm gone as when I'm here. Don't go out alone if you can help it, don't take a fucking Uber, and let your friends know where you're going if you leave the house."

"And don't go to the grocery store after eleven at night, right?" she teased.

"Exactly. Nothing good happens after that time, and if you need a head of lettuce, you wait until it's light outside."

Gillian grinned up at him and somehow kept the tears she could feel at the back of her eyes from falling. "Got it. I'll be careful."

"I need to go," Walker told her.

Gillian nodded, and he gave her one last long hug.

"Ms. Romano?" someone asked from nearby, and she recognized the voice of the young man who'd been bringing issues to her attention all day.

"Be safe," she whispered to Walker.

"I'll let you know the second I get back," he said with a nod.

Forcing herself to let go and step back, she gave him a lame smile and pantomimed shooing him away. "Go on. Git. Before I latch onto your ankle and make you drag me along the sidewalk as you try to leave."

He smiled, but it didn't reach his eyes. "It's never been this hard to leave before," he admitted.

"What's the saying?" she asked. "The sooner you leave,

the sooner you'll get back? Go kick some bad-guy ass, honey."

"Honey," he said quietly. "I like that."

Gillian rolled her eyes. She wanted to tell him she loved him, but felt awkward about it, so she kept quiet.

Walker backed away from her, not taking his eyes from hers until the very last second before he had to go around a corner. One second he was there, and the next he was gone.

Gillian wanted to fall apart, but the man who'd been helping her all day was there with another issue.

"One of the guests' teenage daughters is freaking out in the bathroom because she just got her period and thinks she's dying. The mom isn't dealing well, and...um...do you think—"

"I'm on my way," Gillian said, thankful for the distraction. She'd have time later to break down over Walker leaving. For now, she needed to put her event planner hat on and make sure the rest of the day went off without a hitch.

CHAPTER FOURTEEN

Ten days.

Ten of the longest days of her life.

That's how long it had been since Walker had left.

Gillian had coped pretty well the first week, but the night before last, she'd had a nightmare that Walker had been killed somewhere and no one would tell her. She'd caved and called his friend, Fletch, who reassured her that he was still on his mission, and that he wasn't lying dead in some foreign country somewhere.

His deployment wasn't easy, but like Gillian had told him once, she had a busy life that didn't stop just because he was gone. She continued to sign clients for events and was kept occupied by calling hotels and reserving meeting spaces, as well as figuring out other details for the varied events she put together.

At least once a day she heard from one of her fellow hostages. By now, they'd all gotten the news that there was a seventh hijacker, and her phone had been buzzing with texts and emails from everyone she'd gotten close to.

Everyone was speculating on who it was and what their next plan would be.

Though, ever since her interview with the FBI and DEA, Gillian had begun distancing herself a little from the others. She felt awful about it, but she couldn't help but wonder if one of her friends could actually be a cold-blooded killer. It seemed unlikely, but if someone like Janet, who'd seemed so scared about her daughter, ended up being a hijacker, Gillian would never trust anyone again.

So she'd spent most of her time with her local friends instead of getting any closer to the women who'd been on the plane with her. She'd gone out for lunch with Ann one day, and then joined Wendy and Clarissa for a movie night at Clarissa's house another evening. She'd cried a little and had a bit too much wine, but overall was pretty proud of how well she'd been holding up.

The biggest hurdle was how much she missed Walker. She missed his texts that let her know he was thinking about her. She missed his laugh. She missed falling asleep with him on her couch, or his. It was as if a part of her was missing.

But the other half of the coin was how proud she was of him. She had no idea what he was doing or where he was, but she'd turned to the internet to do more research on Delta Force. They were one of the most secretive special forces units out there. Walker hadn't been kidding when he'd said he'd never be able to tell her what it was he did when he was gone. Hell, she couldn't find any concrete news stories about any group of Deltas at any event around the world. It was almost eerie how they simply didn't seem to exist as far as the press went.

It had taken a day or so to sink in, but Gillian realized she was all right with the secrecy. As long as Walker returned safe, that was all that mattered. He'd probably seen some horrible things in his life, and she wanted nothing more than to give him happiness when he was home. He needed normal. Not a girlfriend who was hysterical when he left and not someone who brought unnecessary drama to his life. She wanted to be that person for him.

It was late on a Thursday night, eleven days after he'd left, when Gillian's phone rang. Concerned, because nothing good came from a phone call after ten at night, at least not in her world, and because she didn't recognize the number the call was coming from, Gillian answered it after two rings.

"Hello?"

"It's me."

Two words, but that's all it took for Gillian's entire body to sag in relief. "Walker," she whispered.

"I'm back, but unfortunately I've got about six hours of debriefing meetings to attend before I'm free to go home. Then, as much as I want to see you, I need to sleep. I've been up for about thirty-six hours as it is."

"It's okay. I'm just glad you're home. Are you...is everyone okay?"

"We're good," he said gently. "I just wanted to call as soon as I could to let you know that I'm all right."

"Thank you. I missed you. More than you'll know."

"That's my line," Walker said. "You okay? Anything weird happen since I've been gone?"

"You mean besides me adopting a family of six and

moving them into my apartment because they had nowhere else to go? No."

"Gillian," Walker said in a mock threatening tone.

She giggled. "No, nothing weird happened. I've been working, seeing my friends, and locking myself in my apartment by nine o'clock every night."

"Good. Gotten any suspicious texts or emails from the other passengers?"

Gillian thought about a recent text from Andrea, about how she'd given up on therapy because it didn't seem to be helping, and she still felt so angry that she'd been the one signaled out by Luis. And the email from Alice, telling Gillian she'd heard Leyton had been detained by Border Patrol when he'd tried to get into Mexico without a passport.

But now wasn't the time to bring all that up. Not when Walker had just gotten home and was exhausted. "Everything's fine," she reassured him. "Go. Do your thing. Maybe I can come up tomorrow evening for the weekend?" she asked tentatively.

"Yes," Walker said without hesitation. "Whenever you can get here in the afternoon will be perfect."

"Okay. Walker?"

"Yeah, Gilly?"

"I'm glad you're home."

"Me too. I'll see you tomorrow. I'll text later when I get back to my apartment before I crash. Okay?"

"Okay. Drive safe. I won't be happy if you made it through whatever you were doing in whatever country you were doing it in, only to get into a car crash your first day back."

He chuckled. "I will. Talk later."

"Bye."

Gillian hung up, but couldn't get Walker out of her mind. Was he really all right? Were Lefty and the others too? He said he hadn't slept in almost two days, so he probably hadn't eaten very well either. Didn't soldiers eat those MRE things when they were deployed?

Springing up from the couch, Gillian headed for the kitchen, a plan formulating in her mind. She knew Walker had meetings he had to attend. Then he had to get some sleep. But he also needed to eat. Something good, and not crappy takeout food or whatever he had in his apartment from before he'd left.

She opened her pantry and contemplated what she could make that would keep until he was done with his meetings. The last thing she wanted to do was push herself on him, especially when he'd just told her he needed to sleep. But she couldn't just sit home and do nothing. She needed to do *something* for him.

Pulling a few ingredients out of the pantry, she nodded in determination. She would make him a casserole that he could easily heat up when he got home and before he slept. Bachelor casserole had always been a favorite of hers, and it was quick and easy to make. She'd just whip up a batch of the noodle and hamburger meal and drop it off for him.

Not caring that it was ten at night and Walker lived forty miles away and it would be close to two in the morning when she got back to Georgetown herself, she got to work.

* * *

Trigger was beyond exhausted. He and the team had finished up their job and headed home without catching up on the sleep they'd lost over the last week and a half. Because they hadn't managed to kill the high-value target —the HVT—but instead had taken out half a dozen of his cronies, they'd had to meet with the base general and debrief. There might be blowback because of their failure to kill the head bad guy—as Gillian would call him—but they were all pretty pleased with the terrorists they had managed to take out of commission.

Not every mission was as straightforward as the one he'd found Gillian in the middle of, which was frustrating, but Trigger had learned how to compartmentalize.

He'd borrowed a phone from one of the Army pilots because he and his team always left their personal cells at home when they went on missions, and he called Gillian the second they'd descended low enough to the ground to catch the signal from one of the many cell towers they were flying over.

He might've been embarrassed at how happy he was to hear her voice, if she didn't sound just as relieved to hear from *him*.

Their debrief only took four hours instead of six, which Trigger was thankful for. He and the rest of his team were dead on their feet. He knew they'd need to regroup when they'd gotten some sleep and some decent food, but for now, their best bet was going home and crashing.

Trigger wished he could've seen Gillian when he got back to his apartment, but he smelled to high heaven and could barely keep his eyes open. He wanted to be at least semi-functional when he saw her again.

Unlocking his apartment door, Trigger froze.

Something was wrong.

It smelled...homey.

He'd been gone for eleven days. The air in his place should've been stale, but instead, the scent of food surrounded him and made his stomach growl.

It was three-thirty in the morning. What the fuck was happening?

Pulling out the K-BAR knife he kept on his person at all times when he was on a mission, Trigger eased his door shut and put down his duffle bag. He crept into his apartment and noticed a light on in the kitchen. A light he definitely hadn't left on when he'd departed twelve days ago. For a moment, he was a little frustrated, thinking that perhaps Gillian had decided to come up to his place even though he'd said he needed some sleep. It was a shitty thought, but he was exhausted and in no mood to entertain anyone. Not even Gillian.

But the kitchen was empty. Trigger saw a piece of paper on the counter, but ignored it for the moment. He needed to clear the rest of his apartment, make sure no one was lurking in the shadows or Gillian wasn't sleeping somewhere. As irritated as he was at the thought she might've ignored his request to come up the next afternoon, after he'd had a chance to unwind from his intense mission, he didn't want to scare the shit out of her by pulling out a knife if she'd decided to surprise him.

But after a quick search, Trigger found his apartment empty.

Putting his knife away, he walked back into his kitchen. Pulling open his stove, he found a glass dish covered in aluminum foil. He felt the dish and realized it was still warm.

Even more baffled now—had someone broken in and cooked dinner? Of course they hadn't. That was just stupid —he picked up the piece of paper and opened it. Glancing at the end, he saw it was a note from Gillian. He read quickly.

Welcome home!

I know you're tired and I didn't want to bother you. It's not the same thing at all, but I know sometimes after a major event that I've spent weeks planning, I don't want to talk to anyone. I need to go home and decompress without having to think about anyone or anything for a while.

Anyway, I started thinking about how if you were tired, you were probably hungry too. I'm sure they didn't have our favorite takeout place wherever you were.

So I made you a casserole. It's nothing fancy, just noodles, hamburger, cream of mushroom soup, sour cream, and cheese. But I thought maybe it might hit the spot. I didn't want to leave your oven on, because I had no idea when you'd get home, so it might be cold. But you can always warm it up in the microwave.

I'm glad you're back. I've thought about your job a lot since you were gone, and for the record...I can handle it. I don't like not knowing where you are or if you're okay, but I'm one hundred percent sure that wherever you are, you're keeping our country safe from men and women who want to do it harm, or you're helping someone like me...a normal person who somehow got stuck in a situation they never thought they'd find themselves in.

Before I met you, I never really thought much about men like you and your teammates, but now that I've experienced a situation where I've needed help firsthand, I'm as proud of you as I can possibly be.

Eat something. Get some sleep. I'll see you soon.
Xoxo, Gillian

PS. I didn't break into your apartment. I knocked on the manager's door. I don't think he was very happy to be woken up at one in the morning, but after I told him what I wanted and how amazing you were, he begrudgingly agreed to let me into your apartment. He glared at me the entire time, and I think he thought I was going to steal something, but I was only in here for like ten seconds, long enough to put the casserole in your oven, turn on a light so you wouldn't come home to a dark apartment, scribble this note, then leave.

How long Trigger stood in his kitchen, reading and re-reading the note from Gillian, he had no idea. He'd never, in all his adult life, had someone do for him what she'd just done.

When he'd called, it had been after ten. She'd cooked the meal for him, driven up to his apartment, woken up the manager of the apartment complex to get into his place, then driven back home.

She understood that he needed to decompress. She'd *heard* him when he'd said he had to get some sleep. But she'd gone even further, understanding that he probably hadn't eaten very well recently either.

He wasn't happy that she was out driving at night as late as she had been, but he loved that she'd been thinking about him.

Eventually, he turned and took the casserole out of the

oven. He scooped some onto a plate and ate it standing up right there in his kitchen.

The meal was delicious. It was lukewarm, but he was too tired and impatient to wait for it to heat up, even if it only took a minute or two in the microwave. He ate way too much, his stomach protesting after the lean rations it had gotten over the last week and a half, but Trigger didn't care. That meal was made with love, for him, and he appreciated it more than he'd ever be able to put into words.

He put the leftovers into the refrigerator and headed to his bedroom. He took a ten-minute shower to wash the rest of the dust and dirt from his mission off his body, then dropped into bed. Right before he fell asleep, dead to the world, he reached for his phone and typed out a quick text.

Trigger: I'm not thrilled that you came up here in the middle of the night, because it's not safe, but that casserole was literally the best thing I've eaten in my life. Thank you, Di. You really are Wonder Woman. MY Wonder Woman. Be ready, we're both sleeping in my bed this weekend. I'm done waiting. You're mine, and I intend to show you how much you mean to me over and over, until we're both so exhausted we can't move.

Knowing that Gillian was asleep, he didn't wait for a response. He put his phone face down on his bedside table and fell into the sleep of the exhausted.

CHAPTER FIFTEEN

Gillian couldn't believe how nervous she was. It was ridiculous because she'd been ready to make love with Walker for weeks now, but reading the text he'd left her last night had knocked her for a loop.

She was thrilled that he wasn't really mad she'd essentially broken into his apartment, but was a bit surprised about his change in demeanor when it came to moving their physical relationship forward.

He'd been adamant about moving slow, making sure they were both on the same page, but that text she'd received had been the opposite of tiptoeing into a physical relationship. She knew exactly what Trigger wanting her in his bed meant.

And while Gillian had been chomping at the bit to move their relationship to a more physical level, now she was freaking out.

She stood in front of the mirror in her bathroom and tried to objectively evaluate herself. She'd put on a matching cream bra and panty set that made her feel good.

But now that she was looking at herself in it, she wasn't so sure. Walker was the epitome of hot. He had muscles on top of muscles, and even though she hadn't seen his stomach, she'd felt it. She was guessing he had at least a six-pack, and probably those V-muscles that pointed down to his groin.

Gillian wasn't anywhere near his league when it came to physical attributes. She had a nice set of boobs, but her stomach was a bit too poofy and her thighs touched when she walked. She burned a bit too easily and hadn't ever found joy in lying in the sun and baking, so she was very pale.

She fluffed out her hair and had to admit that it was one of her best features. She also liked her green eyes.

Blowing out a breath, she turned away from the mirror. She was who she was. Just because she carried more weight than was deemed acceptable didn't mean she wasn't attractive. Walker certainly didn't seem to see what *she* did when he looked at her.

She pulled on a pair of jeans and a cute ruffled cold-shoulder pink shirt. She went a little heavier on her makeup, simply because she hadn't seen Walker in almost two weeks and she wanted him to see her at her best. He'd certainly seen her at her worst in Venezuela, and in her "I'm lying around the house not expecting company" clothes as well.

Still feeling nervous, she packed an overnight bag and got ready to leave her apartment. She'd spent the morning working on the anniversary party for the Howards. She'd talked to the staff at The Driskill and finalized some small details about the food that was going to be served and how to set up the ballroom. It was good to keep busy as it kept her mind off Walker...mostly.

For some reason, as she left her apartment, Gillian had the fantastical thought that when she returned, her life would be different. Which was insane. Having sex with a man wasn't exactly life-changing. Women did it all the time. But she had a feeling that sex with Walker would definitely not be run-of-the-mill.

The drive to his apartment seemed to take forever, and it didn't help that there was an accident on the road that slowed things down as well. She called him when she got into town.

"Hey, Gilly. You close?"

"Yeah. Finally. There was a wreck and it took forever for me to get past it."

"It's okay. I'm just glad you're almost here."

"Me too," Gillian told him, feeling shy.

"Drive safe and I'll see you soon."

"I will. Bye."

Walker hung up without another word, and Gillian couldn't help but feel nervous all over again. This was crazy. She was just going to see Walker. He was the same man he was two weeks ago when she'd last seen him.

But was he? Just from the text he'd sent the night before, Gillian had a feeling he was different, and she had no idea what to expect from him.

She pulled into his parking lot and grabbed her bag before she headed for his apartment. To her surprise, he was standing outside waiting for her. Without thinking, Gillian started to jog toward him. Talking and texting with him wasn't the same as seeing him in person.

He looked good, the same as he had before he'd left.

No bandages, no black eyes, no sign of any kind of injury. A part of Gillian had wondered if he'd been hurt and just didn't want to tell her. But he looked tall and strong, and it was such a relief, she threw herself into his arms as soon as she got close.

"You're really okay," she mumbled as she buried her face in his neck.

His strong arms wrapped around her, taking her off her feet as he hugged her back. "I told you I was fine," he said with a laugh.

He put her on her feet and stared down at her with a look so hot, Gillian had to force herself to swallow. "Hi," she said awkwardly.

Walker huffed out another chuckle. "Hi," he returned.

Gillian put one hand on his cheek. "You look good."

"Did you expect me to come back with green skin and all my hair shaved off or something?"

She grinned. "No, but I don't know you well enough to know if you saying that you were fine *really* meant that you were fine, or if it was manspeak for 'I took a couple bullets but they didn't kill me so I'm good.'"

He stared at her for a heartbeat before throwing his head back and laughing so hard, she could feel his body shake against her own. The sound was beautiful. All the more because she was witnessing it in person, and he really was all right after his mysterious mission.

When he'd gotten himself under control, Walker leaned down until his lips were almost brushing hers when he spoke. "I might downplay how I feel when I talk to you, but I won't lie. If I get shot, I'll tell you I got shot. But you have to understand that unfortunately, getting injured kind of comes with my job. You can't freak if I come back to you with a few scrapes and bruises."

"I can and will," Gillian retorted. "*You* have to understand that the thought of you being hurt turns my stomach and makes me want to march out into the world and beat the crap out of anyone who dared lay a hand on you. I'll do my best to control myself, but you're just going to have to work extra hard to be careful so I don't lose my mind when you come home."

She couldn't interpret the look on his face. But when he said, "Okay, Di. I can do that," she relaxed in his arms.

Walker stared down at her for so long, she started to get concerned. But just when she was about to ask him what was wrong, he moved. He bent and picked up her bag with one hand, keeping his other arm around her waist. He moved them toward the building without another word.

He didn't let go of her for even a second as they made their way to his second-floor apartment. He unlocked the door and led her inside.

The second the door shut behind them, he dropped her bag and Gillian found herself backed up against the wall in the foyer with Walker looming over her.

"Thank you for the dinner last night...well, this morning."

"You're welcome," she said, holding onto his forearms as she stared up at him.

"What time did you get home?" he asked.

Gillian shrugged. "Around two."

"While it was appreciated, don't do that shit again. It's not safe to be driving and walking around at that hour."

"I wanted to make sure you ate," she said softly.

Walker put his hand in one of his front pockets and pulled something out.

Looking down, Gillian saw a shiny silver key in his palm. She looked back up at him in confusion.

"I had a talk with my manager this morning. Told him that you were always allowed in my apartment, and he shouldn't give you a hard time about letting you in no matter what time it is. But I figured it would be easier if I just gave you a key, that way you won't have to wake him up again and deal with his attitude."

"You're giving me a key to your place?" she asked, her brows furrowed.

"Yeah."

She didn't reach to take it. This seemed like a huge deal, and she was having a hard time processing it.

Walker had a small smile on his face and he moved his hand, tucking the key inside the front pocket of her jeans. Then he leaned in closer, forcing Gillian's head back farther.

"You get the text I sent early this morning?"

She nodded.

"Anything about what I said that you don't understand or want?"

Gillian licked her lips nervously. "No, it was pretty clear," she told him. "But...I'm not sure what happened in the last two weeks to make you change your mind from the whole 'going slow' thing and 'I can't sleep in a bed with you' to now."

"I finally got my head out of my ass," Walker said with no hesitation. "I suppose I wasn't being fair to you, but I've seen too many relationships with my friends crash and burn when their girlfriend couldn't handle the uncertainty that comes with our kind of job."

Gillian was a little disappointed with his answer, but she couldn't really blame him. He went on before she could say anything.

"And everything I told you before was true. I was afraid to get tied any closer to you because if you decided you couldn't handle what I do, it would've killed me. As far as I'm concerned, you're perfect. You have your own friends, you're smart, funny, employed, and you've got an innocent soul. And I want all that for myself. I don't want to corrupt you, or change you in any way, but I know that if you're with me, I'll end up doing just that. I guess that's why I was holding back. But when I got home last night, dead on my feet and completely exhausted, and I saw that you'd gone out of your way to respect my need for space to clear my head after the mission *and* to feed me, it hit me."

When he didn't go on, Gillian asked, "What did?"

"That I've been an idiot," Walker said gently. "I was keeping you at arm's length when I should've been doing everything in my power to tie you closer to me. I know it's only been one deployment, and it was a relatively short one at that, but do you think you can handle what I do? Being left on your own for unknown periods of time without having any idea when I might be back or what I'm doing?"

"Yes," Gillian said simply. She wasn't fond of being left in the dark, but if that was the only way she could have Walker, she'd deal. He was hers. She felt it in her bones.

"Fuck, I don't deserve you," Walker muttered before his head dropped.

Gillian didn't have time to think about anything other

than how his lips felt on hers. He physically tilted her head with his hands and the second she opened to him, he was there.

How long they kissed against the wall just inside his apartment, Gillian didn't know, but when she felt his hands at her waist, pulling her shirt up, she gasped and pulled back.

"Arms up," he ordered.

Bemused, she did as he requested and within seconds, she was standing in front of him in her bra. His gaze immediately dropped, and she heard him groan before his hand came up, pulling one of the cups of her bra down, exposing her rock-hard nipple. Then his mouth was there, sucking hard, making her back arch and her fingers spear into his hair, holding him against her.

One of her legs came up and Walker caught it in the hand that wasn't at her chest. He pulled her into him, throwing her off balance. But she knew she wasn't going to fall. No way would Walker let that happen.

His mouth moved up and he sucked on the fleshy part of her breast as his fingers pinched and rolled the nipple he'd just had in his mouth. She looked down and inhaled sharply at the eroticism of what she saw.

Walker's slightly stubbled jaw was working as he sucked on her flesh. "Are you giving me a hickey?" she managed to get out between pants.

He lifted his head and grinned. "Yup."

"How old are you?" she teased.

"Thirty-seven," he answered as if she'd asked a serious question. "And I want to see my mark all over you. I'm claiming you right here and now, Gillian. Tell me to stop if you don't want this. I'm a possessive and protective bastard. If we do this, you're going to have to be all right with that."

His eyes were serious and piercing in their intensity.

"Do I get to claim you right back?" she asked. "You won't get upset if I put handsy bitches in their place when they try to touch you? Or have a stare-down with a pushy chick in a bar? Because I don't share. If you cheat on me, I'm done. You'll get no second chances."

Instead of being concerned over what she'd said, Walker grinned. "I can't *wait* for you to get all possessive on me in public. And as I told you before, I don't cheat. Why the fuck would I when I've got this?" he asked, but it was a rhetorical question, because he once again lowered his head to her chest and ate at her nipple as if he were starving.

Gillian's head fell backward against the wall with a loud thump.

"Ow," she whispered, not really feeling the slight pain, but it was enough for Walker to move. He immediately brought his hand up to the back of her head and turned them so they were walking—more like stumbling—down the hall toward his bedroom.

The second they entered, Gillian inhaled deeply, smelling Walker's unique scent, and she knew her nipples had just gotten harder. She'd fantasized about being in here with him.

At the edge of his bed, he stopped her and reached around for her bra clasp. Within seconds, it was undone and falling to the floor. He didn't stop there; he undid the button of her jeans and lowered her zipper. Then he put his hands against her sides and pushed both her panties and jeans down at the same time.

"Step out," he whispered when they fell to her ankles.

Gillian managed to toe off her sandals and kick off her clothes without falling on her face. But then she realized that she was completely naked, and Walker still had on all his clothes. It was uncomfortable, but also kind of hot.

He stood a foot in front of her, completely immobile. His eyes ran down her body, from her head to her toes, then back up again. His chest was heaving with his breaths, as if he'd just run five miles.

Forcing herself to stand still, Gillian waited for him to say or do something. When he didn't move, she began to feel self-conscious.

"Walker?" she whispered. "What's wrong?"

"Nothing," he said with a croak. "Not a damn thing. You're beautiful. Way too pretty for the likes of me."

Gillian rolled her eyes. "Please," she said. "If anything, the opposite is true."

He put a finger over her lips and his gaze met hers. "Don't put yourself down," he ordered. "I won't tolerate anyone saying anything unfavorable about you, and that goes for yourself as well." His finger dropped from her lips, but didn't break contact with her body. He drew it over her chin, down her collarbone to her left breast. He swirled the digit around her hard nipple then down her side, where she squirmed away from him a bit when it tickled.

His lips quirked up, but he didn't stop. His finger traced her hip bone, then he brushed the curls between her legs. Gillian locked her knees but couldn't stop herself from inhaling sharply as he brushed against her clit. She wasn't sure if he'd done it on purpose or not, but when his smile grew and he did it again, she realized he knew exactly what he was doing.

Gillian reached for him and frowned when her hands touched his T-shirt instead of his skin. "If I'm naked, you should be too," she complained.

His finger continued its teasing, and he used his other hand to reach behind his head to remove his shirt. One quick movement and the cloth was on the floor at their feet, forgotten.

Gillian was having a hard time concentrating as Walker's finger had dipped lower between her folds, but she couldn't help sighing at the sight of his chest. He was ripped, and had both the six pack and those sexy-as-hell V-muscles she'd fantasized about—but it was the large bruise on his side that caught her attention. It was in the ugly green and yellow stage, but it was obvious something had hit him hard.

Without words, she ran her thumb over it gently.

"I'm okay," he said quietly.

Gillian nodded.

"Look at me," Walker ordered.

But she couldn't tear her eyes away from the mark on his side. She kept trying to imagine what in the world could've happened to bruise him so badly, but couldn't come up with anything.

One hand gripped her hip, and the other went under her chin to force her gaze away from his side.

"I'm okay," he said firmly.

Inhaling deeply through her nose, Gillian nodded. This was what he was talking about earlier. "Okay. You're good," she said. "But that doesn't mean that I'm happy. It doesn't mean that I don't want to inspect every inch of you to see where else you're hurt. To kiss every bruise. Every scrape to make it better."

He smiled. "I'm okay with that," he told her. "In fact, I think we should make it tradition. Whenever I come back from deployment, my own nurse has to do a very personal inspection of my body from head to toe."

"Deal," Gillian agreed immediately. "But I can't do that if you're wearing clothes. Strip, Army Boy."

Walker barked out a laugh and Gillian smiled. This was what had been missing from her relationships in the past. Laughter. The few times she'd had sex, it had been quiet and serious the entire time. Being with Walker was fun. It was exciting and nerve-wracking, but she'd never made a man laugh like this in bed.

Walker leaned over and pulled back the covers. Once again, his woodsy scent rose from the linens, and Gillian practically dove onto the mattress. She wanted to roll herself all over the sheets, imprinting his smell onto her body as if she were a wild animal, but she restrained herself. Barely.

Trying to figure out the best way to lie to appear the most seductive, she soon forgot all about positioning herself as Walker made quick work of his pants and stood by the bed, naked as the day he was born.

Inhaling sharply yet again, Gillian squirmed on the bed. She could feel her body readying itself to take him. She was so wet between her legs, and she wanted nothing more than to feel him inside her...finally.

"Walker," she breathed.

He smiled, then slowly joined her on the bed. Instead of lying next to her, he straddled her legs and hovered over her, his weight on his forearms on either side of her head.

She could feel his hard cock brush against the curls between her legs, and she immediately tried to shift, to open her legs wider, but his knees prevented her from moving like she wanted.

Whimpering, she ran her hands up and down his sides, wanting to touch him everywhere at once.

"Last chance," Walker told her.

In response, Gillian moved one hand between their bodies and grasped his hard-as-nails cock. She realized that her hand barely closed all the way around it, and she only managed one quick up and down stroke before Walker had grabbed her hand and moved it away from his dick.

Gillian pouted. "Hey, not fair," she complained.

He chuckled, and once again Gillian realized how much she liked hearing him laugh.

"There'll be time for that later. If you touch me right now, I'm going to go off like an untried boy. It's been thirteen long days for me, sweetheart. Cut me some slack."

"I guess you can't really masturbate while you're on a mission, huh?" she asked.

"No. And I was too tired last night to do more than eat, shower, and fall into bed."

"I suppose you're right," she told him with a smile. "I mean, I was able to take care of myself last night when I got home, so it's only fair."

Walker groaned. "Seriously, woman? That was just cruel."

Gillian smiled. "Hey, a girl's gotta do what a girl's gotta do."

"You think about me while you got yourself off?" he asked.

"Of course."

"Was I touching you?"

"Yes."

"Tell me," he ordered.

Gillian blushed. She wasn't afraid to admit that she masturbated, but telling him about it was a bit daunting.

"Was I touching you here?" he asked, seeing that she was shy. He shifted above her and one hand cupped her breast.

"To start with," she said breathlessly.

For a moment, he teased her nipple, then his fingers brushed down her belly. "Here?" he asked.

Gillian nodded as his fingers brushed her clit. She saw that Walker's head was lowered and he was watching his own fingers as they played with her soaking-wet slit. She sighed and put her head back down on his pillow. She gripped one of his arms tightly as her hips began to undulate under his ministrations.

Then he moved down, until he was on his belly between her legs. He pushed her thighs apart, using his broad shoulders to keep her spread open for him.

Any conversation they'd been having about what she'd been thinking when she'd masturbated had stopped. He was concentrating too hard on what he was doing—and Gillian was too lost in the pleasure he was giving her.

Using one hand to spread her lower lips, Walker leaned down and inhaled deeply. Gillian blushed but didn't have time to complain as the man between her legs groaned then licked her from bottom to top.

"Fucking heaven," he muttered before he did it again. Then again.

Gillian writhed and put her hands on his head.

"*Mmmm*," she murmured as he closed his mouth around her labia and used his tongue to give her the most intimate kiss she'd ever received.

Walker took his time. Kissing, sucking, and licking every inch of her pussy. By the time he slowly inserted one finger into her tight sheath, Gillian thought she was going to die. She lifted her hips off the mattress to try to take him deeper.

"You are so sexy," Walker said as he lowered his mouth once more. But this time, instead of licking her, he latched onto her clit. He sucked at it like he'd done to the flesh of her breast.

"Walker!" she exclaimed, and tried to buck him off. But he put his free arm across her belly and held her down as he continued his assault on her extremely sensitive bundle of nerves.

Gillian felt her orgasm rising hard and fast. It felt different from any that she'd given to herself. She wasn't in charge. She had to lie there and take what Walker was giving her. When she felt herself getting close to the edge, she usually backed off the speed of her vibrator and eased into the orgasm.

But Walker wasn't backing off. He was sending her hurtling toward the edge with no parachute. She was going to fall, and fall hard.

Gripping his short hair, Gillian tried once again to pull away from his mouth. But he wasn't letting her go. In fact, he eased another finger inside her body and began to thrust them in and out. The sounds his fingers made were loud in the quiet of the room. Gillian knew she was soaking wet but wasn't feeling any kind of embarrassment at that moment.

Just when she thought she was going to explode, Walker stopped sucking. He didn't lift his head, or remove his fingers, he just went still between her legs.

Gillian hung on the precipice, torn between being glad he'd stopped and pissed way the hell off.

"Walker?" she croaked.

Then, just as she thought she'd lose the orgasm she'd been climbing toward, he moved. He sucked harder than he had before and used his tongue to lash her clit at the same time he turned his fingers inside her and pressed against her G-spot. His pinky finger also brushed against her anus, stimulating the nerves back there.

She was stunned by the simultaneous assault on her senses, and immediately was lost in the throes of the most intense orgasm she'd ever experienced. She bucked and thrust her hips up toward Walker and threw her head back, screaming out his name. Her muscles shook as the mind-blowing pleasure went on and on.

Gillian had no idea when Walker had changed position. He was now on his knees, putting on a condom he'd produced out of thin air. Thankful that he was coherent enough to use protection, she could only moan when he lifted one of her legs and hooked it over his shoulder. He then put his arm under her other knee and leaned over her.

She was spread wide open beneath him, and she inhaled deeply when she felt the head of his cock brush against her still very sensitive folds. Looking up into his eyes, she saw his pupils were dilated and his nostrils were flaring with every breath he took.

"Tell me you're mine," he ordered in a low, gruff voice.

"After that mind-blowing orgasm? I'm totally yours," she told him.

He grinned briefly, then groaned when he pushed inside her.

It had been a while for her, and because he was so big, she winced as he entered her body.

He noticed, but didn't stop until they were fused together so tightly, she had no idea where she stopped and he started. Then he reached under her and palmed her ass, pulling her butt cheeks apart and pushing inside her even farther.

At first, she felt as if she were being torn apart, but after a second of adjustment, the pain morphed into complete ecstasy. Gillian clenched her inner muscles and was rewarded with a groan from Walker.

"I know I hurt you, but I couldn't stop," he said after a moment. He hadn't moved once since getting inside her, letting her adapt to his entry.

"It's okay."

"It's not," he countered. "But you were so fucking beautiful. Tasted so good, I couldn't stop myself. I'm sorry."

"Stop apologizing," Gillian scolded. She reached down and grabbed hold of his butt and kneaded the rock-hard flesh there. Then she tightened her stomach muscles and leaned up so she could reach his head. She nipped at his ear, then sucked the lobe into her mouth.

She felt him lurch inside her, and it gave her such a feeling of power, she did it again. "You like that," she said.

"I like every fucking thing about you," he returned.

Then he moved his hand farther up on the mattress, taking her leg with him since it was resting on his arm, which opened her even more. Gillian felt her inner thighs protest at the stretching, but she didn't care. She felt sexy as hell all spread out under him with his cock deep inside her.

"Move," she ordered.

"Are you sure? I don't want to hurt you, and I don't think I can go slow."

"Walker, I just came harder than I've ever come in my life. I'm wetter than I've ever been as well. I'm good. Fuck me."

That was all the permission he needed, apparently, because before the last syllable was out of her mouth, his hips were moving. Slow at first, as if he didn't really believe that she wasn't in pain anymore. But with every slow slide into her body, he got more and more confident, until he was hammering against her so hard, the sound of their bodies slapping together was loud as it echoed around the room.

At first, Walker stared into her eyes as he made love with her, but after a while, he looked down between their bodies. Gillian's eyes dropped too, and the sight of his cock disappearing into her body, then reappearing, shining with her juices, was erotic as hell. He must've thought so too, because a muscle in his jaw tightened and he groaned.

Gillian did her best to participate, to lift her hips into each thrust, but it was awkward with the way her ankle was resting on his shoulder and her other leg was in the crook of his elbow.

But her hands were free. So she brought them up and pinched one of Walker's nipples as he fucked her.

"Damn," he said as he thrust harder into her.

Smiling at his reaction, she did it again, played with his

nipples much as he'd done to hers earlier. When she noticed he was staring at her chest, she looked down to see her tits bouncing with every thrust he made inside her.

Gillian had never felt this powerful. Yeah, he was on top of her, and she couldn't move much, but she knew with a bone-deep conviction that she was in control. All it would take was one word from her and he'd stop.

She brought a hand to his nape and tugged him down toward her. His rhythm stuttered as he did as she requested. Aware that it wouldn't be good for him to go back to work with a big ol' hickey on his neck, she settled for latching her mouth onto one of his pecs. In about the same spot as he'd marked her earlier. She didn't mess around, sucking on his skin as hard as she could. He wasn't thrusting into her now at all. His entire body had gone still, allowing her to do as she wanted.

When she was sure she'd broken enough blood vessels under his skin to leave a hickey, she playfully nipped at him before pulling back. She stared at the mark on his chest with a satisfied smile.

"You did say you were possessive," Walker remarked with a chuckle.

"If I'm yours, you're mine," Gillian told him.

Without a word, Walker pulled out of her body.

"Walker! No!" Gillian complained. But he had her turned and on her hands and knees before she could blink.

Then he was pushing back inside her. He felt even bigger like this, if that was possible.

She fell her to forearms, her ass in the air, and Walker groaned.

"You have no idea how good you feel," he said.

Gillian couldn't answer as he fucked her hard from behind.

"I can't stop," he said apologetically.

"Good," she breathed out.

He awkwardly reached around and tried to manipulate her clit once more, but Gillian moved her arm down, shoving his fingers out of the way as she began to finger herself.

She liked this position because she could reach her clit without any issue, and she could also use her other hand to caress Walker every time he pulled out of her soaking sheath.

"Fuck, that's so sexy, make yourself come, Gilly," he croaked. "I want to feel you explode around my cock."

More turned on than she'd ever been in her life, Gillian buried her head into the mattress and inhaled Walker's scent into her lungs as she frantically worked herself up to another orgasm.

"That's it. I can feel you tightening around me. Fuck, I'm not going to last much longer. Hurry, sweetheart."

Feeling his urgency, Gillian did her best to obey. She was on the edge when she felt him spread her cheeks and press his thumb against her ass. He didn't penetrate her there, but the carnality of his touch had her hurtling over the edge before she had time to prepare.

"Yessss," Walker hissed as every muscle in her body clenched.

He thrust into her twice more, then pulled her hips hard against his and grunted and groaned as he finally orgasmed.

For a second, Gillian thought she'd gone blind, but eventually her sight returned and she realized she still had her face buried into the mattress. She turned her head and took a deep breath. Her chest was heaving in and out and her ass was still up in the air. Walker's cock was still deep inside her body, and he was holding her so tightly she had a feeling she'd have little finger-size bruises on her hips in the morning.

"Fuck," Walker whispered. "You killed me."

Gillian couldn't help it. She giggled. The movement made Walker's now soft cock slip out of her body, and they both moaned.

He helped her roll onto her side then pulled the sheet up and over her. "Stay right there. Don't move," he ordered.

"I couldn't even if I wanted to," she mumbled.

Walker's weight left the bed and she figured he was going to take care of the condom. He was back within seconds, climbing under the sheet with her and pulling her against him. Gillian rested her cheek against his chest and lifted one thigh to rest over his.

"I meant it," Walker said after a long moment.

"Meant what?"

"You're mine now. I'm not going back to sleeping chastely on the couch anymore."

"Okay."

"And if you thought I was protective and annoying before with my warnings to be careful, you're probably going to be unpleasantly surprised at how intense I can be about your safety from here on out."

Gillian didn't even tense. "Okay."

"I'm serious, Di. You're strong as fuck and independent to boot, but no more driving up here in the middle of the night. I want you to text me whenever you leave your apartment and when you get home."

"Are you going to start telling me who I can spend my time with and what I'm allowed to do when I'm not with you?" Gillian asked.

"No."

"Then I'm okay with you wanting to know I'm safe."

She felt him let out a long breath. Picking up her head, she looked him in the eyes. "I won't let you take control of my life. I'm still going to hang out with Ann, Wendy, and Clarissa. I'm still going to run my business the way I see fit. But I've waited forever to find you, Walker. I don't mind that you want me safe. That you worry about me. I'm okay with you coming to the events I plan when you can. I like having you by my side. You being concerned about me feels good. Just don't turn it into a controlling thing, and I'm okay with it."

"I don't want to control you," Walker said immediately, running his hand over her head. "But I know the evil that's out there. And the thought of it touching you makes me crazy. Somehow you still have this innocence about you, despite what happened in Venezuela, that I want to protect. I don't want anything else to happen to you. Ever."

Gillian put her head back on his chest. "Okay."

"Okay," Walker agreed.

Gillian knew it was only like four-thirty in the afternoon, but she was exhausted. She hadn't slept well last night after her impromptu trip up to Walker's apartment. And the two orgasms she'd just experienced had blown any desire to get up and do anything to smithereens.

"Tired," she whispered.

"Then sleep," Walker told her.

"Do we need to do anything?"

"No."

"Walker?"

"Yeah, sweetheart?"

"I'm glad you're home."

She felt him smile against her head. "Me too. Now shut up and take a nap. I haven't had nearly enough of you, and you still need to examine me from head to toe to make sure I'm not injured anywhere besides my side."

Gillian huffed out a breath. "I'm going to regret agreeing to that, aren't I?"

"Never," Walker promised.

Gillian wanted to talk some more. Wanted to ask how the other guys were and if they had been hurt as well. She wanted to ask what came next with them, how they were going to make this semi-long-distance relationship work, but she was too tired.

One second she was thinking that it didn't feel weird at all to be completely naked in bed with Walker, and the next she was fast asleep.

* * *

"She knows, and she's talking to the Feds," the mysterious seventh hijacker told Alfredo Salazar.

Salazar was the son of one of the leaders of the Sinaloa Cartel. His father had sent him to Texas when he was ten years old to learn the business and to eventually run the operation from the other side of the border. He was now twenty-five, and one of the most feared men in the Austin area. Salazar was in charge of millions of dollars' worth of meth and cocaine that was delivered from Mexico. It was his job to distribute it around Texas, and up into the rest of the country as well. He was as ruthless as his father and didn't tolerate any threat to his business.

He was at the top of the pile when it came to the US operations. He also kept a close eye on the lieutenants, hitmen, and falcons under him. He had lieutenants who were ultimately responsible for supervising the hitmen and falcons, who could also carry out some low-profile executions without his permission, but *nothing* happened in his organization without Salazar's knowledge.

The hitmen were important to the operation because they were the security for the cartel. Their main task was to defend their turf from rival groups, police, and the military. They stole, kidnapped, extorted, and assassinated where necessary to keep the cartel running smoothly.

The falcons were at the bottom of the cartel hierarchy. They were the eyes and ears for the gang and reported back to the hitmen and lieutenants the activities of their rivals, police, and others who were actively working against them.

Salazar didn't usually communicate with falcons directly, he had lieutenants who listened to their grievances and dealt with their issues. But today, he'd agreed to meet with this particular falcon because of what had happened a few months ago in Venezuela.

"Are you sure?" Salazar asked.

"Positive. She had a meeting in Austin with that pain-in-our-ass DEA asshole Calum Branch, and some FBI shithead as well. She was there at least four hours. They're already trying to crack down on our operation here in

Austin because of what happened in Venezuela. The last thing we need is that bitch telling them anything else."

Salazar leaned back in his chair and eyed the low-level minion in front of him. He hadn't been opposed to the hijacking scheme because it was a means to an end. Namely, getting rid of Hugo Lamas, who'd been a pain in his father's ass way before he'd been thrown in jail. The Sinaloa Cartel hated the Cartel of the Suns. And anytime they could take out one of those assholes was a good day.

It was unfortunate that they'd lost six of their own in the process, but he'd had a hand in personally picking the men who'd carried out the hijacking. He'd chosen them because they were expendable. He didn't mourn their deaths, but he didn't want any more of their brethren to die as a result either. Their deaths were honorable, but their sacrifice shouldn't bring negative attention to the cartel.

If Sinaloa had additional pressure put on their operation here in Austin, it wouldn't be good. They were already losing too much product because of crackdowns at the border, and he couldn't afford to lose any more.

"Bring her to me," Salazar told the only member of the group to survive the hijacking. "I'll figure out what she knows...and if she needs to die."

"But I can take her out easily. One tap to the head and she won't be an issue anymore," the falcon protested.

Salazar raised one eyebrow. "Are you disagreeing with my order?" he asked in a deadly even tone.

"No, of course not."

"Good. Then go get her and bring her here. I want to talk to this bitch myself. I'll find out what she told the Feds. If she needs to disappear for good, *I'll* make the order for that to happen." He leaned forward and pinned the falcon with a deadly gaze. "You aren't a hitman. I'm giving you this task as a reward for your loyalty, and because of the good job you did in fooling everyone in Venezuela. But when Gillian Romano is standing in front of me, I expect her to be unharmed. Understand me?" His threat was clear.

The falcon grimaced, but nodded. "*Si, Senor.*"

"Good. Now get the fuck out."

Salazar had forgotten about the falcon as soon as the door to his office closed. He had more important things to worry about than one fucking woman. Like the twenty-five-million-dollar shipment of cocaine that was supposed to arrive that afternoon.

CHAPTER SIXTEEN

The last two weeks had been idyllic for Gillian. The only thing that would've made them better was if she'd been able to see Walker during the week. They spent the weekend he'd returned from his mission together, and it had been harder than she'd thought it would be to leave to go back to Georgetown on Sunday night.

But they both had work they had to get done. Their phone calls and texts were much more intimate after they'd spent the weekend making love, and Gillian loved the change.

Walker hadn't been kidding, he was very protective and concerned about her. But it hadn't been a hardship to send him quick notes letting him know when she left her apartment and when she returned.

He didn't care where she was, as long as she returned home safely afterward. It had actually been Gillian who'd suggested that maybe they could both download a tracker app on their phones. He'd agreed in a heartbeat.

So now at any time of day, she could click on the app

and see exactly where Walker was, and vice versa. It felt a little stalkerish, but Gillian couldn't deny that it made her feel safe that he knew where she was at all times.

The Howard anniversary party was quickly approaching and because it involved over three hundred guests, it was taking up most of her time and energy. She had a few small parties and gatherings that she was also planning and executing, but those were pretty straightforward and didn't take much effort.

Today, Gillian was meeting the Howards' daughter downtown at a catering company so she could taste different kinds of cakes and make the final decision on what she wanted at the anniversary party.

Since the meeting was at ten, Gillian hoped the Austin traffic wouldn't be too bad getting into the city. She'd already scoped out the area and there was a parking garage within a block of where they were meeting, which was a relief. She hated trying to find parking downtown.

Gillian knew Walker was busy that morning with meetings, but she decided to give him a quick call just to say good morning. He'd told her that she could call whenever she wanted, he'd always pick up as long as he wasn't busy.

"Hey," he said after only two rings.

"Hi," Gillian said happily. She didn't always get to talk to him in the mornings, so she was pleased when she'd been able to catch him.

"Did you have a good morning?" he asked.

"No."

"No? Why not? What happened?" Walker asked worriedly.

"I didn't get to shower with my boyfriend," she said

with a pout. "And I had to get my own coffee, and my Wonder Woman coffee mug was dirty."

"Oh, you poor thing," Walker said, the relief that she'd been kidding easy to hear in his tone. "Sounds like your boyfriend is being a slacker."

Loving their banter, Gillian beamed. "I don't know, he more than makes up for not being around during the week when we get together on the weekends."

"Yeah?"

"Oh, yeah," Gillian said with feeling. "How was your morning? How'd PT go? Did you run a marathon this morning for fun?"

He chuckled. "Only six miles. Then we hit the obstacle course and ran through that a few times."

"A few?" Gillian asked. She knew he and his friends had probably done it at least twenty times in a row. And had probably put on their rucksacks for half of those rotations. Walker and the others were serious about staying in top physical shape. She knew it wasn't easy for Walker, since he was getting close to forty, but she'd seen him work out...there wasn't a doubt in her mind that he was just as fit as his friends who were years younger.

"You on your way to Austin?" Walker asked, turning the conversation from him.

He did that a lot, and at first it irritated Gillian, because she thought he was trying to avoid talking about himself. But eventually she realized that he wasn't trying to dodge her questions, he just wasn't self-centered in any way, shape, or form. He told her once that he asked her a lot of questions because he was more interested in *her*. If he couldn't be with her, he wanted to know everything about what she was doing and thinking. It made him feel closer to her. How could she argue about that?

"Yeah. I left about ten minutes ago. There's a bit of traffic, but it's not too bad."

"You can't wait to eat cake this early in the day, can you?" Walker asked with a chuckle.

Gillian smiled. Walker had found out all about her sweet tooth during the weekends they'd spent together. Her ideal breakfast was coffee and a sticky-sweet doughnut. "Hey, it's a tough job, but someone has to do it," she told him.

"True."

"What's on your plate for today?" she asked.

"Meetings this morning, then me and the guys are headed over to one of the elementary schools on base to volunteer. We're reading to the kids, things like that."

Imagining Walker sitting on a too-small chair reading to a bunch of kids who would be enthralled by whatever story he chose to read to them made Gillian's panties damp. She wasn't ready to have kids, but she couldn't deny the thought of Walker holding a small baby made her ovaries go into overdrive. "Sounds fun," she told him.

He huffed out a laugh. "Kids scare the crap out of me," he admitted.

It was Gillian's turn to laugh. "Why?"

"Because I'm afraid I'm gonna say the wrong thing and they'll go home saying some bad word they learned from me and will be scarred for life. They're like little sponges, absorbing everything around them, and I know I'm too intense. The last thing I want is them learning any bad habits from me."

"Walker," Gillian scolded. "You're intense, yes, but not

in a bad way. I'm sure they see you watching out for them. Being friendly with your guys. Being respectful to their teachers. Not tolerating bullying. Greeting the smallest kid in the class with a special handshake. They're not stupid, they know when adults are bullshitting them, and you're the last person to do that."

"Thanks, Di," he said softly.

Gillian heard someone say something to him in the background, and he told them he'd be right there. She wasn't surprised when he came back on the phone and said, "I have to go."

"I heard."

"Thanks for calling. I needed to hear your voice this morning. I might be busy, but you'll let me know how the taste test went this morning and when you're on your way home?"

"Of course. I'm leaning toward the double chocolate cake, it should appeal to the greatest amount of people, but we'll see how everything tastes when we get there," Gillian said. "You're still coming down this afternoon, right?"

"Wouldn't miss it. If possible, I'll see if I can leave a bit early and get there in time for dinner. That okay?"

"Of course. You're always welcome here." Gillian had given him a key to her apartment the weekend after he'd gifted her with the one to his place. Since he'd returned from being deployed, their relationship had moved forward at warp speed, but Gillian wasn't complaining. She just hated having to be apart from him during the week. They hadn't talked about moving in together, but every Sunday night when she had to say goodbye, it got harder and harder.

She knew it wasn't feasible for him to move to George-town to live with her, so if they were going to move their relationship to the next level, she'd have to be the one to go to him. It would be difficult for her business, and she'd have to put a lot of miles on her car, but if Walker asked, she'd move in with him tomorrow.

She'd had a long conversation with Ann about her relationship with Walker and even though she'd been afraid her friend was going to tell her she was crazy, and that she was moving way too fast, Ann had asked her one question.

"If you got a phone call with the best news you'd ever heard in your life, who would be the first person you'd want to tell?"

The answer was easy. Walker. Gillian felt bad about that since she'd been friends with Ann for so long, but the other woman simply chuckled. "That's the way it's supposed to be when you love someone. They're the first person you should want to turn to when something good happens, *and* something bad. You know I love you, as do Clarissa and Wendy, but you told us from almost the second you got back from Venezuela that you thought he was it for you. Moving in with him, being in a relationship with him or anyone else, doesn't mean you love us less, it just means we have more to gossip about when we get together."

"Gillian?"

She blinked and realized that she'd been daydreaming and not paying attention to Walker on the phone. "Sorry, I'm here."

"Drive safe, and be careful walking to and from the caterer."

"I will," Gillian said. "I've got the pepper spray you got me, and I'll make sure it's out and ready."

"Good."

"Although it's not even ten in the morning. I'm sure the homicidal maniacs are still sleeping from being up and causing mayhem until the wee hours of the morning."

Walker didn't even chuckle. "There's no timeline for bad shit happening."

"But you always tell me nothing good happens after midnight."

"Which is true. But that doesn't mean that assholes can't be drunk at nine in the morning, or looking for an easy mark to get some cash for the drugs they need to get them through the day."

"Okay, okay, okay. I get it. I'll be careful, Walker. Promise."

"Good."

"Say hi to your friends for me."

"I will. I'll talk to you later."

"Walker?"

"Yeah?"

He sounded distracted and Gillian knew he needed to go, that he had to get into a meeting. She'd wanted to tell him how much she missed him and how important he was to her, but while he was rushed didn't seem like the best time. "Have a good day," she said somewhat lamely.

"You too. Bye."

"Bye."

Gillian clicked off the phone connection and sighed. She loved talking to Walker. They never seemed to run out of things to say to each other. But now she needed to concentrate on the other cars around her and finding her way to the right address downtown. With all the one-way streets, she frequently got turned around.

But this time, she was able to figure out where she was going without any issues and she pulled into the parking garage with plenty of time to spare before her appointment. Gillian chose to park at the top of the garage, near the elevator doors. There were fewer cars at the top of the structure, but that was all right with her. Gillian had seen a documentary once on how shoddy architects had designed a parking garage and it had collapsed, trapping and squishing people on the lower levels. It seemed safer to park at the top. Yeah, it was a longer fall down, but at least she'd be on the top of all the debris.

Her friends gave her shit about being so paranoid, but Gillian didn't care. She'd get the last laugh when she was standing on top of the pile of rubble that used to be a parking garage.

She took the elevator down to the first floor and headed for the caterer.

An hour and a half later, and full of sugar from all the cakes she'd tasted, Gillian headed back to her car. They'd settled on two cakes for the party, one the double chocolate cake Gillian had guessed would be a favorite choice, and a simpler vanilla cake with chocolate frosting for the other.

Gillian was thinking about all the things she still needed to do to finalize everything for the Howards' anniversary party as she stepped out of the elevator on the top floor of the parking garage—and didn't see the two men in masks running toward her until it was too late to do anything.

The pepper spray Walker had given her was inside her

purse, but even if it had been in her hand, she wouldn't have had time to do anything other than brace.

One of the men grabbed her around the waist and clamped his hand over her mouth.

Gillian screamed, but the sound barely traveled further than the next car over.

The second man grabbed her legs when she began to kick and fight. They shuffled her over to a white panel van —how cliché—and stuffed her inside when the door was opened.

There were no seats in the back of the van and it was full of all sorts of tools. Gillian had watched enough crime shows to know if the men managed to take her out of the garage, she was as good as dead. They could bring her to the middle of nowhere. Lord knew there were plenty of places in Texas that were totally isolated, even around Austin, that she didn't have a hope in hell of escaping.

Panicked, she fought as hard as she could. She knew she'd made contact with her kidnappers because there was a lot of grunting and swearing.

"Hold her down!" one man said.

"I'm trying!" the other answered.

"Hit her!" a third voice ordered.

The third voice registered in her consciousness as being female, which was a shock, and for a second, Gillian thought it sounded familiar, but then she couldn't think about anything other than the pain as a fist landed on her cheekbone.

Momentarily stunned, she stopped fighting. The door slid shut and she heard the engine rumble as it started.

No!

She tried to fight some more, but because of her

momentarily lapse, the men had gotten the upper hand. One grabbed her wrists and the other zip-tied them together. He tightened them so much, she squeaked in pain.

"Shut up," one of her kidnappers growled into her face.

She spit on him.

He swore, and the last thing Gillian remembered was his fist coming toward her face.

* * *

Trigger couldn't concentrate on the book he was reading to the group of second-graders gathered around him. He'd been set up in a corner of the classroom with five kids, and he loved their enthusiasm and the way they hung on his every word. But he couldn't stop thinking about Gillian.

It was two o'clock, and she should've been done with her appointment at the caterer and back home well before now.

But every time he checked the app on his phone, it indicated she was still in the parking garage near the caterer. He figured she'd forgotten her phone in her car and maybe she'd taken her client to lunch after they'd chosen which dessert to offer at the anniversary party in a couple weeks.

But that didn't really make sense. Gillian *always* had her phone with her. As a small-business owner, she relied on email and phone to talk to new and current clients. She might silence it when she was in a meeting, but she never left it behind. And seeing that blinking icon on the app that said her phone hadn't moved—long *after* her meeting should have ended—made no sense to him.

He hadn't even been able to check in on her until noon, when he and the team had been released to grab a quick bite before heading over to the elementary school. At first he hadn't thought much about where her phone was pinging, until he'd zoomed in and realized her phone was in the parking garage.

It wasn't fair to the kids, but Trigger read the book in his hands as fast as he could. He couldn't let this go. When he was finished, he stood and spent a moment praising each of the kids around him, then he strode toward the door. He flashed the "danger" sign to Lefty before he slipped out of the classroom.

He didn't bother with texting; he clicked on Gillian's name and brought the phone up to his ear. With the way his skin was crawling, he didn't really expect her to answer. And he was right, she didn't. Her voice mail kicked on after five rings. He left a quick message telling her that he was worried about her and asked her to please call him as soon as possible. He then sent a text telling her the same thing.

By the time he was done, Lefty and Grover had joined him in the hallway.

"What's wrong?" Lefty asked, all business.

"I don't know. It's Gillian. She had an appointment downtown this morning and she should've been done by now. The tracking app shows she's in the parking garage nearby. At least her phone is."

"You tried calling her?" Grover asked.

Trigger nodded. "No answer."

"Cops?" Lucky asked.

"You know as well as I do that they'll just tell me she's an adult and she doesn't have to report her every move to me. She'll have to be missing for twenty-four hours before they'll consider taking my report," Trigger said.

"But they could do a welfare check, right?" Grover asked.

"Maybe. I'm headed down there now."

"You want us to come with?" Lefty asked.

Trigger nodded. "If nothing's wrong and I'm overreacting, we can all have dinner or something. I've got my bag in my car already, since I was headed down there later anyway."

"But if something *is* wrong, we'll be there to have your back," Grover said. He then opened the classroom door and signaled to the rest of the team that they needed to move out. Within five minutes, Trigger was surrounded by men who hadn't thought twice about coming to his aid, even if they didn't know what the issue was.

Lefty explained the situation and within five minutes, they'd all piled into both Trigger's and Doc's vehicles to make the trip down to Austin.

Trigger knew he was driving too fast but didn't care. The closer they got to Austin, and with every call that went unanswered by Gillian, he knew deep in his gut that something was very wrong.

She'd been very good about letting him know her whereabouts. The situation in Venezuela had scared her, but Trigger didn't think it had fundamentally changed the way she looked at the world. It was one of the many things he loved about her.

Fuck. He loved her.

From the first moment he'd pushed inside her body, she'd been his in a way no woman had ever been before.

Gillian still saw the good in people. In the world. She

273

had an intrinsically positive outlook on life and felt as if everyone had good in them, that everyone was redeemable. Trigger knew differently, but he found her innocence refreshing.

He just hoped it hadn't gotten her killed.

* * *

Gillian regained consciousness in a blink. She wasn't confused, knew exactly what had happened, but couldn't understand *why*.

Squinting, she looked around her—and her blood froze.

She was in some kind of rundown house. She had no idea where. There was trash and debris all around her, along with some shabby furniture. She was sitting in a very uncomfortable wooden chair with her arms secured behind her back. Her ankles were also tied to the legs of the chair.

But the most frightening thing about her situation was the plastic tarp under her feet.

She wasn't an idiot. She'd seen *Dexter*, she knew what that meant. They were doing their best to contain her DNA so there would be no trace she'd been here.

Her limbs started shaking but Gillian couldn't stop. She whimpered in fear.

Just then the door opened, and she stared at the men who entered and felt herself shake even harder. With just a look, she knew the man in front wasn't someone who felt any sympathy for her. He was Hispanic, with dark hair and bottomless dark eyes. It was if they looked right through her. He didn't see Gillian Romano, he saw an enemy.

Being so loathed and hated wasn't a feeling Gillian was familiar with. She was a nice person. She went out of her way to make others comfortable and to make them like her. What she could've done to this man to make him hate her so much, she had no idea.

"So you're Gillian," the man said after he'd stopped in front of her.

Licking her lips, she nodded. Feeling thankful that she hadn't been gagged, Gillian couldn't seem to make her voice work.

"I hear you've been chatting with the Feds and DEA."

She blinked in surprise. She'd had no idea why she'd been snatched out of the garage, but that wasn't what she thought the man would say.

When she didn't respond, the man tilted his head and studied her. After a moment, he asked, "You have no idea who I am, do you?"

Gillian shook her head.

"Does the name Salazar mean anything to you?"

Gillian wracked her brain, but couldn't think of anyone she'd ever met with that last name, and she eventually shook her head once more.

The man chuckled, but it wasn't exactly a humorous sound. "I think you're the only person living within a thousand miles of Austin who hasn't heard of me," he said.

Gillian hated feeling at a disadvantage.

"I'm sorry, Mr. Salazar, I'm usually very good with names and faces. If we've met before, I've forgotten the circumstances."

If anything, her apology seemed to amuse him more.

"My name is Alfredo Salazar." He paused as if gauging whether knowing his first name would jog her memory.

When she didn't say anything, he continued. "I'm the leader of the Sinaloa Cartel here in Texas...and really, all of the southern US."

Gillian's eyes widened. *Oh shit. Shit, shit, shit.* She didn't watch the news much, it was too depressing. But she'd recently had a very thorough education on the Sinaloa drug cartel, thanks to her plane being hijacked and a few internet searches.

"I see that's ringing some bells," Salazar said. "Let's start again. I have it on good authority you've been talking to the Feds and the DEA about us."

Gillian tried to swallow, but her mouth was too dry.

"I want to know what you told them. What you know. And if I think you're not being honest with me, then I'll have to have my friend here," he nodded to one of the men who had walked behind her to stand at her right shoulder, "remove one of your fingers. Then if I think you're still holding back, maybe I'll take an ear. Or a toe. I can play this game all day," he said, and Gillian had no doubt he'd do what he threatened. "So...what did you tell them about us?"

"No-Nothing," Gillian stammered. "I mean, they didn't really ask about you, about your organization."

Salazar nodded at the man standing behind her and before she could blink, he'd grabbed her hand and had a huge knife pressed against the base of her thumb.

"I'm told it hurts like a son of a bitch," Salazar said matter-of-factly.

"I swear, they didn't ask about the cartel at all!" she cried. "They wanted to talk to me about the passengers on the plane. That's it! I had to look at pictures of every single passenger and tell them what I remembered about them. They're trying to figure out who the seventh hijacker is. That's all!"

The man with the knife still held it against her thumb; he hadn't cut her yet, but Gillian knew she was only one second from losing a digit. The cold steel against her flesh was tricking her brain into thinking he *was* cutting her, especially since she couldn't see her hands where they were bound behind her.

"And who do you think it is?" Salazar asked.

"I don't know," Gillian wailed, scared out of her skull. "Maybe Leyton. He acted really weird and gave me the creeps. But as I told *them*, I didn't spend any time with the men so I couldn't tell them much."

"But you spent a lot of time with the women, didn't you?" Salazar asked.

Gillian nodded. "Of course. They kept us separated."

"You think maybe it's Alice? Or Janet? Maybe Maria Gomez?"

Gillian had no idea how this man knew who the other passengers were, but it shouldn't have surprised her. Whoever the seventh hijacker was had obviously passed along the information about what went on inside the plane.

"I don't know," she said again. "I'm just an event planner. Not an investigator."

Salazar studied her for so long, Gillian was afraid to even breathe. The man holding her hand had an iron grip, and she knew she couldn't do a damn thing if Salazar decided to cut off her thumb.

"What were you doing in Austin today?" Salazar finally asked.

"I had a meeting with a client to decide what kind of cake to serve at her parents' anniversary party."

"You weren't meeting with the Feds again?"

"No! I haven't heard from them since I met with them a month or so ago," Gillian said.

"And I suppose you don't know that the caterer you visited is located smack-dab in the middle of drug central, downtown Austin?" Salazar drawled.

Gillian blinked in surprise. She *hadn't* known that. She had no reason *to* know that little fact.

"Christ," Salazar said with a shake of his head. "You're like the epitome of white privilege, aren't you?"

Gillian had no idea what he was talking about, so she didn't agree or disagree, feeling that was the safer thing to do at the moment.

"You live in your lily-white world, never worrying about being shot at because of the color of your skin. Never having to bother your little head about finding yourself in the wrong part of town because your blonde hair and green eyes will save you somehow. Even in the middle of a fucking hijacking, you came out on top, being picked as the chosen one to talk to the authorities." He shook his head. "You ever done drugs, Ms. Romano?"

Gillian shook her head.

"Not even smoked a little pot?" Salazar insisted.

She shook her head again.

"Ever been tempted?"

Again, she silently answered in the negative.

"There's always a first time," Salazar said smoothly. He crouched down a few feet in front of her, not touching the plastic sheeting that had been laid at her feet. "Everyone says that drugs make you feel like shit. That they're bad.

But what you don't know is how fucking *amazing* a little cocaine can make you feel. It's the best feeling, euphoric. There's nothing like that first high. You'll spend the rest of your life chasing the feeling you got the first time you shot up. You don't want to feel good, Gillian?"

She hated the way her name sounded on his lips. On the outside, Alfredo Salazar was good-looking. But she could feel that he was evil through and through. He wouldn't hesitate to have her killed. He loved money and power, that was it. All she could do was stare at him in terror. She didn't want him to force cocaine on her. Or any other kind of drug. She didn't want to be addicted. Not when everything in her life was going so well.

"Look at you, your heart is beating out of your chest. You're like a feral dog, too scared to move, but terrified to stay where you are as well. You honestly have no clue who the bad guy was on that plane, do you? Out of all the people you befriended, you have no idea who wants to see you and everyone else dead."

"No," Gillian whispered.

"And you told the authorities that too, right?"

She nodded.

"Bet that pissed them off," he muttered.

"They weren't thrilled," Gillian said hesitantly. She'd hated letting them down, but she'd told them everything she could think of. She knew nothing she'd said had helped in the slightest. They'd been polite and thanked her for her insights, but deep down, she was aware she'd disappointed them.

Salazar shook his head and muttered more to himself than her, "Fucking bitches and their drama." Then he lifted his chin at the man holding the knife to her hand

and he let go. Gillian breathed a sigh of relief. But it only lasted a heartbeat, because the man behind her then wrapped his hands around her head and tilted it backward.

Gillian lost sight of Salazar and struggled in the man's grip. But with her hands tied behind her and her legs immobilized, she had no leverage. No way to protect herself.

"Relax, *chica*," Salazar said. "I believe you. I apologize that you were inconvenienced today. I should've done a bit more looking into the situation before believing one of my falcons. But that doesn't change the fact that I can't simply drop you back into your world of ignorance."

"Please, don't kill me," Gillian whispered as she stared up at the ceiling. "I won't say anything about what happened. Hell, I don't even *know* what happened, or why."

She heard Salazar chuckle. "I'm sorry, but I don't believe you. You'll tell someone. A friend, a boyfriend, the cops, someone, then I'll have to worry about that shit, along with all the other crap piled up on my plate at the moment. But...I can't help but be intrigued by the innocence and goodness you wear like a fucking cloak."

Gillian shivered as she felt a finger trace along her vulnerable throat. Salazar had obviously gotten up and approached her. With her head forced back like it was, she was completely at the mercy of this man. "I was like you... once. But that ended on my ninth birthday when I was introduced to the way my life was going to be. I saw my first man killed that day. He deserved it for snitching on the Sinaloa, but it was...jarring, to see a man's blood spurt out of him and watch as he writhed on the floor, begging for mercy."

Gillian couldn't stop the tears that fell out of her eyes. She wanted to be brave. Wanted to be the kind of person who could kick ass like the ones in the books she read. But she wasn't. She was tied up and helpless. She had no idea if Walker or anyone even knew she was missing at this point.

"In a second, you're going to be offered a drink. You're going to drink it without fuss. All of it. Every drop. Understand?"

She didn't want to. She knew whatever was in the cup was probably poisoned and this was literally her last seconds to live.

"I can see your mind working overtime. It won't kill you. It's Rohypnol. It'll relax you. In fifteen or twenty minutes, you'll fall asleep. You won't remember what happened here. You won't be able to tell the cops anything about me or what we talked about. It'll be as if it never happened. This is in your best interest. It's this...or my lieutenant slicing your throat and you bleeding out."

Salazar leaned over her until Gillian was looking up into his steely brown eyes. "But this is your only free pass, Ms. Romano. If I hear you've somehow remembered our little talk today, and you've snitched, it won't go as well for you a second time. And I understand you have some good friends in the area too, right? You wouldn't want your friends—Ms. Pierce, Ms. Reed, or Ms. Thomas—to have an accident, would you?"

The thought of Ann, Wendy, or Clarissa being in the hands of this cold-hearted monster made her physically sick. Gillian shook her head as best she could.

"Good. So we're on the same page. Now, drink up."

Before she could agree or not agree, a plastic cup was pressed against her lips and the goon who held her head pressed on an area of her jaw that made her cry out in pain. With her mouth open, the second man tipped the glass and she had no choice but to drink.

It tasted horrible and burned as it went down her throat. For a second, Gillian thought they'd forced her to drink acid or antifreeze or something, but when she inhaled through her nose as she swallowed, she knew it was some kind of alcohol. Tequila maybe.

She sputtered and choked, but the men didn't relent. By the time they let go of her, she was soaked from her chin to her belly button. She tried to breathe, but gagged instead.

A huge hand covered her mouth from behind and she stared up at Salazar as he said, "If you throw it up, you'll have to swallow it back down. Can't let good roofies go to waste."

Forcing herself to take a big breath through her nose, Gillian tried to tamp down the need to puke. When the man finally let go of her, she immediately inhaled and asked, "What now?"

"Now? We wait for you to go to sleep. Then my men will find a nice quiet place to drop you off. Wouldn't want any big bad drug dealers to find you passed out now, would we? They might not be as nice to you as I've been."

Gillian wanted to scratch his eyes out, but she couldn't do anything but sit there and listen.

"Just because I made a mistake in believing my falcon and having you brought in doesn't mean I'm not keeping an eye on you. Be a good girl, go back to your white world of privilege and stay there. Understand?"

Gillian had no idea what he was talking about with a falcon, but she nodded anyway. She was still terrified of what was going to happen to her when she went unconscious. The alcohol was going straight to her head, but it was the drug he'd forced her to ingest that worried her the most.

She knew all about women being roofied at clubs. It was an infamous date-rate drug. She didn't want to forget what happened here. It seemed very, *very* important that she not forget.

As the minutes ticked by, she repeated the words over and over in her head in the slight hope that maybe when she woke up, her unconscious mind would be able to recall them.

Salazar, falcon, Salazar, falcon, Falazar, salcon...

The room was beginning to spin.

"That's it, Gillian. Close your eyes and go to sleep. When you wake up, this will all be a bad dream."

She did as ordered, feeling as if her body belonged to someone else. *Salafar, fanzar...*

Gillian tried to hang on, tried to memorize what she needed to before she lost it completely, but it was too late.

Salazar waited until he was sure the bitch was out before motioning to his lieutenants. "Bring Vilchez to me as soon as she can be found. First, I told her to bring Gillian to me unharmed. Those bruises on her face are gonna piss her man off, and that's the *last* thing we need. Secondly, this meeting was unnecessary and potentially dangerous to our organization. She's already on the Feds' radar, and her new boyfriend is one of the men who took out Luis and the others. I've done as much damage control as I can do here, but there's still a chance she'll remember something and talk. Vilchez has a *lot* to answer for."

"*Si, Senor*," the men said in unison.

"Where do you want us to put her?" the man who'd forced the roofied drink down Gillian's throat asked.

"Don't care. Somewhere without cameras," Salazar said impatiently, then turned and left the room. He was pissed he'd wasted his time on this shit today. He had more important things to do—namely, distributing the millions of street dollars' worth of cocaine he'd just had delivered the day before.

Vilchez would be dealt with one way or another. Making sure his falcons knew their place was imperative, and disciplining Vilchez would serve as a reminder of how they were supposed to be serving Sinaloa. Watching and reporting so they could stay under the radar. Not lying about what they'd seen or heard to serve their own vendettas.

Sinaloa came first, period. When a falcon agreed to work for Salazar, he or she was putting their own needs second to those of the cartel. A reminder of that would be good for everyone.

The falcons would be scared into thinking before they acted.

The hitmen would have a chance to practice their interrogation techniques.

And the lieutenants would learn to think twice before bringing stupid shit to his door.

Shaking his head, Salazar strode confidently to the car that was waiting at the curb. His Mercedes was out of place in the rundown neighborhood, but no one would say a word, he was sure of that. He owned this part of town.

Half the residents were working for him and the other half needed the drugs he supplied.

Putting thoughts of Gillian Romano out of his head, Salazar settled onto the leather seat of his car and nodded at his driver. This little meeting might've been an amusing break from his normal routine, but it was also annoying, because now it meant he had to deal with the reason it had come about in the first place.

"Fucking bitches and their drama," he murmured for the second time that afternoon, before picking up one of his many untraceable cell phones and dialing another one of his lieutenants. Time to get back to work making money and selling drugs.

CHAPTER SEVENTEEN

Five hours.

That's how long it had been since Trigger figured Gillian had gone missing.

He and his team had gone straight to the parking garage where her phone was pinging and, after driving through it, had found her car on the top level. Her purse, with her phone and pepper spray inside, was also there, kicked underneath a car near the elevators.

The app had said the phone had been there since eleven thirty-three and it was now four-thirty. He felt sick and at the moment had no idea what to do next to try to find her. They'd called the police as soon as they'd found her purse and realized she was missing, but searching for someone took time. Time Gillian might not have.

He'd told the cops as much as he could about Gillian being a hostage a couple months ago and how the seventh hijacker hadn't been identified, but knew none of that was any help. Lucky had called the DEA agent who'd interviewed Gillian, and he'd been in contact with the FBI, but again, nothing happened fast with those bureaucracies, and the thought of Gillian being in the hands of the drug cartel who'd had no problem killing innocent civilians on the plane ate away at his soul.

"We're gonna find her," Grover said quietly as he stood next to Trigger on the top level of the garage. Trigger hadn't wanted to leave since it was the last place Gillian had been. The surveillance cameras were on a timer, and at the exact moment his woman had been taken, the fucking things had been pointed at the other end of the garage. By the time they'd swung back around, Gillian was gone.

He'd promised to keep her safe, but how the hell could he do that when he had no idea who to keep her safe *from*?

"Trigger? Did you hear me?" Grover asked.

He nodded. The words were merely platitudes. They both knew there was no way Grover could promise that they'd find her. Thousands of people disappeared off the face of the earth every day. Killed by strangers, or even by people they knew and loved, their bodies buried or dismembered and thrown away like trash.

The thought of his Gillian being discarded like that hurt like hell.

"Holy shit, Trigger!" Lefty exclaimed, running toward him and Grover at a dead sprint from the other end of the garage, where he'd been looking for clues.

Trigger's heart stopped.

"A woman's been found on the other side of the city," Lefty told him excitedly. "She was lying unconscious in a parking lot between two cars. They think it's Gillian!"

"Is she alive?" Trigger forced himself to ask.

"Yes. She's being transferred to St. David's, north of here."

Trigger was on the move before Lefty had finished talking.

Gillian was alive. That was the only thing that mattered to him at the moment.

Brain got behind the wheel of Trigger's Blazer and drove like a bat out of hell to St. David's. He didn't bother to park, but pulled up outside the emergency room entrance to let everyone out.

Trigger made a mental note to thank him later, but for now, all his attention was focused on getting to Gillian.

He strode up to the desk and noticed that the woman's eyes widened in alarm at his approach, but he didn't slow down.

"Gillian Romano," he barked. "She should've just been brought in. She was found unconscious in a parking lot. Where is she?"

The woman cleared her throat and said, "I'm sorry, sir, if you'll just take a seat, I'll see what I can find out about her. Are you family?"

"Yes." The lie came out without hesitation. "I'm her fiancé."

She looked skeptical, but didn't call him on it. "Okay, as I said, if you'll take a seat, I'll be with you as soon as I can."

"No," Trigger said with a shake of his head. "I need to be with her now. She has to be scared out of her mind."

The woman opened her mouth, probably to deny him once again, when a commotion sounded behind them.

Turning, Trigger immediately recognized Gillian lying on the stretcher that was being wheeled into the emergency room. Somehow they'd beaten the ambulance to the hospital.

Without hesitation, Trigger headed for the woman who held his heart in her hand.

"Step back, sir." He heard someone say, but he didn't. He couldn't.

"Gillian?" he called when he got close.

Her head turned—and the second he caught sight of her, Trigger wanted to fucking kill someone. She had the beginnings of a black eye and her cheekbone was bruised.

But it was the clear finger marks on her neck that had him seeing red.

"Walker?" she croaked and held out a hand to him.

Both the paramedics' heads swung toward him at the same time security closed in on the group. Trigger knew his team had been at his back the entire time, and they probably made quite an imposing sight to the employees in reception.

But before he could be hauled away from Gillian, one of the paramedics held out his hand. "He's fine," the man barked, stopping the security officers in their tracks. "She hasn't said much since she came to in the ambulance. But she recognizes him. Let him through."

Grateful for the reprieve, Trigger didn't hesitate, he went right up to Gillian's side and gripped her hand in his. He tried to assess her, but when she whimpered, he couldn't look anywhere but into her eyes. "I'm here, Di," he told her softly. "You're okay. I'm here."

"Walker," she said again.

"Move with us," the paramedic ordered, and without looking away from Gillian's dilated pupils, Trigger nodded.

"You're okay," he repeated as he walked alongside the gurney with Gillian's hand in his. They didn't get a chance to say anything else as the paramedics wheeled her into a room and got to work transferring her from their gurney to the bed. The grip Gillian had on his hand was almost painful, but there was no way Trigger was going to complain.

She looked okay, beyond the bruises on her face and throat. He turned to listen to a paramedic as he briefed the doctor who appeared inside the room.

"Patient's name is Gillian Romano, age unknown, as she didn't tell us anything other than her name. She was found unconscious in a parking lot on the south end of town. Other than the superficial bruising, we haven't found any other obvious injuries. No broken bones and no pain anywhere that we can tell. Her heart rate and blood pressure are high, but that's most likely because she didn't seem to know where she was or what was happening when she regained consciousness. We started an IV, but we suspect she's high or has ingested some sort of drug within the last few hours because of her dilated pupils."

Trigger listened with a bizarre mixture of horror and relief.

The doctor nodded. "Nurse, please do a complete blood panel and we'll see if we can get her to tell us what she's taken. I'd also like a rape kit done, just in case. She might need an MRI to make sure she didn't hit her head at any point. Gillian, can you look at me? What happened?"

Instead of looking at the doctor, Gillian kept her eyes glued to Trigger's. He hated, *hated*, the look of terror in her eyes. "It's okay, sweetheart. You're safe now. Can you tell us what happened?"

She shook her head.

"You're safe," he reiterated.

"I don't remember," she whispered. "I'd tell you if I

could, but I don't remember anything. All I know is that I woke up in an ambulance and my head hurt."

Trigger's stomach rolled. "What's the last thing you remember?"

Gillian swallowed hard and closed her eyes. After a moment, she opened them and said, "Talking to you on the phone in my car."

"You were going to the caterer to taste cakes for the Howards' anniversary party," he prompted.

She blinked. "I don't remember anything about that. Did I make it there?"

"Yes. You parked in the garage nearby and met with the Howards' daughter. You guys picked out two different cakes." Trigger knew all this because he'd talked to the caterer himself to verify that Gillian had actually made it there.

"I can't remember," she whimpered.

Trigger touched the backs of his fingers lightly to her face. "Does this hurt?"

She shook her head, but winced when she pressed against his fingers. "My throat hurts though, and I feel as if I'm hungover."

"If you'd please step back, we need to examine her," the nurse said impatiently.

Trigger reluctantly let go of Gillian's hand and stepped to the side.

The second he let go of her hand, Gillian started to shake. Trigger wanted to go right back to her, but he forced himself to stay where he was. He knew he was lucky to be allowed to remain in the room, and he didn't want to do anything to force the doctor to kick him out.

He watched as Gillian's clothes were removed and placed into a bag for the police to collect later.

"Damp," the nurse said as she cut Gillian's shirt off. "Smells like alcohol too. Were you drinking earlier?" she asked.

Gillian shook her head, but kept her eyes closed as her body was manipulated by the medical personnel.

"She's got ligature marks around her wrists and ankles," the nurse added. "Looks like they're bruising, but the skin's not broken."

"We'll need pictures for the detective assigned to her case," the doctor said.

They were talking as if Gillian wasn't there. As if she couldn't hear every word they said. It infuriated Trigger, but he kept quiet.

That was, he was silent until it came time for the nurse to do the rape kit, and she tried to kick him out of the room. "You'll need to step outside, sir," she told him firmly.

Doing his best not to lose his shit, Trigger stepped up to the bed and took hold of Gillian's hand once more. "Do you want me to leave, Gilly?" he asked quietly.

Her eyes popped open and she shook her head frantically. "No! Don't go! Please!"

"I'm staying," Trigger told the nurse firmly.

She pressed her lips together but didn't force the issue.

"I was raped?" Gillian asked fearfully as she looked up into Trigger's eyes.

He eased himself into a chair near her head and put his hand on the uninjured side of her face. "It's just a precaution."

"But was I?" she asked. "I can't remember anything. I

don't hurt...down there. Did someone touch me when I was unconscious? I don't think I would've gotten drunk in the middle of the day...but I guess I did?"

"*Shhh*, sweetheart. Don't get yourself all worked up."

"I can't remember!" she repeated in a tone full of agony.

"They took blood. They'll find out what you were given. Until then, you can't panic, Di."

Gillian squeezed her eyes shut and did her best to control her breathing as the nurse put her legs in stirrups and began the rape test.

"I'm not Wonder Woman," Gillian whispered. "I'm scared to death. My head and neck hurt, and apparently I was tied up. How come I can't remember any of it? That makes no sense!"

"You being scared doesn't make you any less amazing or kick-ass, Gillian. And not remembering makes sense if you were given something to help you forget," Trigger soothed.

"But why?"

"Why what?"

"Why didn't they kill me?"

Trigger had been wondering the same thing, but he didn't let on. "Maybe because whoever took you realized how amazing you are, and killing you would put a black mark on his soul he'd never recover from."

For the first time since he'd caught her eye as she was being wheeled in, Trigger saw something in her expression other than absolute abject terror. "Yeah, I'm sure that was it. Must've been my wicked sense of humor."

Trigger was overwhelmed with gratitude that his woman had managed to break free of the tight hold fear had on her.

"We're going to figure this out," he told her, looking intently into her eyes as he said it, so she'd believe him. "Brain and the rest of the team is on this. I want you to come and stay with me until whoever did this is caught."

"And if they can't catch him? It's not as if I can give any information about what happened," she said.

"Then you'll just have to stay with me forever." Nothing felt as right as the thought of going to sleep every night with Gillian by his side and waking up to the same.

"If you're feeling responsible for whatever happened to me, and that's why you're asking, then my answer is no," she told him.

Trigger opened his mouth to protest, but she went on before he could.

"But if you're asking because you truly want me there, if you might think you could someday love me as much as I love you, then my answer is yes."

They were in the middle of an emergency room. A nurse had just put Gillian's legs down after doing a rape test, and Trigger was overwhelmed with her bravery.

"I love you. When I realized you were missing, it felt as if my heart had been ripped out of my chest. It only started beating again when we got word that you'd been found and were alive. I want you to live with me so I can see your smiling face every day. So I can feed you coffee and doughnuts every morning and hear your sigh of contentment. I want to laugh with you and argue as well... simply so we can make up afterward. And yes, I want to keep you safe, but eventually this hard time will pass, and I'll still want to wake up to your gorgeous face every morning."

"Damn, that was beautiful," the nurse mumbled as she busied herself off to the side, preparing slides for the labs.

Gillian huffed out a laugh. "I'm not quitting my job. I've still got events to organize and finalize."

Trigger frowned, but nodded.

"How about this—I finish with the events I've got planned right now, then I switch my focus to the Killeen area. That doesn't mean I'm going to stop working in Austin, because I have a lot of contacts here already and repeat clients, but I'll do my best to stay closer to home."

"I'd move if I could," Trigger told her honestly.

"I know. But what you do is important, and you have to be as close to the base as possible."

She hadn't said anything that wasn't true, but it still smarted. He nodded.

The doctor came back into the room. "How do you feel, Ms. Romano?"

Gillian shrugged. "I'm okay."

"On a scale of one to ten, where ten is the most pain you've ever felt in your entire life and one is no pain whatsoever, where would you put yourself right now?"

"Three?" Gillian said with a shrug. "My head and throat hurt, but that's about it."

The doctor nodded approvingly. "You'll need to talk to the detective when he arrives, but I don't think there's any need to keep you overnight. Your pupils are still a bit dilated, but other than not remembering what happened, you don't seem confused or disoriented."

"I'm not," Gillian told him.

"Do you have someone who can stay with you?"

"Yes, she does," Trigger said immediately. "She's going to be staying with me. I'm in the Army and have enough medical knowledge to watch over her. I can bring her to the hospital if her condition or pain level changes."

The doctor nodded again. "Good. I hope they find whoever did this to you."

"Me too," Gillian said.

Then the doctor smiled distractedly and spun on his heels and left the room, his attention already on his next patient.

Trigger knew they needed to wait for the police detective to get there, but he wanted nothing more than to wrap Gillian up and take her home. He was well aware that he'd almost lost her. He had no idea what happened, but he had a gut feeling it had to do with the hijacking. Someone wanted information, and they'd decided to snatch one of the people who might have it. He made a mental note to call the FBI agent and make sure the other passengers were on high alert.

Gillian had been kidnapped, probably questioned, then given something to make sure she didn't remember anything before being dropped off at a random location, largely unhurt and unmolested. It was more than odd, and it didn't make sense...which made it all the more worrisome.

The rest of the afternoon and early evening was spent talking with Gillian's friends and making sure they knew she was all right and where she'd be living for the foreseeable future. The detective also arrived, and it was painful and frustrating—on all their parts—to have to listen to Gillian say over and over again that she didn't remember anything about her abduction.

The detective left with no more information than they'd had before. He'd also confirmed Trigger's suspicion that if they didn't get any DNA from her clothes, and if she hadn't been assaulted, there wouldn't be much the police could do to find the perpetrators unless Gillian remembered something.

Trigger knew she was frustrated and exhausted, and when the doctor finally signed her discharge papers, he couldn't get her out of there fast enough. She was wearing a pair of scrubs a nurse had scrounged up and she fell asleep almost the second he started driving north.

His teammates had been there with him the entire time. Bringing them food for dinner and doing their best to keep Gillian's spirits up.

Lefty and Brain were with Trigger. The others had left with Doc, back to the parking garage to retrieve Gillian's car, which they'd drop off at Trigger's apartment complex.

"I've been researching," Brain said after they'd been driving for fifteen minutes and they were all sure Gillian was asleep. "The doctor suspects Rohypnol, and I agree. In some cases, people are able to remember bits and pieces of the time right before they were dosed."

Trigger grunted. It would be helpful if Gillian remembered something, but it wouldn't change what had happened to her.

"Who do you think is behind this?" Lefty asked.

"Honestly?" Trigger asked.

"Of course," Lefty said.

"Sinaloa," Trigger replied with no doubt in his voice.

"Yeah, that's what I was thinking too," Lefty confirmed. "Roofies are easy to get in Mexico. They're legal down there, so it wouldn't be hard to put some into a drink and force her to ingest it."

"But kidnapping her doesn't make a lot of sense," Brain

added. "Why now? I mean, they've had months to make their move and take her out if they wanted. And why release her without any real harm?"

"I'm guessing they heard about her visit with the FBI. Maybe they wanted to know what she told them. If she knows who the seventh hijacker was," Lefty mused.

"And when they found out she had no clue, they decided it wasn't worth the risk to kill her," Brain concluded.

Trigger's jaw ticked in frustration. Everything his team-mates were saying made sense, but he hated that it was *Gillian* they were talking about so unemotionally. This was what they did with every mission. They talked it through... but it felt wrong this time.

"Guys?" he asked.

"Yeah?"

"What's up?"

"Can we please drop it for now? The last thing Gillian needs is to subconsciously hear us talking about her," Trigger said tightly.

"You're right, sorry," Brain apologized.

"Yeah, sorry, we should've waited," Lefty added.

Trigger took a deep breath and tried to relax, which was impossible.

"So...you're moving her in, huh?" Lefty asked, and Trigger could hear the smirk in his voice even if he couldn't see him from the driver's seat.

"Yup."

"She realize that she's never going back to her apartment in Georgetown?"

Trigger smiled for the first time in hours. "Don't know. Don't care."

His friends chuckled.

"You need help moving her stuff from her place to yours?"

"Would appreciate that," Trigger said gratefully.

"She gonna lose her mind when we show up with her shit?" Brain asked.

"Don't know," Trigger said again. "But in the long run, she'll be okay with it. I love her, she loves me back. She was meant to be mine. There's no way she's living anywhere other than by my side until I know for sure she's safe from whatever is threatening her. And afterward, I'm hoping she'll be so comfortable, she won't even think about leaving."

"Your place is pretty small," Brain observed. "I bet you could find something bigger. Maybe a three- or four-bedroom condo or something."

"It's on my radar," Trigger admitted. Just last week, he'd perused the internet looking for places to rent around the base that were bigger than his apartment. "But for now, my place will do. It's small but safe. And I'd rather not worry about being distracted with moving until the threat to her is over and done."

"Agreed. Happy for you, Trigger," Lucky said.

"Thanks."

"I'd complain about things not being the same, now that you've found a woman, but after seeing Ghost and his team fall—and fall *hard*—and how their relationships have all weathered the changes, I don't mind so much," Brain said.

Trigger agreed. The other Delta team had proven that, with the right women, having a family and a life as a Delta soldier could go hand in hand. He hadn't been looking for love, but it had fallen into his lap, and he'd be damned if he'd give up Gillian because of fear of making a relationship work.

His and Gillian's souls were linked and nothing was going to take her from him. Nothing and nobody. He'd do everything in his power to make sure of it.

CHAPTER EIGHTEEN

A week later, Gillian was feeling much more like herself. The first few days had been rough. She'd been sore and she felt extremely vulnerable. She hated not being able to remember what had happened to her. She'd finally been able to recall being at the caterer and tasting the different kinds of cake, but everything after she'd left the building until she'd woken up in the hospital was still a blank.

It felt good to be able to hole up in Walker's apartment and hide from the world. She knew without a doubt that he'd keep her safe. She hadn't even been upset when his team had shown up with a whole hell of a lot of her stuff from her apartment. Things were cramped in Walker's place now, with her stuff comingled with his, but he'd never complained.

For the first two nights, he'd held her all night long, reassuring her when she woke up with nightmares. But after that, she'd gotten tired of him treating her like a fragile piece of glass. She wanted to be Diana Prince for him again. Be the tough woman he'd nicknamed her after.

So the third night, she'd made her move before they'd climbed into bed. He wanted to continue to coddle her, but she knew she'd get her way when she got down on her knees in front of him, and he didn't protest. Her face had still been sore, but that didn't mean she couldn't show him without words how much she loved him.

He hadn't let her linger too long, much to her disappointment, but he'd more than made up for it when he picked her up, placed her on her back on his bed, and proceeded to give her two of the most intense orgasms she'd ever had. Then he'd made love to her...there was no other word for it. He was tender and gentle, and he looked her in the eyes the entire time he moved inside her.

Her third orgasm had been less intense than the previous two, but just as earthshattering. When he'd finally let himself go, she couldn't take her eyes away from the pulse pounding in his neck as he'd thrown his head back and groaned through his orgasm.

She'd thought their lovemaking would be a turning point, that things would go back to normal and he'd loosen up a bit on his protectiveness. But she'd been wrong.

Now Gillian was torn. While she loved the fact he was so concerned, he refused to let her go anywhere by herself. She quickly felt as if she was losing her independence.

Ann, Wendy, and Clarissa had visited once, and Walker had only left when her friends had promised not to leave her alone. Of course, her friends had thought it was romantic and sweet, but Gillian was starting to get frustrated.

Yes, she'd been kidnapped and roofied.

Yes, she was still freaked about the whole thing.

But that didn't mean she'd suddenly turned into a five-year-old who had to be supervised at all times.

As the first week rolled into the next, Gillian became more and more irritated. Walker was being *too* protective. It was stifling, and even though she knew he loved her and *why* he was loath to have her out of his sight, it had to stop.

His latest decree was the last straw. He'd overheard her talking to the Howards' daughter and reassuring her that the party would go on as planned the upcoming weekend. As soon as she hung up, he'd started in.

"I don't think it's a good idea for you to go to Austin this weekend."

Gillian did her best to control her temper before she turned to face him. "Walker, I have to. This is my livelihood. I've spent nearly three months working on this party. I'm not missing it."

"You've done all the leg work, it'll happen just fine if you're there or if you aren't," he said in a maddeningly calm tone.

"You have no clue," she said a little harsher than she'd intended. "You were there at the zoo. You saw what I do. There are a million little details that need to be dealt with. Things go wrong and someone has to be there to redirect everyone."

"You can hire someone to do that. You should probably hire an assistant anyway," Walker said reasonably.

"Are you serious right now?" she asked, putting her hands on her hips.

"Yeah. I am. *You* can't seriously be thinking about going back to Austin already? Your face is still bruised and you were kidnapped a little over a week ago. Why would you think it's a good idea to go back there?"

Gillian had been holding back her frustration for a few days—and she couldn't do it anymore. "I love you, Walker. I do. But I can't be the kind of woman who's happy sitting at home waiting for her man to come back from deployment. I need to work. I love what I do. I thought you understood that?"

"I do," he said immediately, stepping toward her.

Gillian wasn't ready to be placated, so she backed up so he couldn't touch her. They both knew that was her weakness. That when he put his hands on her, she melted like a piece of chocolate on a hot day.

Walker straightened and his lips pressed together before he spoke again. "Fine. We haven't talked about this, so now's as good a time as any. When I realized you were missing, it was the worst day of my life. Worse than any mission I'd been on. My world stopped. I didn't know what to do or where to even start looking for you. Even worse was the fact that you'd already been missing for a couple hours. I know better than anyone how easy it is to kill someone. You might've already been dead before I knew you were missing. I wasn't there for you when I'd promised you'd be safe, and it almost destroyed me."

Gillian's defenses began to crumble at the evidence of his heartbreak. "Walker," she whispered.

He shook his head and spoke before she could continue.

"We'd done everything we could and it wasn't enough. The Feds had no idea where you might be, the surveillance cameras hadn't caught anything. Your phone, purse, and car were still there in the parking garage. We literally had no clues. *Nothing.* You could've been in Mexico already for all we knew. Then, by some miracle, we got the call that you'd been found alive. My heart started beating again at that moment, and I swore that I'd *never* let you down again."

"You didn't let me down," Gillian insisted. "There was nothing you could've done. Walker, I could get hurt or die walking down the street outside your apartment. Or driving to the grocery store. Or I could have a heart attack."

"Can you please stop talking about you dying?" he begged. "I can't take it. Not with you standing there with the bruises still on your face and you not letting me touch you."

"Okay, Walker."

"I'm not sure you realize how much of a miracle it is that you're standing in front of me right now. Every day, hundreds of people go missing, never to be seen again. And from everything Agent Tucker has found out, and what me and the team suspect as well, you were taken by the Sinaloa. The most ruthless and dangerous drug cartel the world has ever known. They hijacked a plane, for God's sake, in order to get back at a rival drug gang.

"Not only were you left alive, but they didn't sexually abuse you, they didn't break any bones, they didn't send body parts to me in the mail, threatening to do more if I didn't do what they wanted. You should *not* be standing in front of me right now. It makes no sense. None.

"I know I've been overbearing and an ass for the last week, but it's because I love you so damn much, and the thought of someone deciding they made a mistake and you shouldn't have been set free, and recapturing you, makes me absolutely crazy. I can't go through that again. I can't! It's unfair for you, and it makes me look like a domineering boyfriend when I can't leave your side for two minutes without making sure someone is watching over you, but I literally *can't* do anything else.

"I'll get better, I promise. But all I want is for you to be safe. I want to marry you. Have a family. Grow old with you. I know you're independent. I love that you have your own life, that you don't need me to be happy. If you ever decided you didn't love me anymore and you left me, it would suck, but ultimately, I'd be okay...because I'd know you were alive and well. But if you were killed, I wouldn't be able to survive.

"You were meant to be mine, Gillian. I need you like I need air to breathe. You've changed my life in such a short time it's almost unbelievable. I used to live for the Army. For my teammates. But now I live for *you*. Now that I've had a taste of what my life can be with you, I can't go back. Please tell me you understand."

Gillian's eyes were filled with tears. She'd known Walker was on edge and worried about her, but she hadn't realized to what extent. She took a step toward him, and before she realized that he'd moved, she was in his arms.

"I love you, Walker. I understand, I do. I'm not saying I want to jaunt off to Austin by myself. I don't think I'll be able to go there by myself ever again. I assumed you'd be *with* me." She looked up at him. "I swear I'll be careful. I won't complain if you dog my every step during the party. I just...I've worked hard to build up my business. If I flake out on this event, it'll hurt. Clients will lose confidence in me. It doesn't matter that I was possibly kidnapped by a drug cartel; people are selfish. They want what they want.

They might be sympathetic toward me and what happened, but they still want their party."

"I'll want the rest of the team to be there as well," Walker said after a moment.

Gillian nodded. "I have no problem with that."

"And you aren't to go *anywhere* without one of us with you."

"Even to the bathroom?" she teased.

Walker didn't crack a smile. "One of us will scope it out before you go in, and no one else will be allowed in while you're in there."

Gillian took a breath. She wanted to protest. Tell Walker that he was being paranoid. But then she remembered how scared she'd been when she'd woken up and realized she had no idea what she was doing in an ambulance, and why she was hurting so bad. "Okay," she told her boyfriend solemnly.

Walker put his hand on the back of her head and brought it to his shoulder. "Okay," he whispered.

They stood like that in his kitchen for quite a while, Gillian staring out the window that led to his balcony, watching the birds flying from tree to tree outside.

Falcon.

She abruptly pulled back and looked up at Walker. "Falcon!" she said urgently.

"What?"

"Falcon. I don't know what it means, but it has to do with my kidnapping."

He raised an eyebrow, but his expression hardened. "You sure?"

Gillian nodded. "Yeah. I don't know why, but...yes."

Walker ran a hand over her hair, then brushed the

backs of his fingers over her healing cheekbone. "I'm proud of you, Di. You are every inch a Wonder Woman."

"But it makes no sense."

Walker shook his head. "Doesn't matter. I'll call Agent Tucker and let him know. He can research and see if he can figure out what it means."

Gillian closed her eyes and willed her brain to recall something else.

Falcon, falcon, falcon. She repeated the word over and over in her head.

Then another word popped into her brain.

"Salazar!" she blurted.

This time, he looked shocked.

"What?" Gillian asked. "Who is that?"

"Alfredo Salazar is the head of the Sinaloa Cartel here in Texas. Calum Branch, the DEA agent you talked to, claims he's headquartered right in Austin. I don't know why you're remembering that name, but if he was the one who took you, or had you taken, then it's even *more* of a fucking miracle you're standing here in my arms right now."

"Why?" Gillian asked, not sure she wanted to hear the answer.

"He's ruthless. He started as a part of the gang when he was still in elementary school. Killed his first man around age ten. Everyone knows that if they cross him, they're dead. It's said he has no mercy. That he killed his own *sister* when he thought she'd betrayed the cartel."

Gillian's eyes widened with every word from Walker.

"I need to call Tucker," he said.

Gillian nodded. "I know."

"Maybe I'll see if Ghost and his crew can come to Austin with us as well," he muttered.

As scared as Gillian was, she thought that was a bit overkill. Having fourteen men following her around during an anniversary party would be a bit much. But she'd fight that battle later. Maybe when they were both replete after a few orgasms.

"Walker?"

"Yeah, sweetheart?" he asked distractedly.

"I trust you."

That got his attention. He raised an eyebrow.

"If something else ever happens to me, I trust you to get there in time. You've changed my life too. I always felt as if something was missing, even though I have great parents, amazing friends, and a job I love. Now I know it was you. *You* were missing."

He leaned down and kissed her gently.

"We're going to get through this," she told him. "Neither of us is used to living with someone else. Throw in close quarters, me being hurt, and you dealing with the fact that you couldn't help me...we're bound to fight. Thank you for not shutting me out or storming off. It's not easy to talk about what's bothering us, but I appreciate you doing just that."

"I've been a bachelor for a very long time, but nothing feels as right as waking up with you in my arms, Gilly. I can't promise to always be happy and in a good mood, but I do promise to never take what's bothering me out on you. I'll do my best to talk things through before we go to bed. I never want to go to bed mad."

"Me either. And, Walker?"

"Right here, sweetheart," he said with a smile.

"I haven't missed that your friends moved practically my entire apartment here this week."

He smiled. "Wasn't keeping it a secret."

"So now that I'm better, I'm assuming you don't want me to go back to Georgetown?"

"Absolutely not," he said immediately. "And not just because I'm worried about your safety. I like you hogging the covers at night. I like watching you brush your teeth in my bathroom...*our* bathroom. My sheets and towels smell like honeysuckle, and I freaking *love* it. I like bringing you coffee while you get ready in the morning, and I love looking up from whatever I'm doing and seeing you. I love *you*, Gillian."

She practically melted in his arms. "I love you too, Walker."

"You're okay with moving in...permanently?"

"Do I have a choice?" she asked cheekily.

"You always have a choice," he said without cracking even the smallest smile. "I'd never force you to do anything you don't want to do."

"I want to live with you," she told him.

"Good. Eventually, we'll get a bigger place. We're stuffed in here like sardines. I don't mind it, but after a while it might get to be a bit much. Now, as much as I hate to let you go, I really do need to call Tucker. You remembering even those two small words is a good thing. It might not mean anything to us right now, but the fact that you're strong enough to break through the chemicals that fucked with your memories just reinforces my thought that you *are* fucking Diana Prince."

And with that, Walker kissed her on the forehead and turned to grab his phone.

Gillian gave him some space, heading into their bedroom. She didn't need to hear his conversation. She had no idea what falcon and Salazar meant, and she could admit that she kinda didn't *want* to know. She had a few more last-minute details to work out for the Howard party, and she needed to talk to their daughter and reassure her that she'd be there on Saturday night.

* * *

"It's not much," Gary Tucker told Trigger.

"I know, but I wanted to let you know as soon as possible that Gillian had remembered something."

"Hmmm. All right, I agree with you about the name Salazar. Although it's probably unlikely that she actually saw him in person. He's elusive and doesn't get involved with extortion and kidnappings."

"I might not be an expert on drug kingpins," Trigger said, "but I'm guessing he's more involved than everyone thinks. I mean, I know there's a hierarchy in organizations like that, but wouldn't he be aware of everything that's happening? Who's targeted and why?"

"Holy shit," Agent Tucker said suddenly.

"What?" Trigger asked in alarm.

"Hang on...I'm calling Calum. As DEA, he knows a lot more about the Sinaloa than I do."

Trigger waited impatiently as the FBI agent patched in the other man.

"You here, Branch?" Tucker asked after a minute or so.

"Yeah," the other man answered.

"Trigger?" Tucker asked.

"Also here," he confirmed.

"Right, so, Calum, Trigger called to tell me Gillian remembered two things from her kidnapping."

"That's great," the DEA agent said.

Trigger was glad to hear the sincerity in his voice.

"The first was the name Salazar."

Calum whistled long and low.

"Yeah. Trigger and I were having a conversation about him when something occurred to me."

"What's that?" Calum asked.

"We were talking about how unlikely it was that Salazar himself had any direct contact with Ms. Romano. I told Trigger that he probably left the kidnappings and assassinations to the lower members of his organization."

"That's probably true. Drug lords usually don't bother themselves with that sort of thing. They've got highly trained and trusted members of their organizations who do the dirty work."

"Exactly. Which brings us to the other thing Gillian remembered."

"Well? What was it?" Calum asked, when Gary hesitated.

"She remembered the word 'falcon.'"

"Wow. Okay, that makes sense. I just wish we knew what the context was," Calum said after a moment.

"Would one of you please fill me in?" Trigger asked impatiently. He had no clue what falcon could possibly mean, but obviously it had some relevance, based on what the two men were saying.

"So, in cartels like the Sinaloa, there are different levels of players," Calum explained. "At the top are people like Salazar, the drug lords. They're the ones ultimately in charge. The head of the snake, if you will. Under them are lieutenants. The people at that level are in direct contact with the drug lord and are highly trusted and valuable, as they supervise a lot of the lower-level people in the organization. Next come the hitmen; I think their job is self-explanatory. But under *them* are the members known as falcons. It's the lowest position in the gang, and most of them work hard to gain the trust and favor of the hitmen and lieutenants with the goal of moving up the ladder someday."

"So, what does Gillian remembering the word falcon mean in this context?" Trigger asked.

"Normally, I'd say we're not sure. It could be that whoever had her kidnapped referred to a falcon in one way or another. Or it could mean that she saw a bird flying overhead after she was dumped and her brain simply conjured up the word 'falcon.'"

"Then why was Tucker all fired up to bring you in on this call?" Walker asked.

"Because remembering the word falcon all by itself means nothing. But remembering it in conjunction with the name *Salazar* means she was definitely in the hands of the Sinaloa Cartel. There was a reason she was taken, but there was probably a bigger reason she was let go relatively unharmed...which I don't have to tell you is very, *very* rare. I can count on one hand the number of people who've escaped the Sinaloa Cartel's clutches after being kidnapped," Calum said.

"Of the people you know who have escaped...how many have been retaken by the cartel?" Trigger asked.

"None," Calum told him without hesitation. "There's only been one situation where we know for sure what happened. We had a UC—sorry, an undercover—imbedded with the cartel, and he reported that the hitmen had kidnapped someone who they'd thought was snitching. Turns out they grabbed the wrong man. They had the same name, but the poor schmuck who ended up in front of Salazar was a guy who happened to be in the wrong place at the wrong time. He was let go after a severe beating and a warning not to say a word about what had happened to him. The guy ended up moving to Canada with his family, and he still lives there to this day."

Trigger let out a long breath. "So what are your thoughts on all this in reference to Gillian?" he asked. "And give it to me straight. Why was she taken, what are the odds she's still in danger, and do we have to look over our shoulders for the rest of our lives? Do I need to request a PCS move to Alaska?"

"Honestly, I'm not sure what to think," Calum said, and Trigger tensed once more. "I mean, the fact that she was let go unharmed is a good thing."

Trigger wanted to argue the "unharmed" thing, but let it go.

"But nothing about this is normal. The hijacking was an extreme and bold move, and the fact that we still don't know who the seventh hijacker was means there are a lot of loose ends. Ms. Romano had a very active role in that whole thing, she was picked out of all the passengers to be the spokesperson between the hijackers and the negotiators. She was also right there when the hijackers were killed as well. So it could be the Sinaloa was just trying to find out what she knows about who the other hijacker might be."

"We're headed into Austin this weekend for an event she's planning," Trigger told the men.

"Do you think that's a good idea?" Tucker asked.

"No," Trigger said emphatically. "But I can't keep her locked up forever. If she's brave enough to get back on the horse after she was bucked off, then I'll be right there by her side. Me and my friends."

Trigger knew the two men understood what he was saying when they both murmured their approval. They knew he was Delta Force, and that he'd be on security duty.

"Let us know if you notice anything that looks off," the FBI agent said.

"I will," Trigger reassured them.

"Thanks for letting us know what Gillian remembered," Calum added. "I know it doesn't seem like much in the scheme of things, but the fact she remembered anything at all is pretty damn amazing."

"That's what I told her," Trigger agreed. "I'll stay in touch."

The three men hung up, and Trigger stood in his living room, staring outside for a long moment. In some ways, the phone call made him feel better about Gillian's safety, but he was also still uneasy. He figured he'd be nervous about her for a long time coming.

When she'd been missing, and he'd realized they had absolutely no clues as to where she might be, he'd almost lost his mind. It wasn't often he felt helpless, and he hated the feeling.

He wanted to keep her locked in his apartment safe and sound forever, but knew that wasn't feasible. Besides, with his luck, someone in a nearby apartment would start a grease fire and the damn building would burn down. He'd learned throughout his career that sometimes the safest place was actually the most dangerous.

He had to let Gillian fly, but that didn't mean he couldn't be there to catch her if she fell.

He looked down at his phone and clicked a button to call Lefty. He needed to let his team know they'd be going to Austin for a party on Saturday.

CHAPTER NINETEEN

Gillian looked around the large ballroom at The Driskill with satisfaction. Everything looked absolutely beautiful and the event was running incredibly smoothly so far. She'd arrived at the hotel earlier that afternoon to make sure everything was set up to her specifications. She'd put on the only dress Walker's teammates had brought over from her apartment; luckily it was dressy and appropriate for the event. She'd bought the light green dress one day while shopping with Ann. Her friend had said it made the color of her eyes pop, and in a moment of weakness, Gillian had bought it.

When she'd come out of the bedroom with it on, she'd thought for a second Walker was going to bend her over the sofa and take her right then and there. She wouldn't have been opposed, although it would've meant she'd have been late getting to the hotel.

Instead, he'd restrained himself, whispering in her ear that when they got home later that night, he was going to

SUSAN STOKER

fuck her so hard she'd feel him inside her for at least a week.

Gillian's knees had gone weak, but she'd merely replied that she couldn't wait.

Walker had followed her around the hotel as she'd met with the various members of the staff to make sure everything was ready for the party. He hadn't been intrusive, standing off to the side, but he refused to let her out of his sight. She'd had several people ask about him and his friends, and she'd explained them away as being security. He and his teammates looked like models in their dark suits. None of them wore a tie, but their white shirts under black suits made them look like they were straight off the set of *Men in Black* or something. She'd gotten a few weird looks at her "security" explanation, but no one had questioned her further.

Lefty and Brain had studied the guest list she'd received from the Howards' daughter and hadn't found any names that had caused alarm. Two hours ago, the couple of the night had arrived for what they'd thought was an intimate dinner for two arranged by their daughter, and had been pleasantly surprised at the huge party being thrown in their honor.

The cakes had been well received and devoured within an hour. The drinks were flowing from the open bar and the DJ was playing music that everyone, no matter their age, could appreciate and dance to.

Overall, the evening had been a success, and Gillian was relieved it was finally winding down.

"Ms. Romano?" a staff member of The Driskill said from behind her.

Gillian turned. "Yes?"

"*Erhm*...there's been a problem with the credit card used to pay for the Howards' room for the night."

"Oh, I'm sure it's just a misunderstanding. I'll come with you and take care of it and make everything right with my client later. Walker," Gillian said, turning to him. "I'll be right back. I'm just going to go to the front desk real quick."

"I'm coming too," Walker said.

Gillian wanted to roll her eyes and insist she could probably make it to the front desk and back without him watching over her, but since she truly didn't mind, she simply nodded.

She followed the employee through the throng of people in the ballroom and out into a hallway. The hotel was older, and the hallways were narrow. Because there were so many people, and it was a Saturday night, it felt as if they had to fight their way to the front desk.

The front desk staff was slammed with all the people checking in and needing this or that, so she handed her card over to the employee and stood off to the side, waiting for her to return. Walker was standing across the room, against the wall. She caught his eye and smiled, loving how his face gentled as he smiled back at her.

A ruckus at the other end of the lobby made him turn his head, and Gillian looked in that direction. A man and a woman were yelling at each other, and the man reached out and shoved the woman's shoulder. Gillian watched as Walker pushed off the wall and headed for the couple.

Of course he would. There was no way he'd stand by and watch as someone assaulted a woman.

"Gillian!"

Hearing her name, Gillian turned her head—and gaped at who was standing there.

It was Andrea. And she looked absolutely horrible.

She had makeup on, but it couldn't hide the deep bruises on her face. One arm was in a sling, and she had a huge bandage on that hand as well.

"Holy shit, Andrea, are you all right?" Gillian asked, rushing over to the woman she hadn't seen since they'd been rescued in Venezuela.

Andrea grimaced and nodded. Then winced at the movement.

"What happened?"

"I had to come warn you. I didn't know where you lived but remembered you talking about this party when we were texting. The cartel kidnapped me and wanted to know all about the hijacking. They said they were going to come after you too."

"They already did," Gillian admitted.

Andrea's eyes widened. "They did?"

"Yeah."

Andrea seemed to sway on her feet. "Oh, shit, I don't feel so good," she moaned.

"Come on, let's find you somewhere to sit," Gillian said, putting her arm around the other woman's waist.

"I shouldn't have come. I found a place to park in the first row of the lot. Can you believe that? Just help me out there, and I'll get out of your hair."

"Should you be driving?" Gillian asked in concern as Andrea turned them toward one of the many hallways off of the lobby.

"Probably not, but I had to come see you. I didn't want

to say anything over the phone in case they were listening."

Gillian looked back into the lobby for Walker. She wanted to make sure he saw where she was going, but he was busy trying to control the inebriated man at the other end of the large room. The woman wasn't helping the situation, as she kept trying to hit her husband or boyfriend or whoever he was.

Thinking she'd just be gone for a minute or two, and Walker wouldn't even know she was missing, Gillian helped Andrea limp down the hallway toward the exit. They went outside, and Andrea pointed at the far end of a line of cars. "It's in the first row, down at the end," she said.

"I'm so sorry this happened to you," Gillian said.

"Me too," Andrea agreed.

When they got to her car, Gillian kept her arm around Andrea's waist as she led them to the door. "Give me your purse, I'll open the door for you."

"Thanks."

Gillian let go and dug into the small purse for the keys.

She'd just clicked the door locks when she felt something push into her side.

"Get in," Andrea said in a tone Gillian hadn't ever heard from her before.

She looked down in confusion—and was shocked to see a gun in Andrea's hand. She'd shoved it against her side and was pressing it into her flesh aggressively.

It took a second for Gillian to comprehend what was happening. "What?" she asked in disbelief.

"Get in the car," Andrea repeated. "Do it. Or I'll fucking blow a hole in your side."

"Why are you doing this? Did they put you up to it?"

"They? The cartel? Fuck them! I did *everything* they wanted. And for what? Nothing, that's what! I urged Luis to volunteer for the job in Costa Rica. Salazar told us it would be a piece of cake. Sinaloa supporters would deliver weapons to the plane and it would be easy to take it over. And it was. That asshole Lamas was killed, just as we planned...but then *you* fucked everything up!"

Gillian was still trying to wrap her mind around what she was hearing. "Luis? The hijacker? You *knew* him?"

"He was my husband!" Andrea spat.

"But...you have different last names."

"Which doesn't mean a damn thing. It wasn't hard to get false documents. Let me introduce myself properly— my name is Andrea *Vilchez*, not Vilmer. Luis Vilchez was my husband. The love of my life. And you got him killed!"

Gillian's mind was spinning. "Me?"

"Yes, you bitch! We were home free, almost in the getaway plane. We would've taken off and flown under the radar back to Mexico, and we all would've been promoted from our flunky positions in the cartel. But no, *you* had to go and trip Alberto. I don't know why that asshole broke from the plan and decided to take you with us. Then you tripped and gave those assholes a chance to shoot my Luis! You ruined *everything*!"

"But—"

"Get in the car, Gillian, and I'll make your death as painless as possible. If you don't, I'll shoot you in the gut, which means you'll bleed out nice and slow. Then I'll go inside and start shooting the guests at your precious party. I'll save that asshole who killed Luis for last. Before I kill him, I'll make sure he knows that his death is *your* fault."

Gillian wasn't an idiot. There was no way Andrea would be able to kill Walker. Not with her being as beaten up as she was right now.

She *was* an idiot for leaving the hotel, even though she'd thought Andrea was a friend. But the very last thing Gillian was going to do was get in that car. If she did, she knew without a doubt she'd die a horrible, painful death, no matter what Andrea promised.

And suddenly, a phrase popped into her head.

Fucking bitches and their drama.

Gillian knew she'd heard that when she'd been kidnapped.

"You told Salazar that I knew more than I did, didn't you?" she asked.

Andrea smirked. "Of course I did. And he did just what I wanted—he approved your kidnapping." Her face contorted with rage. "But then you had to go and make him believe you didn't know shit!"

"I *didn't* know shit," Gillian insisted.

"He was supposed to fuck you up! Take off a few fingers. Torture you the way *I've* been tortured every day since my Luis was shot!" Andrea hissed.

"Is that what happened to you?" Gillian asked, looking down at Andrea's bandaged hand.

"He didn't like that I'd lied," Andrea said in a way-too-calm tone. "Told me he was making an example of me. Took three of my fingers and beat the shit out of me. Then he threw me into the basement of one of his trap houses. Hoped I would bleed to death, but if I didn't, he was sending another falcon—a fucking newbie at that—the next day to finish what he'd started. I was to be her first kill. But I got the fuck out of there. I've been in hiding for the last week, just waiting for tonight and the chance to get my revenge."

Gillian wanted to feel remorse that Andrea had been beaten so badly, but she couldn't. Not when she was there to kill her.

Then something else occurred to Gillian—and she felt like the most gullible person ever. "Luis didn't assault you on that plane," she said flatly.

Andrea smirked again. "Nope. I gladly sucked him off. And it was *awesome*."

Gillian felt sick. She shook her head. "I'm not going with you," she told Andrea.

"Yes, you are. Get in," Andrea demanded.

"No," Gillian said, taking a step back. She had no idea how many minutes had passed, but Walker had to have realized she wasn't standing by the front desk anymore. He'd find her. She just had to give him enough time.

Andrea lifted the gun and aimed it right between Gillian's eyes. "Get. In. The. Car."

Gillian was tired of being scared. Tired of looking down the barrel of a gun.

She had no idea what came over her—but she was done being a victim.

"I cried for you," Gillian said in a steely tone. "I felt horrible that you had been treated so badly on that plane... or what I *thought* was badly. I even talked to the other passengers about doing something to help you out. And the entire time you were probably laughing at us. You didn't care about those passengers who were killed. You were cheering on those monsters the whole time! I have more respect for Alfredo Salazar right now than I do for *you*."

Andrea didn't even flinch. "I don't give a shit about anyone but myself. I cared about Luis, but now he's gone. Because of *you*. One more chance. Get in the fucking car!"

Gillian stared into the eyes of a woman she'd thought she knew. A woman who'd witnessed the most traumatic experience of Gillian's life.

Andrea wasn't who she'd thought. She was a cold-blooded killer.

At the same time she heard a shout from her right, Gillian moved.

Instead of reaching for the gun aimed between her eyes, she swung her fist and hit Andrea's bandaged hand as hard as she could.

The gun in Andrea's hand went off, and Gillian felt an immediate rush of fire in her upper arm. She dropped to the ground even as something went flying over her head. She caught a flash of black, and then someone pulled her backward and threw himself over her.

Struggling under the heavy weight, Gillian did her best to fight.

"Easy, Gillian, it's me," Lefty said into her ear.

She immediately stopped moving, and instead gripped his sleeve with the hand on the arm that didn't hurt.

"Just give him a second, and then we'll move," Lefty said.

His words didn't make much sense, but Gillian remained still, trusting him.

* * *

Trigger was more irritated with the fighting couple in the lobby than anything else. He stepped in when the man shoved his girlfriend, but the woman didn't back off, even when her man had been subdued. It had taken way too long for hotel security to get there and take over, separating the couple and calling the police to straighten everything out.

It had only been minutes, actually—but it seemed like longer when Trigger looked back to where he'd last seen Gillian, only to find the space near the front desk was empty.

For the second time that month, his heart stopped beating in his chest.

"Where's Gillian?" he asked Lefty when his friend came up beside him.

Within moments, his entire team was in the lobby, trying to figure out where she might've gone.

It didn't take long for one of the guests milling in the lobby to tell them she'd seen someone in a knee-length green dress with her arm around another woman—who looked as if she'd recently been beaten up—heading down a hallway toward a back door.

Trigger had no idea who the woman was, but the hair on the back of his neck was standing straight up. He'd never ignored his instincts before and wasn't going to start now.

He and the rest of his team headed down the hall. They couldn't draw their weapons, not in the middle of a crowded hotel, but they were just as lethal without them.

The second they exited the hotel into the parking lot at the back of the building, Trigger saw Gillian. She and another woman were standing face-to-face at the far left side of the first row of vehicles. It looked like they were simply talking, which made the butterflies in his stomach relax.

But then the mystery woman raised a gun and pointed it at Gillian's face.

Trigger was moving before he'd even thought about it.

His team was well trained, and they immediately fanned out. Doc, Oz, and Lucky split off to the right to come up behind Gillian and the woman, and Lefty, Grover, and Brain followed Trigger.

He couldn't hear what was being said, but it didn't matter. No one pointed a gun at his woman. *No fucking one.*

As he got closer, he heard the other woman say, "One more chance. Get in the fucking car."

He opened his mouth and let out an almighty roar that he hoped would shock the woman into turning and looking at him. Gillian seemed to move at the same time. He didn't see what she did, but the other woman screamed and a gunshot sounded in the quiet Texas night.

Trigger leapt over a now crouched Gillian and tackled the woman. She fell backward, her head hitting the pavement with a loud thump. He wanted to turn and check on Gillian, but he trusted his team to pull her away to safety and administer first aid if needed.

The sound of the gunshot still ringing in his ears, Trigger's adrenaline was flowing through his veins as he subdued the woman under him. She struggled weakly in his grasp, and as he stared down into her bruised and battered face, he realized that he recognized her.

"Andrea Vilmer?" he asked in shock.

"It's *Vilchez*," she hissed, then tried to spit in his face.

It all clicked then. She was the seventh hijacker.

Vilchez was Luis's last name, and she was obviously related to him. Sister, wife...it didn't matter.

Blood was seeping through the bandage on her hand, and Trigger spared only a brief thought as to what might've happened to her. He was more concerned about making sure she never got a chance to hurt Gillian again. She'd done enough. More than enough.

He hauled her upright and quickly secured her hands behind her back with a zip-tie. He had a feeling Gillian might make fun of him later for having the damn things on his person, but he'd learned the hard way on a mission to always have a way of securing the enemy.

It was only then that he looked back at Gillian. Lefty was on top of her, looking back at him. Lucky and Doc come up next to Trigger, and he immediately let them take control of the spitting-mad woman he'd tackled.

"The police are on their way. And Brain's calling Branch and Tucker," Lucky told him.

Trigger heard his friend's words, but he couldn't look away from Gillian as Lefty slowly moved off her.

Blood. It was staining the ground under her, but he couldn't tell where it was coming from. Feeling as if he was moving in slow motion, he went toward her. Gillian blinked. Then blinked again. But this time it took a moment for her eyes to re-open.

Everything in Trigger's world stopped. "No," he said in a choked whisper as he went to his knees next to Gillian.

"I'm sorry," she said in a rasp he could barely hear. "I shouldn't have left the lobby with her."

"Don't talk," he ordered, terrified out of his mind, any and all medical knowledge he had going straight out the window. This was his woman lying there bleeding—and he couldn't think of one damn thing to do about it!

"It's Andrea."

"I know," he said. "Please, don't talk."

Her eyes closed again. "Salazar beat her up because she lied and told him I knew who she was, and was telling the authorities."

"Don't leave me!" Trigger begged. "I can't live without you."

Her eyes opened again, and she looked up at him in confusion.

"Save your strength. The ambulance will be here any second. Just hang on."

"Walker—" she began, her brow drawing into a frown.

"*Shhh*," he ordered.

"I'm not dying, Walker," she told him firmly.

He looked at the blood under her and pressed his lips together.

"I'm not," she insisted. "My arm hurts like hell, and I think Lefty squished all the air out of my body when he jumped on me to protect me from stray bullets, but I'm not dying. At least...I don't think I am."

Trigger blinked, took a breath—and everything suddenly came into focus. The blood under her was only on one side. Her pupils were reacting to light, and her breathing was a little fast but even.

"Fuck," he said, sitting back on his heels. "Fuck, fuck, *fuck*!"

He heard Lefty and Grover chuckling from next to him.

"Shit, man, you seriously thought she was dying?" Lefty asked.

"Shut up," Trigger grumbled.

"You did!" Grover crowed. "Hey guys, Trigger saw a little blood and freaked out!"

He tuned-out the ribbing his team was giving him when he felt Gillian touch his arm. He immediately leaned closer and grabbed hold of her hand.

"I'm okay," she told him quietly.

Trigger nodded. "Now that I can think straight, it looks like it's just a graze. But you're still going to the hospital," he said sternly.

"Okay, but only long enough for them to sew me up. I'm exhausted. I've worked my ass off today, and you promised to do dirty things to me when we got home."

He barked out a laugh and closed his eyes as he shook his head. When he opened them again, he saw tears in Gillian's eyes. "I'm sorry about Andrea."

"Me too," she agreed.

Trigger knew Gillian would have some hard days ahead of her. They'd both known the seventh hijacker was one of the passengers, but to have been betrayed by someone she'd thought was her friend had to hurt. He'd do whatever it took to erase the pain and betrayal from her eyes. He also knew spending time with her true friends—Ann, Wendy, and Clarissa—would help as well.

But he had no doubt his Wonder Woman would straighten her shoulders and be back to her usual brave self sooner rather than later. As sirens sounded in the distance, Trigger vowed to be by her side every step of the way.

EPILOGUE

Gillian held on to the couch with fingers that had turned white with strain as Walker took her from behind.

It had been three months since Andrea had tried to kidnap and kill her behind The Driskill. She'd had to throw away the green dress Walker had liked so much, but she'd gone shopping with Wendy and Clarissa, and had found the dress she'd worn tonight.

It was shorter than the one she'd worn all those weeks ago. Cut low, showing off her cleavage, and she'd hoped after Walker had seen her in it that *this* was how their night would end.

She'd met him at the restaurant for dinner, since he'd had to work late, and his reaction to the dress, and her in it, had been everything she'd hoped for. His eyes had widened, then his pupils had expanded, and he swore low under his breath.

Throughout dinner, he couldn't keep his hands off her, his fingers frequently straying into indecent territory on her leg as they sat next to each other on the same side of the booth in the steak restaurant. He wasn't as chatty as usual either.

It was probably a good thing they both had their cars and had to drive separately to their apartment, because otherwise, Gillian had a feeling she would've been naked and he would've been on her in the car.

As it was, the second the apartment door was shut behind them, Walker had grabbed her, pulled her into him, and kissed her as if he hadn't just that morning had his wicked way with her.

Now she was bent over the side of the couch as he took her from behind, just as she'd imagined he'd do after the Howard party when they'd arrived home.

She was still fully dressed, except for the white silk panties he'd ripped off her right before he'd entered her from behind. They'd stopped using condoms a couple weeks ago, and Gillian still couldn't believe how amazing Walker felt inside her.

His hips sped up as he neared his climax. One of his hands pushed under her belly and down, and he roughly strummed her clit as his cock slammed in and out of her.

"Come for me, Di," he ordered.

Gillian had tried to explain to him once that just because he ordered her to orgasm, didn't mean it was going to happen, but tonight she was right there with him. She'd been soaking wet and ready for him before they'd gotten home, and seeing him completely lose it, unable to hold back, had pushed her close to the edge.

As usual, he didn't back off manipulating her clit when she got close. One second his touch almost hurt, and the next, she closed her eyes, arched her back, thrust her ass against him and came. Hard.

She felt him slam inside her once more then hold himself as far inside her as he could as he came, as well. His groan echoed around them, but his fingers didn't let up on her clit. Gillian tried to squirm away from him, but it was no use.

"One more," he croaked. "Let me feel you squeeze my cock."

That did it. Another, smaller orgasm ripped through her, every muscle in her body tightening. She swore she could feel him still throbbing inside her.

They stayed like that for just a moment, their hearts beating out of their chests, sweat dripping from their brows.

"Holy crap," she muttered when she could get her brain to work.

Walker chuckled and slowly pulled out of her soaking folds. Gillian felt a rush of his come slide down her inner thigh.

"I know it's inconvenient for you, but I'll never get sick of seeing that. It's sexy as fuck," Walker told her. "Come on, I'll help you get cleaned up."

He helped bring her upright and kissed her gently before putting his arm around her waist and walking her down the hall to their bedroom.

Cleaning the evidence of their lovemaking away and changing for bed didn't take that long, and within ten minutes, they were snuggled together in their bed.

"In case I forgot to tell you, which I think I did, you looked beautiful tonight," Walker told her.

"Thanks. I'm glad we finally got to do the whole bent-over-the-couch thing," she told him honestly. "I was beginning to think you'd treat me like a fragile piece of glass for the rest of our lives."

She felt Walker shudder, and even though she knew he didn't like talking about that night, she needed to.

"You're the strongest person I know, Di. Seriously. But I just…that night…fuck."

Gillian smoothed a hand over his chest. "I know."

"No, you don't. When I saw her lift that gun and point it at your head, my life flashed in front of my eyes. I don't get scared a lot, just ask the guys, but at that moment, I was terrified."

Gillian got up on an elbow so she could look him in the eyes. "I *know*. I think I was more scared that night than on the hijacked plane. Maybe because of the hatred I saw in Andrea's eyes. She legit despised me. It was a hard thing to reconcile in my brain because of how nice she'd been to me since the hijacking, and how bad I felt because of what I'd thought had happened to her while we were on that plane."

"How do you feel about what happened to her?"

"About her being killed in prison?"

"Yeah."

Gillian tried to sort through her feelings before she answered. "Relieved," she said after a beat. "I know that's bad, but—"

"It's not bad. I celebrated with the team today when I heard," Walker admitted. "I was so damn glad she was dead, and you wouldn't have to testify, and that hopefully any threat her connection with the Sinaloa Cartel might've caused you is now over and done with for good. It's not as if the authorities don't already have the cartel on their radar, and since it's not a secret that Andrea was the seventh hijacker anymore, there's no real need to be concerned about Salazar coming for you."

Gillian lay back down, her head resting on his shoulder once more. "The news said she was targeted at the prison?"

"Yeah," Walker said. "She'd been in isolation, but someone fucked up, or maybe they did it on purpose, and she was let out into the yard with the general population. My guess is that someone connected to Sinaloa took the opportunity to take her out. She wasn't exactly on their good list. They have long memories and a certain code they live by."

"I *do* feel bad for her," Gillian said on a sigh.

"Uh-uh," Walker said, shaking his head. "She gets none of your goodness. None of your sympathy."

"But her husband was killed," Gillian protested.

"They *chose* that life," Walker said as he rolled her onto her back and loomed over her. His eyes were intense as they stared down into hers. "No one forced them to get involved with the cartel. No one forced them to be drug dealers. Luis was a murderer. It's not like he was on an innocent business trip and was killed in a car wreck. She doesn't deserve one ounce of your goodness."

"Okay, Walker."

"I mean it, Gillian. She got what was coming to her."

"I said, okay."

She watched as he took a deep breath and relaxed when he rolled back over and pulled her back into his side.

"I'm proud of you, Di," Walker told her. "I wasn't thrilled to have to leave you a month after it happened, but you were tough as hell through that deployment."

"I wasn't thrilled either, but I hung out with my girls

SUSAN STOKER

and got a lot of work done on the few upcoming events I was planning."

"I almost begged my commander to let me stay back stateside, before I figured it would be just as hard to leave you the next time we got called out, so I bit the bullet and went. But I thought about you every second."

"Which isn't safe," Gillian scolded.

Walker chuckled. "The guys knew I wasn't one hundred percent and made sure I didn't take point on anything."

Gillian wasn't sure what that meant, and she didn't really want to know. "They're good guys," she murmured.

"They are." Walker moved then, reaching over her to a drawer in the small table next to the bed.

She grunted as she was mushed against his chest for a second before he lay back down. "What the hell?" she grumbled. "Sniffing armpits is not sexy, Walker."

Before she could shift and get comfortable again, Walker had taken hold of her hand, which had been resting on his chest. Her eyes got huge as he slid a beautiful, perfect princess-cut diamond ring onto her ring finger.

"Wha—"

"I love you, Gillian Romano. I can't imagine spending my life without you. Will you marry me?"

The proposal came out of nowhere...but then again, it didn't. They'd settled into living together so easily it was as if she'd lived with him forever. She'd officially canceled her lease for her apartment in Georgetown, and the stuff that wouldn't fit into his apartment was sitting in storage, waiting for them to find a bigger place to live. Walker told her, and showed her, every day how much he loved her, and they'd had a long conversation one night about souls and how he truly believed they'd known each other in another lifetime, and that was why they'd clicked so immediately.

"Of course I will," she told him with a huge smile. "On one condition."

"Name it," Walker said.

Gillian loved the carnal look in his eyes and knew she was about to get thoroughly ravished...again. "I'm not planning our wedding. I don't want something big. I have to think logistics and plan parties every day of my life. I want something low-key and stress-free. I just want to get it done, hang with our friends, and get on with the rest of our life."

"Will your parents freak if they don't get to participate in a huge wedding for their only daughter?" he asked.

Gillian loved how respectful he was of her parents. They'd once again flown out to Texas when they'd learned she'd been shot, and although it wasn't how she would've wanted Walker to meet them, she couldn't have been happier with how that had turned out. Her parents loved Walker immediately, which wasn't surprising.

"No," she told him. "Will *your* parents be upset?"

"No. I think they're just happy I finally found someone to put up with me. So whatever kind of ceremony you want, you'll get," he said. He picked up her hand, kissed the ring he'd just put there, then gently pushed her onto her back. "Anything else you want to talk about before you can't think anymore?" he asked as he slowly inched his way down her body, pushing the covers down as he went, exposing her to his burning gaze.

Gillian eagerly spread her thighs, giving him room as she shook her head. "No, I think I'm good."

"Oh, you're gonna be good, sweetheart," Walker said with a gleam in his eye.

It was at least an hour and a half later—and three orgasms; two for her and one for him—before Gillian could think once again. Walker was curled up against her back, holding her, and Gillian gazed down at the beautiful diamond on her finger. She thought about her friends, and Walker's team, about how lucky she was to have escaped death not once, but twice, and vowed right then and there to be happy.

No matter what happened in her life from here on out, she had a man who loved her, good friends, and a job she enjoyed. Life wasn't perfect, but hers seemed pretty damn close at the moment.

* * *

"These babysitting jobs are my least favorite," Doc grumbled as part of the team stood outside a room in a nondescript building in Paris, France. Doc, Trigger, and Lefty were on duty at the moment, and Grover, Oz, and Lucky would take over later. Brain was on patrol duty, hanging around outside, listening to the chatter of the people gathering near the building and watching for anything that might compromise the safety of the officials inside.

Normally, Lefty would agree with Doc about babysitting, but earlier that day he'd seen the Assistant Secretary for Insular and International Affairs, Walter Brown, arrive —and he knew that meant his aide was probably around somewhere.

Kinley Taylor. He'd met her the last time they'd been tasked with bodyguard duty in Africa. Her boss had been there, and he hadn't given even the littlest shit about his assistant. He'd sent her back to his hotel to pick up something he'd forgotten—in the middle of a fucking protest. She'd almost died, and if it hadn't been for Lefty slipping out, following her, and making sure the asshole protestor who had his hands on her regretted picking her out of the crowd to mess with, she would've been killed.

He and Kinley had spent the rest of the trip meeting on the sly whenever they could. She was funny. And petite, which appealed to his masculine side. He'd always been drawn to smaller women. He'd wanted to wrap his hands in her long black hair and pull her close every time he saw her, but they'd kept things professional and aboveboard.

They'd had a lot of fun on that trip. Laughing and joking with each other, but even as she teased him, he'd sensed an underlying sadness in her. It made each smile she shared with him even more rewarding.

When that summit had ended, and thus Lefty's bodyguard job, she'd promised to keep in touch, but he hadn't heard from her again.

It had taken him quite a while to get over her. He didn't know what he might've done that made her change her mind about keeping in touch, and that bothered him.

But now they were once again in the same place at the same time, and Lefty wanted answers. Wanted to know why she'd so coldly ghosted him when he'd thought they were actually friends.

Delta Force was used every now and then to watch the backs of high-ranking government officials when they went overseas. This time, their job was covering the Deputy Secretary of Agriculture. Important political members from countries all over the world had been invited to Paris, and like usual, having that much power in one place attracted the crazy, the unhappy, and the people who just wanted to protest against something.

Kinley's boss was being protected by another Delta team out of Fort McNair in Washington, DC. Lefty had met the men a couple of times on other ops, and he knew they were good operatives and would do whatever they could to protect not only the Assistant Secretary for Insular and International Affairs, but his assistant as well.

But that wasn't good enough for Lefty. He wanted to watch over Kinley personally.

"What's wrong?" Trigger asked.

Lefty mentally swore. He knew one of his friends would notice his odd behavior sooner or later.

"She's here," he told Trigger.

"Kinley?" his friend asked, knowing exactly who he was talking about.

Lefty nodded.

"She still working for that asshole?"

"As far as I know."

"You talked to her yet?" Trigger asked.

Lefty shook his head.

"We'll make sure you've got time to make that happen," Trigger said.

"'Preciate that," Lefty told him. And he did. They were here for a job. There wasn't time for fun. No romantic dinners at a charming café and no visits to the Eiffel Tower. But everyone knew how upset he'd been when Kinley hadn't responded to any of his emails or texts. His team would do what they could to make sure he got the closure he needed.

Lefty could remember his last conversation with Kinley as if it were yesterday.

"Thanks for being a stalker and following me into that mob of people."

"You're welcome. I hope this isn't goodbye for good. I like you, Kinley. I'd like to keep in touch...if that's okay."

"It's more than okay. I'd really like that. I don't have a lot of friends. Living in DC is...tough. People are always using others to try to climb the political ladder."

"And you don't want to do that?"

"No way! If I had my choice, I'd be living on a farm in the middle of nowhere with only animals to keep me company. They're honest. They don't lie or try to hurt you."

"Who's hurt you?"

"Oh...I was just saying. But yes, I'd love to keep in touch."

He'd thought about that exchange again and again for over a year, since he'd last seen her, and it bothered him more and more, especially after he'd never heard back from her. He'd tried to blow it off and tell himself she was just being polite when she said she'd keep in touch, but he didn't think so. Something about the entire situation seemed off.

And now Lefty had another chance to get to the bottom of the mystery that was Kinley Taylor. He couldn't wait. If she thought she could blow him off again, she was insane. No one had fascinated Lefty as much as she had. A part of him wanted to know what he'd done that had made her ghost him, but another part was worried.

They'd clicked. That never happened to Lefty. Ever.

Something had scared Kinley away from talking to him, he was sure of it. He wanted to know what it was.

For the first time in his life, he was grateful for bodyguard duty.

I hope you're ready to give me some answers, Lefty thought to himself, his eyes constantly roaming the hall for potential threats to the men and women inside the room behind him. *Because I'm not willing to let you go so easily this time. I want to know everything about what's behind the sorrow I saw in your eyes...and fix it.*

*

Find out what Kinley's hiding and if Lefty can break through her protective walls in *Shielding Kinley*!

Want to talk to other Susan Stoker fans? Join my reader group, Susan Stoker's Stalkers, on Facebook!

JOIN my Newsletter and find out about sales, free books, contests and new releases before anyone else!!
Click HERE

Want to know when my books go on sale? Follow me on Bookbub HERE!

Would you like Susan's Book Protecting Caroline for FREE?
Click HERE

Also by Susan Stoker

SEAL of Protection: Legacy Series
Securing Caite
Securing Brenae (novella)
Securing Sidney
Securing Piper
Securing Zoey
Securing Avery (May 2020)
Securing Kalee (Sept 2020)

Delta Team Two Series
Shielding Gillian
Shielding Kinley (Aug 2020)
Shielding Aspen (Oct 2020)
Shielding Riley (TBA)
Shielding Devyn (TBA)
Shielding Ember (TBA)
Shielding Sierra (TBA)

Delta Force Heroes Series
Rescuing Rayne
Rescuing Aimee (novella)
Rescuing Emily
Rescuing Harley
Marrying Emily (novella)
Rescuing Kassie
Rescuing Bryn
Rescuing Casey
Rescuing Sadie (novella)

Rescuing Wendy
Rescuing Mary
Rescuing Macie (novella)

Badge of Honor: Texas Heroes Series

Justice for Mackenzie
Justice for Mickie
Justice for Corrie
Justice for Laine (novella)
Shelter for Elizabeth
Justice for Boone
Shelter for Adeline
Shelter for Sophie
Justice for Erin
Justice for Milena
Shelter for Blythe
Justice for Hope
Shelter for Quinn
Shelter for Koren
Shelter for Penelope

Ace Security Series

Claiming Grace
Claiming Alexis
Claiming Bailey
Claiming Felicity
Claiming Sarah

Mountain Mercenaries Series

Defending Allye
Defending Chloe

Defending Morgan
Defending Harlow
Defending Everly
Defending Zara
Defending Raven (June 2020)

SEAL of Protection Series

Protecting Caroline
Protecting Alabama
Protecting Fiona
Marrying Caroline (novella)
Protecting Summer
Protecting Cheyenne
Protecting Jessyka
Protecting Julie (novella)
Protecting Melody
Protecting the Future
Protecting Kiera (novella)
Protecting Alabama's Kids (novella)
Protecting Dakota

Stand Alone

The Guardian Mist
Nature's Rift
A Princess for Cale
A Moment in Time- A Collection of Short Stories
Lambert's Lady

Special Operations Fan Fiction

http://www.AcesPress.com

Beyond Reality Series

Outback Hearts

Flaming Hearts

Frozen Hearts

Writing as Annie George:

Stepbrother Virgin (erotic novella)

ABOUT THE AUTHOR

New York Times, *USA Today* and *Wall Street Journal* Bestselling Author Susan Stoker has a heart as big as the state of Tennessee where she lives, but this all American girl has also spent the last fourteen years living in Missouri, California, Colorado, Indiana, and Texas. She's married to a retired Army man who now gets to follow *her* around the country.

She debuted her first series in 2014 and quickly followed that up with the SEAL of Protection Series, which solidified her love of writing and creating stories readers can get lost in.

If you enjoyed this book, or any book, please consider leaving a review. It's appreciated by authors more than you'll know.

www.stokeraces.com
www.AcesPress.com
susan@stokeraces.com

facebook.com/authorsusanstoker

twitter.com/Susan_Stoker

instagram.com/authorsusanstoker

goodreads.com/SusanStoker

bookbub.com/authors/susan-stoker

amazon.com/author/susanstoker

CPSIA information can be obtained
at www.ICGtesting.com
Printed in the USA
LVHW042321060420
652382LV00017B/573

9 781644 990117